RELOADED

Matt Rogers

ISBN: 9781519094971
ISBN-13:

"Only the dead have seen the end of the war."

- George Santayana

CHAPTER 1

After a harrowing amalgamation of third-world war zones, terrorist strongholds, biological weapons facilities, corrupt prisons and extreme environments in the most remote corners of the globe — all Jason King really needed was a little sun.

The Bay of Calvi twinkled under a cloudless sky. It was mid-summer on the Mediterranean island of Corsica, and the weather couldn't have been more perfect. A collection of multi-million dollar pleasure yachts — all polished and smoothed until they gleamed — rested in a spacious marina built into one side of the bay. The turquoise water had a clarity that seemed to be the trademark for these kind of exotic locations. It lapped gently at the sandy shore, adding soft background noise to the serene ambience of the bay.

The town of Calvi itself was calm and peaceful. The houses stood almost side-by-side, all sporting traditional thin schist tiles on the roofs. A cluster of restaurants dotted the Quai Adolphe Landry curving past the marina and running along the bay's edge.

It was paradise.

Jason King surfaced noiselessly from the warm ocean and wiped his eyes with a calloused hand. He tread water and took a deep breath. Watching. Waiting. Ordinarily he would be armed, having approached a target with precision, preparing himself to bring death to whoever he'd been ordered to attack.

But this life was very different to his previous one.

He wore swimming trunks and nothing else. His skin was a deep shade of brown from over a month of soaking up the Mediterranean sun. Veins ran along his forearms, like a road map spread across bulging muscles. His current physique had been chiselled out of an intense desire to maintain the physical fitness of years past.

When he'd first landed in Corsica, he imagined he might take a break from rigorous exercise in an attempt to instil a sense of normalcy into his life. But he quickly found that would not be the case. The iron kept his mind at peace when all else failed. He enjoyed it.

And, of course, it had its benefits.

It seemed that he had finally found his peace. He swam gently to shore, taking his time. That was what he relished most.

The freedom.

With no financial burdens to speak of, and the remnants of his career fading piece by piece into memories, he could simply do as he pleased. For the first few months of his retirement, he'd embraced the life of a nomad, a wanderer who moved from country to country with no fixed abode — seeing the sights, enjoying the change of pace.

It hadn't gone as planned.

Two separate incidents in Australia and Venezuela had caused him to reconsider his future trajectory. Whether by fate or coincidence or sheer bad luck, trouble had followed him to the most remote corners of the globe. He'd left a trail of bodies in his wake — the exact thing he'd been attempting to avoid by getting out of the game.

He'd tasted the closeness of death many, many times since stepping away from covert ops. It was a concept he was all too familiar with. An increasingly repetitive action that he knew — if he allowed it to continue — would eventually catch up to him.

Reaction speed could only fend off so much carnage.

There would come a time when he knew his reflexes would kick in a millisecond too slow. Then a bullet would tear his vital organs to shreds and that would be that.

It wouldn't happen.

He wouldn't let it.

He felt wet sand underneath his feet and clambered ashore. His swim trunks clung to his legs. They were a size too small. He'd bought them nigh on twenty days ago — but it seemed such a drastic change of lifestyle had enabled him to focus all his intensity on the gym. With no-one to shoot at and nothing to worry about, he'd needed somewhere to take out the primal urges that often coursed through him.

Already at an unimaginably high level of fitness, it seemed his body had reacted to the concentrated training by tightening and hardening. Regular beach-runs in the summer heat every morning kept his pores open and his body fat percentage in the high single digits.

It sure drew attention. He stuck out like a sore thumb amidst the hordes of soft-bodied middle-aged tourists that flocked to these parts in the summertime. But he didn't mind.

Sometimes, that sort of attention created hedonistic advantages.

Women noticed.

He crossed the sand, heading for the towel he'd laid down a few minutes prior. He'd just finished a quick five-mile run and the wash-off in the bay had closed his pores. He dried himself, meeting the eyes of several nearby beachgoers who couldn't seem to keep their eyes off his physique.

He smiled at them — something he'd found himself doing more and more lately.

Happiness was a sensation that he hadn't had much time to experience over the last ten years. In this place, he was beginning to grow accustomed to the feeling.

After all — what was there to possibly be unhappy about?

He gathered his belongings — a small rucksack containing a change of clothes, a mobile phone, a wallet and a set of keys — and made for the town. He slung the bag over one shoulder and drank in the sun as he walked. Changing attire could wait. There was no rush.

He passed between buildings painted pale shades of orange and yellow. Most were multi-storey. The seaside town had an air of relaxation about it. King had been to many places on this planet. Not many induced anything close to comfort.

Most were plagued by a distinct sense of aggressive hostility.

He found the same narrow stairway made of cobblestone that he'd ascended a hundred times already, carving between two tightly-grouped buildings near the water. He took the steps two at a time, his bare feet finding relief on the cool surface. The shade cast by the neighbouring roofs meant that the stairway formed one of the only reprieves from the Corsican heat.

As he walked, he couldn't help but smile again. It had been strange to transition into retirement, especially given what he'd been through. Despite the risks that had come with being thrown into a corrupt third-world prison in South America and facing an army of mercenaries in the backwoods of Australia, it pained him to admit that he'd felt more at home during those times than the periods in between of travel and rest. He'd decided to give an uneventful life one last shot. That was what this was.

It seemed to be working. He hadn't felt this way since his childhood.

He stepped out into a small courtyard atop a hill. A low brick and mortar fence curved around the edge of the courtyard, facing out over the Bay of Calvi. The ground was loose gravel and the view was picturesque. King had taken a shortcut, but the main road leading to the courtyard lay empty. A single car was parked in front of a low one-storey building with large fold-out windows and a cozy but spacious atmosphere.

Previously a residential building, the place had been converted into a bar long ago. The interior walls had been knocked down to create a sprawling single room, complete with a dozen tables and an enormous oak countertop at one end. Hundreds of bottles of alcohol lined the walls behind the bar, each at varying levels of completion.

It was a nice place.

More importantly, it was his.

CHAPTER 2

King passed the car — a Mercedes-AMG C63 S Coupe — and double-checked that it was locked. He'd purchased the vehicle on a whim upon landing in Corsica, finally deciding to dip into his considerable savings.

In certain situations, violence paid.

Two men loitered outside the bar's front entrance, waiting patiently on cheap stools dotting the patio. They were both elderly, which meant they'd long ago realised that there was no need to force unnecessary conversation where none was needed. They sat in silence, soaking in the morning sun, thoroughly content. King had grown to know both men over the length of time that he'd owned the bar, and had quickly decided that they were a stellar example for enjoying life in their older years. One day, he strived to be like them.

'Morning, gents,' he said as he stepped up onto the deck.

'What took you so long?' Benédict demanded. The man was in his sixties, previously a real estate developer in Cairns before retiring to Corsica with enough money to buy the island itself if he wanted. His English was impeccable, with only a slight trace of an accent — a necessity given the high-profile Caucasian clients he'd assisted over the years. He enjoyed the simple things in life — like a drink on a Sunday morning.

King checked the Rolex he'd looped over one wrist on the walk up through Calvi. 'It's two minutes past ten.'

'And you open at ten.'

'You're certainly right,' King said. 'I'll do better next time.'

They exchanged grins and King moved to slot a key into the bar's double doors. He nodded to Franc, a similarly-aged retiree who spoke little English but knew how to order a scotch on the rocks — as proven by his repeated visits. The doors creaked open and King stepped through, striding across the timber flooring.

'You know,' Benédict said, 'I never did ask. How much did you pay for this place?'

King raised an eyebrow as he stepped behind the bar and dropped his rucksack on the floor underneath the counter. 'There's a reason you don't ask those questions, Benédict. That's very forward.'

'Ah, nonsense,' the old man said, dismissing the statement with an exaggerated wave of the hand. 'We're big boys. I'm sure you can handle it.'

'I paid a hell of a lot more than I'm ever going to make back from it,' King said.

'Then why on earth did you buy it?'

King pointed out the window. 'You like the view?'

Benédict nodded. 'Who wouldn't?'

'Exactly. I liked the view. So I bought it.'

'If you have enough money to afford this place, why would you waste it? You'd have to be business-savvy to get to where you are now. Rumours are you got yourself a cozy place up in Calenzana too.'

'Rumours are correct,' King said, fetching a bottle of scotch down from the wall. He slapped two glasses on the table and scooped ice into each. 'The usual?'

Benédict and Franc nodded in unison.

King spread his arms wide. 'What can I say, Benédict? I'm enjoying retirement.'

'*Chançard,*' Benédict muttered, shaking his head, clearly perturbed by the fact that a man as young as King could afford such a lavish lifestyle. 'So you buy the bar because you enjoy the work?'

King nodded. 'There we go. You're getting it. Needed to keep myself occupied.'

'Why this?'

'I visited a similar set-up in Australia. Liked the place a lot. Felt jealous of the owner. And hey — I could afford it. I break even. Life's good.'

'*Oui,*' Benédict agreed. 'Life is good.'

King finished pouring the drinks — making sure to be particularly generous with his servings — and slid them across the countertop. The two men handed over a crumpled five-euro note each. King accepted the exchange with a nod of thanks and dropped the money into a battered till. He fired up the trio of flat-screen televisions spread out across the room and started to prepare for the mid-afternoon rush that would inevitably come, as it did each Sunday. He swung each windowpane out in turn, allowing the warm morning breeze to flow in through the open panes. Then he ventured into the fridge behind the bar and cracked open an ice-cold beer.

Today will be a good day, he mused.

Something he'd been forcing himself to repeat every morning. A mantra of sorts.

He settled into light conversation with Benédict as the morning's first customers began to trickle in.

CHAPTER 3

The day passed in the same way that the last thirty had — full of warm greetings to the patrons and a steady flow of alcohol and soft tropical music wafting from a jukebox in the far corner. King alternated between watching the television on the far wall and conversing with tourists and locals alike.

Through his new life he'd discovered something that greatly interested him — simply listening.

As the days passed by he realised he knew very little about ordinary civilian life. He'd spent an enormous chunk of his own being whisked from danger to danger — always fighting, always killing.

It hadn't afforded him the luxury of living anything close to a normal existence.

As such, he found himself asking open-ended questions to customers and letting them talk. On this particular day, a man from Dallas who wandered in mid-afternoon spent thirty minutes complaining of his soul-sucking 9-to-5 job back home. He sat in a tiny cubicle and managed paycheques for the hundreds of men and women that his firm employed. He said it was draining, and that he felt like nothing more than a mindless drone.

King listened quietly and found himself wondering if his choice of career hadn't been so bad after all.

'Hey,' he chimed in, 'at least it allowed you to come here.'

The man shrugged. 'That's true. Short breaks like this keep me sane.'

'You been here before?'

The guy shook his head and took a swig of beer. 'Never. Only been out of the country once. What about you? This your place?'

King nodded. 'Settled down here only a few months ago.'

'What'd you do before that?'

He paused. 'A lot of shit. None of it pleasant.'

'At least you're living the life now,' the guy said, probably assuming King was talking about manual labour or unpaid overtime.

King stared out the bar's open windows at the afternoon sun glinting off the waves. He shook his head in bemusement. Perhaps it would all work out after all.

By four in the afternoon, King had served dozens of patrons and amassed a fairly respectable total for the day. Of course, it would never be enough to make serious money, but he had no need for that. He could take ten times as much as he was currently earning from the bar and it would leave no sizeable impression on his bank account. That hadn't been the point when he'd decided to make the purchase. It had been an anchor of sorts, something to keep him in one place.

He knew he had to shake free the travel bug if he hoped for any semblance of a regular life.

Benédict and Franc had left a couple of hours ago, probably returning to their disgruntled wives. On that note, King's mind wandered to the possibility of settling down.

He had no shortage of options — rumours had spread quickly throughout the island of a young, wealthy, good-looking American who owned a luxurious villa in Calenzana — but the concept of a long-term relationship was still foreign to him. He'd had flings in his time, but the nature of his previous life had barred all ability to develop an attachment to anyone.

As if on cue, a woman stepped into the bar. King — in the middle of washing a set of used glasses — glanced up as he heard the familiar jangle of a new customer and tried his hardest not to stare. Even though Corsica was home to a plethora of beautiful women, he hadn't seen someone so striking in quite some time. She had Scandinavian roots, evident in her pale blonde hair and blue eyes and softly tanned skin. She wore a loose floral dress that accentuated her curves and carried a small clutch bag.

As King returned his gaze to the glasses, she approached the bar and sat down on one of the stools. She sighed emphatically.

King looked up. 'Long day?'

She nodded. 'Very.'

'Seems that way. What can I get you?'

'Beer, please.'

'Any preference?'

'What do you recommend?'

'I've got a local craft. Called Pietra. It's good.'

She nodded. 'Sounds like it'll hit the spot.'

He cracked one open and passed it across the countertop. 'Swedish?'

She smiled, flashing pearly white teeth. 'How'd you know?'

King shrugged. 'The accent. I've been there a couple of times.'

'On holiday?'

He shook his head. 'For work. Didn't have much time to see the sights.'

'You should go back some time. It's a beautiful country.'

'I'm sure it is.'

He met her gaze for a fraction of a second too long, the type of look between two parties that signified mutual attraction. Noting that the feeling was there, he turned back to the glasses. He didn't want to seem too interested.

Not yet.

'You are American?' she said.

'I am.'

'So what are you doing here?'

King smiled and shook his head. Seemed everyone had that question on their mind. 'I retired very young. Made enough money to get out early. Now I'm just enjoying life.'

'I've heard.'

He raised an eyebrow. 'Oh?'

She took a sip of beer and looked at him. 'You're the talk of the town, Jason King.'

'You know my name,' he noted.

'I've talked to a few friends who've said that you're *quite* the naughty boy.' She spoke sardonically, as if jokingly scolding him for his behaviour.

King snatched up his own half-empty beer and took a swig. He thought he might need it. 'And who are your friends, exactly?'

'Model friends,' she said. 'Well, the ones that live locally. I'm out here on contract. Big magazine shoot along the bay. One week, all expenses paid.'

'Sounds fancy.'

'Fancy enough. I went out on the town last night and found out about you.'

'Your friends seem awfully gossipy.'

'Just the ones you've slept with.'

King shrugged. 'Am I supposed to say no?'

She shrugged back. 'Not my business, is it? I'm Klara, by the way.'

'Pleasure to meet you, Klara.'

'Is it true about—?' She lowered her voice, trailing off, as if she were about to discuss private information that could not be overheard.

King hadn't the slightest idea as to what she was getting at. 'What?'

'The villa.'

'Ah...' he said. 'Yes, it is.'

He should have known that information would spread eventually. Benedict had brought it up, and now Klara. The sprawling complex in the hills above Calvi — positioned in the small town of Calenzana — had gouged a serious dent out of his personal fortune, holding a price tag in the high seven-figures. It was three storeys of luxury — complete with a view over half the island, a rooftop Olympic-sized swimming pool, a home cinema, lush well-maintained gardens and an enormous four-car garage which he'd converted into a powerlifting gym.

It was his own private paradise. He felt he deserved it, all things considered. He'd made the purchase intending to never leave the island again, investing in such an extravagant home to set himself up for decades of comfort and peace.

Of course, he had to make sure that the first — and hopefully last — property he'd ever owned was a special one.

He'd travelled enough for ten lifetimes.

Klara sensed his hesitation. 'You don't want to talk about it?'

'I'm not adverse to it,' King said. 'I just don't like to come off as bragging.'

'I'm the one who asked you,' she said. 'Of course you're not bragging. So — what'd you do?'

King paused and looked at her, his eyes wide. 'What the hell is it with people today?'

She raised an eyebrow.

'Everyone's poking around,' he explained.

She shrugged and leant forward, resting her tanned forearms on the counter. 'Everyone's curious. Wealthy foreigner shows up and throws that kind of money around. Maybe I can be the one to wrestle it out of you.'

He drained the beer from his bottle and tossed it in the trash. 'You want to wrestle?'

She smiled. 'Not like that. I'm here on business.'

'Uh-huh.'

'Are you going to tell me?'

'Why should I?'

'Because I want to know. And I have the afternoon free, so I thought I'd explore the town.'

He noted her exquisite beauty and imagined she didn't often come across a man who told her "no". 'You usually get what you want, don't you?'

'I do,' she admitted.

'And you think I'll tell you where I got all my money because of that?'

'So it's a big secret?'

'Possibly. I don't know you. You could be anybody.'

'Were you a bad man?'

King raised his hands in mock surrender and stood up. 'Can't tell you. Sorry. Why so inquisitive, might I ask?'

'Always been that way,' Klara said. 'I guess you could call me nosy. Or reckless. It's how I got into this job. Parents had me on a different course — but what's the point?'

'Of life?'

'Of doing something you're not passionate about.'

King shrugged. 'Wouldn't know. I've never had that problem.'

Klara did not respond. King had realised long ago what Benédict and Franc had concluded — there was no point forcing conversation. Sometimes, silence was comfortable. They sat on opposite sides of the bar and let the stillness of the late-afternoon wash over them.

'What time do you close?' Klara said finally.

King looked up and noted the patrons beginning to disperse. 'Soon. I keep the evenings free most nights.'

'For?'

'A few different hobbies.'

It wasn't a lie.

His newfound sedentary life had provided King with the one thing he'd been lacking for most of his adult existence — free time. He'd found the opportunity to branch out and dabble in a number of different fields. Due to the conditions of his past life, certain adrenalin-inducing activities appealed to him more than the finer arts. On days where he kept the bar closed, he made the coast-to-coast trip to the commune of Ghisonaccia, home to the island's only skydiving dropzone. The fun jumps were definitely a change of pace from the usual circumstances in which he'd flung himself from planes in years prior. He also owned a pair of quad-bikes which he used to circumnavigate the mountains — usually to clear his head. He found the wind against his face calming, a sensation that he couldn't find in many other places.

Of course, he had a different hobby in mind tonight.

He turned to Klara. 'You seem awfully interested in the villa.'

'Like I said…'

He cut her off. 'Want to see it?'

Her lips parted slightly, as if she were considering responding but thought better of it. She drummed her fingers on the sturdy countertop and met King's eyes. 'That's very forward of you.'

'Is it?' King said. 'I'm just offering a tour to a curious soul.'

'Oh, I'm sure.'

'I'm not forcing you to do anything,' King said. 'Just putting it out there that I'm not adverse to it. It honestly wouldn't bother me in the slightest if you turned and waltzed out of here.'

'Aren't you above all this?'

'Above what?'

'Drinking and chasing women and spending your off days on the beach ... it just seems so blasé for someone with the net worth that you obviously have.'

King tapped the countertop. 'You think I'm a hedonistic douchebag?'

'Not at all,' Klara said. 'In fact, you seem very switched on. That's why I'm questioning it.'

'Why, thank you,' he said. 'Truth is — I don't care what people think. I spent ten years in almost constant pain. The amount of stress I've had to deal with ... it would drive anyone insane. It almost did. I got out before it all caught up to me.'

'You were a soldier? A killer?'

'Something like that. But I spent too long at one end of the scale. I waded through mud and dirt and shit in third-world hellholes. I've been injured more times than I can count. So now I'm experiencing the opposite end. And I'm loving it. And you can call me shallow, but it doesn't bother me. I'm happy.'

'I can see that,' she said, finishing her beer. 'You look happy.'

He smiled. 'What is there to be unhappy about?'

'Not much at all,' she admitted. 'I would love a tour.'

Five minutes later, the last customer of the day exited the bar with a jovial wave. King locked up the till, looped his rucksack over one shoulder and motioned to the door. Klara's stark blue eyes wandered up and down his frame.

'Let's go,' he said.

CHAPTER 4

The eight-cylinder engine of the Mercedes purred as it climbed the hills out of Calvi. Klara sat in the passenger seat, staring out the tinted window at the passing surroundings. King imagined she hadn't been this far inland during her time on the island. Tourists tended to spend their precious vacation time exclusively in the seaside towns. When you headed further into the mountains, the bustle of civilisation vanished and was replaced by a sense of tranquility. King relished that sort of thing.

It was a pleasant contrast to the commotion of Calvi.

They passed a deep ravine of rock and dead grass dropping away from the side of the road. Klara craned her neck to get a better look at it, to no avail. The sun had dipped below the horizon and making out the various landmarks was difficult in the twilight.

'You enjoying it here?' she said.

King gripped the leather steering wheel and spurred the luxury coupe a little faster. 'I don't see how I couldn't be.'

'Maybe whatever you used to do might be bothering you,' she said. 'I don't know. Hard to tell who's happy these days.'

'I'm happy,' he assured her. 'I'm thinking about that stuff less and less.' He paused. 'Does it bother you?'

'Huh?' she said, cocking her head.

'That I used to do some questionable things. I haven't given you much detail.'

'Not really. You seem nice enough.'

'Is it that simple?'

'To me it is.'

'That kind of attitude could get you in trouble.'

'It's worked so far. I can tell someone's intentions the second I meet them. Always have been able to.'

'And what's your opinion?'

'Of you?'

King nodded.

Klara smiled. 'Well, you definitely want to sleep with me. That much is clear. But you seem like a good guy.'

'Right on both counts,' he muttered, just loud enough for her to hear.

She turned away to hide a laugh.

The Mercedes ascended the road into Calenzana. It was a tiny picturesque village set against a backdrop of a looming mountain range. In the winter — King had been told — the peaks became snow-capped. He hadn't been here long enough to experience the sight.

He hoped he would make it that far.

King swept the car through narrow gravel roads and past stunningly beautiful traditional Corsican houses painted the colour of mahogany. They passed through the town in moments and the tyres crawled up a trail leading to a vast gated property. He stopped by an electronic panel on a pole and punched in a security combination through the open driver's window. The steel gate groaned as it swung open. He took the car through and Klara's jaw visibly slackened.

So had King's when he'd first laid eyes on the grounds.

The villa curved in a broad U-shape around a stunning courtyard complete with a fountain and an collection of benches and *Phoenix canariensis* palm trees. Even though they weren't discernible from behind the estate, it was clear that the views of the land sloping down towards the Mediterranean Sea would be stunning. Combined with the warm climate of the late evening, it created one of the more beautiful settings King had ever seen.

The decision to purchase the property had been effortless.

Anyone in their right mind who had sufficient funds would have swept it up in a heartbeat after a single tour.

'It really is something,' Klara said as King coasted the Mercedes to a stop in the wide driveway. 'So what's the bar?'

King looked at her. 'Huh?'

'Clearly you don't make anywhere near enough from the bar to support this lifestyle.'

'I have enough to support this lifestyle for a long time. The bar keeps me busy. Keeps me grounded.'

She paused for consideration. 'You meet a lot of women there?'

'A few,' he admitted.

She laughed. 'Living the life, aren't you?'

'Now I am. It's about time…'

Finally within the confines of a private area, they quickly made their way into the house, barely suppressing the sexually-charged atmosphere. Once they both stepped into a large marble lobby and found themselves alone, King couldn't keep his urges contained any longer. He wheeled Klara around and pressed his lips against hers. She kissed back with a ferocious passion, pressing her body against his. He slid his hands under her paper-thin summer dress, feeling the smoothness of her skin, roaming with his hands.

They didn't even make it to the bedroom.

Fuelled by a wild excitement that had only surfaced once he'd had the chance to settle down, King scooped Klara up and walked through to a wide living room complete with a sprawling suede couch. He dumped her down and she giggled uncontrollably.

They sank into the soft material, fixated by each other's bodies.

King pulled the dress off her with barely any effort at all and pressed his mouth against her full breast. She let out a flutter of pleasure and swung one bare leg over his waist. Increasingly animated, she peeled his clothes away and they settled into a pulsating rhythm.

King kissed her long and hard, wondering just how his life had taken such a drastic turn from the vicious hell of the past.

CHAPTER 5

The evening passed in a blur of physical sensation and emotional joy.

King relished the peace that fell over him when he was with a woman. It kept him in the moment. He couldn't think about anything he'd done in the past, or dwell on things he might have been able to change. Maybe that was why he'd undergone such a radical transformation during his time in Corsica.

The pursuit of women hadn't been important before. He quite simply hadn't had time for it.

Now he found there were benefits to being tall, well-groomed and in impeccable shape. It attracted certain types, which he hadn't realised he enjoyed so much until recently. He thought he might settle down in the future — maybe find someone to create a long-term relationship with.

But not yet.

He wasn't ready.

As night fell over the villa, plunging the view of the coast through the floor-to-ceiling windows into darkness, Klara fetched an expensive robe from the guest bedroom and returned to the couch. She sprawled out next to King and draped a thigh over him.

'They were definitely right,' she said.

King raised an eyebrow. 'Who were?'

'The people I spoke to last night. You're very good.'

He smiled. 'That surprises me. Didn't had much time for this sort of thing before I moved here.'

'Sex?'

'Not just that. Any kind of companionship, really. Being intimate. It just wasn't part of my life.'

'By choice?'

He shook his head. 'I was always on the move.'

'Did you kill people?'

King looked at her. 'That's not something I want to get into.'

She nodded understandably. 'Want me to cook something up for dinner?'

He smiled and kissed her. 'I'll do it. By the way — how long are you here for?'

'Here in your house?'

'In Corsica.'

'A couple more days. Tomorrow's the last day of the photoshoot, then we have a big function at one of the politicians' mansions. I haven't caught up on the details yet, but it's to celebrate the fashion industry. I think they're happy that the big magazines are coming out here more. Brings more money to the economy. That sort of thing. I think it's just an excuse for the old bastards to surround themselves with models.'

King motioned to the eighty-inch television mounted on the wall in front of them, which was set to the evening news. On screen, a French man in his mid-fifties with thick white hair and a plump frame was halfway through a passionate speech, its content unknown due to the mute function. A banner under his chest read "*Yves Moreau addressing political corruption in Ajaccio*".

'Him?' King said.

Klara craned her neck, then shook her head. 'No — not him. He doesn't seem like the type to care about his image. It's probably one of the men he's talking about.'

'I've heard about him,' King said, staring at the lined face portrayed in high-definition, full of emotion and enthusiasm. 'He's taking a stand against corruption? I don't think he has much of a chance.'

'Cleaning up politics,' Klara scoffed. 'That's a joke. Don't know what he's hoping to achieve.'

'Probably trying to get his name out there,' King said. 'Last I heard, he's a minister in the regionalist coalition. Maybe he wants to be Prime Minister some day.'

'Maybe.'

Despite the overall lack of activity throughout the day, King was tired. The sex had started slow and passionate, but their hormones had come through and it had devolved into an intense, largely enjoyable experience towards the end. The plush material all around him and Klara's warm body against his made his eyes grow heavy. Before he knew it, both of them had drifted into an undisturbed sleep.

He didn't dream.

A welcome relief, given his track record.

The day he dreamt of pleasant experiences and feelings of happiness was far off on the horizon. What he'd been through would take more than a couple of months in paradise to wear off.

Because he didn't close the blinds overnight, the dawn woke them both at close to seven the next morning. King's eyes fluttered open and he glanced around, noting his unbroken sleep. Usually he found himself awake and sweating in the middle of the night, tossing and turning, full of unrest. Maybe it was Klara's presence that had kept him calm.

He made a mental note to move *"getting into a relationship"* to the top of his list of priorities and headed for the shower.

He showered cold, as always. It kick-started his energy for the day. He didn't know the science behind it — and hadn't bothered to do his research — but he knew that if the water's temperature was as close to arctic as possible, it eliminated all feelings of grogginess left over from sleep.

He cooked up a quick breakfast of bacon, eggs and sausages, which he shared with Klara.

'I wasn't planning to sleep here,' she said between a mouthful of toast, grinning wryly.

'That casual of a fling?!' he exclaimed in mock surprise.

She laughed. 'Not for that reason. Estelle will be wondering where I am.'

'A friend?'

Klara nodded. 'My best friend. Since childhood. We joined Criterion Management together. Somehow, we always manage to end up getting booked for the same gigs.'

'She's protective?'

'We both are. There's too many pieces of shit in the world.'

King let the statement hang in the air, flashing back to all the carnage he'd wreaked around the world. 'There sure are.'

'I hope it's not too much to ask for a lift back into Calvi. We need to be on the beach at nine.'

'Of course.'

She smiled, leant across the table and pressed her lips against his. They were soft, and full. He closed his eyes and enjoyed the sensation. He'd been focusing on that more and more lately. Living in the moment was a new concept.

Usually his mind was fixated on a plethora of threats to his wellbeing.

But not anymore. Not in this paradise.

'Will I see you again?' he queried. He let the question fall out on a whim. He wasn't ordinarily the type to ask such things.

She smiled. 'Maybe. I have the day off tomorrow. We could see the sights — if you want?'

'I'd like that,' King said.

'Are you free?'

'I work for myself. I'm free whenever I want to be.'

She took another look around the villa's gargantuan interior. 'Must be nice never having to worry about money.'

'Now it is,' he admitted. 'It didn't come easy though.'

'I can't imagine it would have. Shall we go?'

'Let's.'

He slipped into the master bedroom and quickly selected a suitable outfit for the day ahead — outrageous floral shorts and a loose-fitting tank top.

The wonders of owning a bar, he thought.

The four-poster king-size bed was immaculately made, untouched from the previous night. He found himself sleeping in it less and less as the days passed. It was almost too comfortable. Time after time he settled down on the couch or in one of the chairs in the living room.

Some habits — like sleeping anywhere available — were harder to shake than others.

As they exited through the same gate in the Mercedes, King glanced over at Klara, who was enamoured by the scenic view out the passenger's window. He noticed how the dress rested gently on her curves, showing off all the right places, and how her long hair spilled over one shoulder carelessly but somehow managed to look like it had been fixed in place with impeccable attention to detail. She was beautiful. He felt something in his chest that he had barely experienced before.

Excitement for what lay ahead.

He didn't want to reveal that he couldn't wait to spend the day with her tomorrow. It would make him seem like a teenager fawning over his crush, but that was exactly how he felt. He took the luxury coupe through the tight bends with ease, feeling the balmy wind flow in through the open window. He smiled.

Maybe this was the reason he'd forced himself through so many horrible situations.

Because that's what it took to really appreciate life afterwards.

As they descended the hills into Calvi, they spoke about work. Klara revealed she was growing sick of the model lifestyle. It was lavish and extravagant, but ultimately empty. She hated being whisked from place to place, never really being able to stop. King silently related to her. He'd felt the exact same way before settling in Corsica. He thought that maybe a future might actually be possible between the two of them, yet he didn't dare say so. She would almost certainly consider him to be moving too quickly.

Moving fast was the only thing he was used to.

He pulled into the courtyard in front of his bar at three minutes past nine, according to the Rolex on his wrist.

'You may be slightly late to your shoot,' he said.

Klara laughed. 'That's okay. I'm sure they'll forgive me.'

This early on a weekday, Benedict and Franc had yet to make an appearance. They were alone in the lot. Klara leant across the centre console and beckoned for King to do the same. He kissed her ferociously, transfixed by how addictive the experience was. Right then and there he wanted nothing more than to give up the bar and villa, head straight for the airport and spend the rest of his days travelling the world with her. But that was a little too much fantasy, even for him.

They parted and got out of the car. Klara stretched her arms over her head, relishing the morning sun. 'Where to?'

King motioned to the narrow path between two residential buildings opposite the bar. 'That'll take you straight to the beach.'

'Meet you there tomorrow?' she said. 'Around midday?'

'Sounds like a plan. Goodbye, Klara.'

'Bye, King. Thanks for the night.'

She turned and frolicked away without a care in the world. A young, free spirit on a Mediterranean island. King watched her go until she disappeared from sight, then turned and made for the bar, swinging the Mercedes' key fob in a loop around his finger, whistling softly to himself.

Unaware that the illusion of calm would soon be shattered in devastating fashion.

CHAPTER 6

It happened at ten minutes to one.

The morning had been largely uneventful. Patrons trickled in, stopping by for a drink or two before continuing on their exploration of the seaside town. King served them all with a smile, content with his newfound good fortune, letting the positive aura wash off onto every customer he tended to. As usual, the atmosphere was pleasant and vibrant, soothed by the sound of tropical birds and the faint echo of waves lapping at the shore.

Then a man stepped through the open entrance and wandered towards the bar, walking with a pronounced limp in his right leg.

At first, King thought nothing of him.

He was clearly different to most of the people that came in, but that was nothing to be alarmed about. Instead of the carefree nature of a tourist with no particular destination in sight, he carried himself with a certain level of concentration and focus. Like he had somewhere to be, and not a lot of time to get there. It didn't bother King. He must be on the island for work.

He was a little taller than the average, somewhere around six foot. His skin was the colour of mahogany, indicating Arabic roots. He had dressed oddly for the climate, wearing cargo pants and a black leather jacket that seemed slightly too large draped across his slender frame. His long straggly hair had been parted at the middle, falling at random to either side. Thick strands were tucked behind his ears.

His beady eyes — wide and alert — flicked across the room in a measured and deliberate pattern. Scanning every corner for potential threats. Always vigilant, always switched on.

The look of a man accustomed to conflict.

Instantly King noticed this, because he himself had very similar tendencies. He studied the man in a new light. It took the guy eight steps to cross the room and reach the bar. He sat at a stool and nodded to King, who nodded back. The exchange was nothing but a pleasantry. There was nothing behind it.

'Can I get you something?' King said.

The guy cocked his head and looked at him for a moment too long. The sort of prolonged silence that indicated all wasn't as it seemed. Then he shook it off and shrugged. 'Yes.'

'Beer?'

'I do not mind.'

King shrugged in turn and slid a Pietra across the table, the same brand he'd given to Klara. Most people seemed to enjoy it. He found it odd that the man hadn't entered the bar with any idea as to what he wanted. But he recognised the mannerisms.

This guy was clearly some kind of combatant. Either a soldier, or a bodyguard, or something much more sinister. But King didn't think it had anything to do with him. The man simply didn't know how to relax. Something King himself had struggled with for too long.

He sympathised.

The guy picked up the beer with his right hand and took a long swig. His left arm dangled uselessly by his side. King quickly realised it was a prosthetic. The sleeve of his jacket rested in an unnatural fashion against the plastic or carbon fibre or whatever the artificial limb was constructed from. King hadn't noticed it until the man was right near him.

His gaze wandered up to meet the man's eyes, hazelnut in colour. More importantly, they were cold and detached. And they were boring into him. Like the man was trying to connect the dots of a long-forgotten puzzle.

'I'm Jason,' King said.

'Afshar,' the guy replied, his accent thick and heavy.

'What brings you to Corsica?'

'Work. No time to relax.'

'I see.'

'Who are you?' Afshar said abruptly, refusing to peel his gaze away from King's face.

'I'm sorry?'

'I know you.'

'Do you?'

'I recognise you. I am not sure where from.'

Under the bar's heavy countertop, King slowly clenched his knuckles. An inkling of his past began to scratch at the surface. 'Is that why you came here?'

The man shook his head. 'No. I come to get a drink. My business is elsewhere. But you are familiar.'

Then King felt it. A sudden twinge from somewhere deep down, like a hazy memory bubbling its way to the surface. He wasn't sure what it meant, and he didn't have time to dwell on it. But it wasn't good. He knew that much.

'I'm just a bartender,' he said.

The guy shook his head. 'What do you know about Ta'if?'

'Ta'if?'

'In Saudi Arabia. What do you know about that city?'

Recognition crashed over King in a wave. Suddenly he knew exactly what the twinge signified. He knew exactly where he remembered the man from.

And he knew why the man recognised him.

'That life is in the past,' King said, his voice low and controlled. He knew that one wrong step could get him killed. 'I have nothing to do with it anymore.'

'It is not that simple, my friend,' Afshar said. 'It is not luck that I came across you.'

'I'm sorry about what happened.'

'Are you?'

'Yes.'

'I do not think this makes a difference,' Afshar whispered. King heard the sound of the man's teeth gnashing together in rage, grinding the enamel away as he battled to control a wave of emotions. 'It seems you are living the good life now.'

King had nothing to say. He silently clasped his fingers around an empty glass bottle from the bin underneath the counter, ready to smash it over Afshar's head and deliver a staggering right uppercut into the man's throat if such a response was required. For the first time in months, he felt the rush of adrenalin into his chest. His heart rate skyrocketed. His breathing quickened. He would react to the slightest level of hostility.

It would be necessary if he wanted to stay alive.

The two men stared at each other across the bar for what felt like an eternity. It wasn't the first time they had met. King had expected their first encounter to be the last. He hadn't anticipated that fate would bring the man into this very bar.

He had forgotten the guy existed.

Afshar's face had blurred into a kaleidoscope of memories he'd been determined to lock away, mixed into the hundreds of brutal skirmishes that had taken place in the darkest corners of the third world.

'A very good life…' Afshar said in a low tone, casting his eyes around the bar.

'I'm sorry,' King said again. It was the last time he would say it. 'It was business.'

'Of course it was.'

Afshar got off the stool and began to slowly back away from the bar. One hand was empty, and the other was plastic. He was unarmed — clearly telling the truth about the encounter being unintentional.

If he'd known that Jason King owned the bar in Calvi, he would have come armed to the teeth.

He paused by the entrance, refusing to tear his gaze away from King, hate flowing freely behind his pupils. A couple of tourists in their mid-twenties — previously deep in conversation — stopped as their attention was drawn to Afshar.

'Good to see you, Jason,' Afshar said. His voice cracked as he spoke. 'Good to see you…'

He spun on his heel and disappeared from sight, stepping down into the courtyard.

King dropped the bottle back into the trash, leant against the countertop and breathed a sigh of relief.

CHAPTER 7

The day drew to a close without incident.

Tourists and locals alike flowed in and out of the bar, but Afshar did not return. King spent the remainder of the afternoon on edge, his skin cold and his hands clammy. At any moment he expected the man to return with an automatic rifle. King knew he would see the barrel of the weapon first as it protruded through the open entrance. Then Afshar would follow, squeezing the trigger, unloading a few dozen rounds of ammunition across the room. King might see a brief muzzle flash before the lead tore into him and stripped him of his consciousness and his life.

Every time a shadow passed across the front patio, he expected his life to come to an end. However, as the sun touched the horizon and began melting into the ocean, the last customers drifted out of the bar and King found himself alone.

He closed up, his actions filled with haste. He moved with the efficiency of an ex-soldier who had been viciously thrust back into the situational awareness of years past. He found it hard to force the cortisol in his veins away after it had been unleashed. He was ready to fight, but there was no-one to deal with.

You're retired, King.

He locked up and paused on the deck, scanning the courtyard for any sign of activity. Nothing. Not a peep. Convinced that the encounter had been a once-off, he fished the Mercedes' key from his pocket and made to unlock the coupe.

Something stopped him.

He looked out at the beach curving around the bay, bathed in an amber glow by the twilight. Tourists frolicked in the shallow water, laughing and interacting. He decided to watch the sunset from there. Usually he headed straight home, often making it back to the villa before it got dark. But he wasn't afraid to admit that the encounter that afternoon had shaken him. It had been a stark reminder of a past he couldn't just forget.

He wished to reflect.

He left the Mercedes where it was and navigated through Calvi, strolling ambivalently, trying to return to the way things had been. But he couldn't. His mood had shifted. Every time he rounded a corner he assessed the scene for dangers as fast as he possibly could. It had only taken a single moment in time to revert everything to the way it had been. He feared that all the progress he'd made in forgetting the past had been ruined. He found the beach and dropped down to the sand, sitting cross-legged, watching the sun begin to disappear.

He couldn't help but think back to Ta'ir.

The operation had taken place during his second year of working for Black Force, a clandestine wing of the Special Forces that existed on no official documents. Already the money had come pouring in, millions upon millions of top-secret government funds heaped into his account in exchange for the devastating services he could provide, services which had been detected during his time in the Delta Force and quickly made use of. It had only taken a year for his reputation to become something of legend. Sixteen times in that first year he'd been thrust deep into enemy territory, tasked with a wide range of objectives ranging from hostage recovery to elimination of terrorist threats. Each time, he'd succeeded in quick and brutal fashion, leaving a trail of bodies in his wake.

He'd killed ninety-six men that first year. He would never forget that number. It had been the beginning of what would go down amongst those in the know as the most successful military career in United States history.

Shame that those who knew of his feats numbered in the low single digits.

The situation in Ta'ir had surfaced out of nowhere. It had been a matter that required an urgent and unforgiving response, which was why he'd been contacted.

Black Force officials smuggled him into Saudi Arabia under the guise of human traffickers. He'd spent three days buried in the depths of a rickety wagon, barely able to breathe, eating and drinking when he could. Finally, they got him close enough to the Saudi compound to cut him loose. They armed him to the teeth and sent him into a rogue facility containing chemical WMDs.

He could not deny that he had been ruthless. There was no room for speculation in regards to the weapons. They were there, and intel indicated that a mercenary force intended to use them for malevolent purposes.

He had cut a swathe through their ranks, infiltrating their compound through sheer overwhelming force.

Early in his career he quickly found that it wasn't difficult to shatter morale and break the order of things with a few bullets and a lack of conscience. He'd used the same strategy to escape from a corrupt Venezuelan prison not two months prior to arriving in Corsica.

He remembered Afshar clearly.

King was the reason that the man was missing an arm.

Afshar was a soldier of fortune, and at the time he'd been tasked with protecting the WMDs from any enemy forces —

clearly for a hefty sum of blood money. King knew nothing else about the man, but he held no empathy for what happened to men of his moral standing.

King had burst into the laboratory with a trail of bodies left in his wake. He laid eyes on a truckload of nerve agents capable of decimating an entire populated city. Afshar intercepted him from the side, knocking his gun away.

They'd brawled in the cold steel room, wild and violent and animalistic.

King ended up securing the upper hand and — spurred on by the consequences of failure — wrenched a fire safety axe with a fibreglass handle off the wall near the lab's entrance. He had taken Afshar's arm off near the shoulder joint with a single calculated swing.

It had ensured that the man would not put up a fight while King secured the WMDs. The loss of a limb had the uncanny ability to freeze anyone in their tracks. Nothing else mattered in that moment except the enormous pain and shock of such a violent action.

The mission had unfolded without a hitch. King had left the compound an hour after entering it. All the enemy forces had been taken care of. He called in U.S. reinforcements to neutralise the WMDs and disappeared into anonymity in the bowels of Saudi Arabia.

Moving onto the next task.

Never resting.

He hadn't given Afshar a single thought after that day. In his mind, anyone who willingly protected such devastating weapons, keeping them in the hands of terrorists who had every intention of using them, deserved what was coming to them. King had left the man in a pool of his own blood inside the laboratory and thought nothing of it. He'd moved on.

Somehow, some way, Afshar had walked into his bar nine years later, on the other side of the planet. Their paths had crossed again.

King couldn't help but worry that it wouldn't be the last he'd see of the mercenary.

He got to his feet as the sun vanished under the horizon and night began to descend over the Bay of Calvi. Street lights flicked on and a pleasant murmur sounded from the Quai Adolphe Landry as tourists emerged from their hotels and headed into the multitude of restaurants lining the bay. King took a long sweeping look around. He couldn't imagine trouble finding its way into such a peaceful town on such a serene island.

He hoped Afshar would focus on whatever work he had come here for and put the sighting of Jason King well behind him.

King made it back to the Mercedes within moments. The bar lay dormant and dark, locked up until the next day. He made a mental note to erect a sign in the window early the next morning, informing the patrons that the bar would be closing early.

He had a date with Klara that he had no intention of skipping.

He climbed into the leather seat and felt the smoothness of the wheel. He thumbed the "ENGINE ON" button and the coupe roared to life. Luxury cars were an interest he hadn't anticipated, but he'd fallen deeply in love with the German engineering of the AMG. With an incomprehensible amount of funds still stored in his personal account, he imagined an upgrade would be in order down the line. Perhaps a 458 Italia. He reversed out of the space and took off towards Calenzana.

Towards home.

Four miles up the mountain, unbeknownst to King, a trio of hardened men in balaclavas received radio instructions that their target had left the bar. They thumbed the safety off their weapons in unison.

CHAPTER 8

King stayed alert, but it seemed unnecessary. At this time of the evening, traffic was basically non-existent.

He decided — given the tense nature of the confrontation earlier that day — that letting off a little steam was in order. As the street lights of Calvi fell away and the silver coupe glided into a twisting mountain road ascending past rolling hills and craggy ravines, he pushed the accelerator to the floor and let speed take over. Maybe it was fear spurring him on, but he found himself determined to reach the confines of his walled property.

There, he could relax and de-stress after the fragment of his past life had resurfaced.

The engine roared as the speedometer ticked up to eighty miles an hour. He stamped the brakes as he approached a bend in the road and turned hard. The tyres bit into the asphalt and squealed. He straightened the wheel on the other side and let the car correct course, finding purchase on the mountain road and gaining forward momentum.

King let out a hoot of joy and slapped the roof of the coupe. He didn't cut loose often. He'd made a couple of mountain runs before, but never at night. The danger reinvigorated him.

'Don't do this,' he muttered to himself, restoring calm. *'Don't.'*

He knew why the speed excited him as much as it did. He'd lived his whole life skirting perilously close to death. When he strayed too far into normality, he felt like he wasn't *truly* alive. It was a bad mindset to hold, and he'd done his best to eliminate it during his time in Corsica. Taking the C63 to blistering speed would not help him. It would only reintroduce the feeling of living on the edge.

He made the decision to slow down.

Then suddenly his whole world went mad.

With the speedometer rising fast towards the ninety-mile-an-hour mark, he took his foot off the accelerator and moved it across to the brake. Before he pressed down, he tore his gaze away from the road ahead for a split second and checked the speed at which he was travelling.

That was enough.

When he looked up, his headlights illuminated three figures crouched by the side of the road a couple of hundred feet ahead. He couldn't make out a single thing about them, but their hunched outlines were enough to spike his heart rate. There shouldn't be a soul in these parts. He was travelling through the middle of nowhere. A cluster of individuals could only be there for a single reason.

He slammed the brakes with sudden urgency and fish-tailed the Mercedes to the right.

It wouldn't help.

The windscreen exploded in a deafening hurricane of glass. At the speed the coupe had reached, the shards came flying inside the vehicle, whipping around the interior as King swerved violently off the road in the opposite direction to the three men.

He didn't hear the gunshots above the racket, but he'd been through enough to know bullets were tearing the chassis to shreds. With a pounding heart he ducked under the line of sight and kept all his weight pressed firmly on the brake pedal.

Too little, too late.

The coupe slowed as it left the asphalt and bounced viciously off the gravel surface. King felt the wheels shuddering under the uneven ground and quickly realised that would be the least of his problems. In the sudden explosion of noise and confusion he hadn't managed to work out exactly where he was on the mountain trail, but in all likelihood there were ravines and valleys on either side of the road.

He closed his eyes, kept his foot on the brake, and hoped for the best.

Hoping achieved nothing.

The whining of tyres on gravel disappeared all at once and a terrifying moment of silence descended over the Mercedes' interior. King knew he was in serious shit.

Next came the stomach drop as the coupe lurched over the edge of *something*. He wasn't sure what. Blind to how bad the situation was, he sat up to get his bearings.

He swallowed hard and braced for impact.

He knew the drop could easily be fatal, depending on which way the chips rolled. The front end careered off the edge of a steep descent packed with boulders and scrub jutting out at all angles. Enough forward momentum and the car would enter a barrel roll for well over a hundred feet.

But if luck fell on his side…

With a roar that sounded from everywhere all at once, the Mercedes smashed into a boulder, crumpling one side of the hood. The airbag exploded out of the wheel, impairing King's vision. He jerked against his seatbelt. It tore the air from his lungs and punched a thick invisible fist into his sternum, winding him. The car spun horizontally and its tail ploughed into a second rock, demolishing the chassis in a violent explosion of parts. His head flew back, carried by the momentum, and smashed against the headrest. He bit down hard on his tongue. He tasted blood and let out a grunt of pain.

In its final throes, the Mercedes rotated a full revolution, rolling onto its roof and then slamming back down on its wheels. It came to rest wedged in the middle of a cluster of rocks, all the windows shattered, all the tyres burst, most of the chassis nothing but a dented mess.

King let his heart rate settle and sucked in a full breath of air. Droplets of blood made their way down his throat. He coughed and forced himself to calm down. He was badly shaken by the sudden turn of events, but the hundred-thousand euros of German engineering had done their job, protecting him from any significant injuries. A cheap second-hand car might have been torn to pieces by the impact.

He looked out over the deflating airbag, into darkness. Both headlights had been destroyed by the crash. He couldn't make out much more than faint outlines, but they revealed enough.

The car had come to rest at a fourty-five degree angle roughly a quarter of the way down a steep and uneven slope. Surrounded by boulders and dead undergrowth and the occasional laricio pine tree, King found that the coupe had fallen far enough to block the line of sight from the road. He made out several decent areas to take cover from his position in the driver's seat. As the loose parts that had come off the Mercedes during its descent skittered away, the final noises of the crash faded into obscurity.

Silence settled over the hillside.

King heard faint voices from the road above, speaking in Arabic. He had spent enough time in that part of the world to form a rudimentary grasp of the language. He translated as best he could.

'*Did you see that?!*' one man cried.

Another responded, '*You think we hit him?*'

A voice that King recognised as Afshar spoke, a little softer. '*If we didn't, the fool killed himself. Did you hear the sound of that wreck?*'

King undid his seatbelt and gently slipped a hand into the door handle. He swung the battered thing out and shimmied out of the demolished car, a little bloodied and bruised, but overall no worse for wear. Making no noise whatsoever, he crouch-walked around to the rear of the car, taking care to stay in the lee of a nearby boulder despite the night enveloping his massive frame.

'You're going to be fucking sorry you didn't hit me,' he whispered as he noiselessly lifted the trunk and withdrew the fully-loaded Beretta-M9 he kept inside.

CHAPTER 9

Like a bad dream, ten years of experience came roaring back.

So much for paradise.

He thumbed the safety off and slipped a finger inside the trigger guard. A warm evening breeze blew gently down the hillside, ruffling his hair. There were no sounds of wildlife. The slope was barren enough as it was, and the noise of his car hurtling off the edge of the road above would have scared away the few animals that populated the region.

If Afshar had survived this long as a mercenary, then he was a skilled and ruthless bastard. King wouldn't underestimate him. Most employees in his field got rich quick and disappeared, or died trying. Turning the life of a soldier of fortune into a long-term career was an incredibly rare trait to possess. King had done it. He knew a handful of others that had.

Therefore, he placed Afshar in that category of individuals. He knew that dispatching him would be no small task.

They would come down to verify his dead body, without a doubt.

He would intercept them when they did.

He pressed himself against the nearest rock, feeling its smooth texture against his bare shoulders. He became still and listened for the sound of Afshar and his thugs. Three men made noise descending a treacherous slope in the dark — no matter how adept they were at masking it.

Then he felt it. The same feeling he'd experienced a million times before. The feeling he'd worked so hard to avoid.

He felt *true* calm.

This was what he did. It was all he did. *How could he deny that any longer?*

Poised quietly in the dark, waiting for enemy forces to come searching for his head, King felt an unbridled thrill. It started at the base of his spine and worked its way up in an involuntary shiver.

He loved it.

And he couldn't deny it.

A cluster of twigs snapped a few dozen feet up the hillside. King noted the position of the sound and crept around the perimeter of the boulder, taking care in each step, using the limited visibility to scour the ground for anything that might accidentally signal his own location.

He ducked out of sight just as the trio reached the wreckage.

Judging by the sounds they made, the three men approached from different angles, surrounding the car. Their guns would be raised. King kept his breathing low and steady. A soft glow emanated from the edges of the boulder, which meant one of them had lit up a flashlight. That meant...

One of the men cursed quietly in Arabic and shut the light off instantaneously. King smiled wryly. They were good. Most would panic when they found the car empty. These three didn't. They quieted down, probably already in the process of spreading out.

Putting distance between the potential targets.

But they'd made a fatal mistake by bringing the light out in the first place.

The boulder had protected King from direct exposure to the light, so his eyes were still adjusted to the dark. The beam's close proximity to the trio meant that it would take them a moment to re-adjust.

King rounded the boulder fast, not caring how much noise he made. Any shot headed his way for the next few seconds would be entirely blind as their vision became accustomed to the night. He took his chances.

He raised the Beretta and fired three rounds as soon as he made out the shape of a bulky man near the wreckage.

A trio of blinding muzzle flashes tore across the slope, the light illuminating all the surroundings for a brief moment. The guy King aimed at grunted from the first bullet, but the other two shut him up for good. He jerked like a marionette on strings and slapped across the hood of the Mercedes. The sound was wet. Blood had already begun pouring from his fatal wounds.

Before the other two had time even had time to register what had happened, King was gone.

'Ahhh, motherfu—' Afshar cursed in English.

A couple of wild shots tore past the space King had occupied a second ago. But he wasn't there to see it. He skirted round to the other side, hurdling a fallen log, and crashed down into a thick clump of undergrowth. Thorn brambles tore into his calf. He felt warm liquid run down his leg and swore under his breath. But the pain was secondary to what he needed to do.

With twelve rounds left in the box magazine he let off an eight-round volley over the space of two or three seconds. He was just as blind to his targets as they were to him, all disoriented by the muzzle flashes. Hopefully — sheer volume would lend a hand.

Afshar's other friend let out a blood-curdling scream.

King noted his success and dropped into the scrub, pressing his face through a mass of branches and brambles, burrowing his bulky frame as deep as it could go into the undergrowth. He had to disappear to throw Afshar off.

After all, he had no idea what kind of firepower he was facing.

The answer came swiftly.

King recognised the familiar stutter of a HK sub-machine gun sounding from somewhere near the wreckage. Displaced air washed over him as bullets tore across the space above his head. He couldn't work out whether it was an MP-5 or an MP-7, but it didn't matter.

Afshar emptied the entire clip in his direction. King kept his head down and clenched his jaw tighter than he thought possible, riding out the wave of stress crashing through him. His chest constricted and he gasped for breath. Towards the end of the barrage, a single round ripped through the bush he'd burrowed into, coming dangerously close to ending his life.

Then the gunfire ceased.

King figured he could make it to the wreckage in four seconds at a full-pace sprint. He didn't think Afshar could eject an old magazine and chamber a fresh one in that time. It was a complete guess, but he had to act instantly if he wanted a shot.

He burst out of his rudimentary cover and descended the short stretch of hillside with exaggerated, powerful strides. Halfway to the wreckage, he realised he'd gained far too much momentum than he originally anticipated. In fact, he was out of control. He didn't think he could stop himself without collapsing in a heap.

Afshar heard his large frame bounding towards the Mercedes and poked his head out of the wreckage.

King fired the last few rounds in the Beretta before the gun clicked dry. All of them missed. He threw the useless weapon away and leapt with everything he had.

He skimmed across the roof of the wreckage, clearing it with barely an inch to spare. Wildly out of control, he thrust two hands out as he passed over the Mercedes, hoping to seize any kind of grip on Afshar's clothing and drag him along for the ride.

He looped three fingers inside the guy's jacket and held on for dear life.

The mercenary lost his balance as King snatched him and the two of them slammed into the jagged ground, smashing the breath from their lungs. They tumbled down the hillside, unable to slow themselves or get their bearings. King saw flashes of his surroundings mixed with rocks and gravel and branches crushing him, smashing him left and right. Pain flared across his body. Finally, he struck a boulder and lay still. He spat a mouthful of blood onto the ground and staggered to his feet, taking care not to lose purchase on the steep mountainside. Another fall like that would prove disastrous.

Enough damage had been done already.

It had been a while since he'd felt pain so intense. Before he made sense of where he'd landed and worked out where Afshar was, he took a few deep breaths in an attempt to calm his heart rate. His head swam and veins bulged against his skin. Air came in shallow, rapid gasps. It seemed the agony bored into him from everywhere at once, like an old friend returning. Thankfully, he had years of experience dealing with this sort of thing.

Then again, so did Afshar.

The mercenary had come to a halt on the hillside in equally devastating fashion. His real hand was wrapped around a tree root a few dozen feet away. He was covered in dirt and blood. His prosthetic arm dangled uselessly. Traversing this kind of terrain was difficult enough for King. He couldn't imagine trying it one-armed.

He set off fast, moving away from the boulder, groping for handholds on the steep ground, finding temporary purchase as he made his way towards Afshar. The Mercedes' crash site was at least a hundred yards above them, buried somewhere in the scrub, well out of reach. He'd sacrificed his own wellbeing to take weapons out of the equation.

He fancied his chances in a fistfight against a one-armed man.

Perhaps not entirely fair.

But nothing was fair in this world.

As he got closer, he began to make out more details through the darkness. Afshar's face was a bloody mess. His nostrils poured red. His eyes were half-closed. His breath came in rattling waves. King approached warily, wondering if the man was really as injured as he appeared to be.

He wasn't.

King took a final step across the hill, knocking loose dirt down the slope, and came within range. As soon as he did, Afshar activated. The mercenary struck out with a steel-toed boot. The blow came so fast that King could do nothing to avoid it. He felt the blunt tip of the shoe sink into his ribs with considerable technique and force behind it. It hurt like all hell. He stumbled on the hillside and reared back, away from the point of impact, away from the pain. He slipped once, then again. He shot out a hand and found a clump of bushes growing out of the ground. It corrected his balance and he paused for a moment, breathing hard, wincing from the crippling pain coursing through his sternum.

He'd broken two ribs only a few months ago, deep inside an abandoned cruise ship in Venezuela. He knew the feeling well.

This wasn't as severe, but it had certainly stunned him.

Afshar surged at him.

The half-dead look had been a ruse. The man was bloodied and bruised, just like King, but his consciousness had been preserved. He scrambled across the hillside with venom in his eyes, determined to finish what he'd intended to do on the road above.

King grit his teeth and knew he was in for a fight.

'*What about your payment?!*' he roared as Afshar charged at him.

It meant nothing. It was a vague, open-ended question that could have applied to a number of things, none of which King knew anything about. He'd thrown it out there with the sole purpose of creating a second's hesitation, nothing more.

Afshar's pace slowed. A confused look spread across his face for a brief instant — but in King's world that was more than enough.

He used the branches to catapult himself across the space between them. He took two steps on the loose dirt, knowing his purchase would probably give, but that didn't matter. He just had to get within range. He crashed into Afshar, disorientating him. He slipped two hands behind the guy's head and gripped his long greasy hair. Then he smashed the man's forehead into the hillside.

Once.

Twice.

Three times.

Now he was truly incapacitated.

King knew that he had the upper hand. He used the change in momentum to shift his position. He leapt onto Afshar's back and used all his weight to flatten him out against the dirt. At the same time, he wrapped his thighs around the man's waist, known in grappling circles as "sinking the hooks in". Afshar was going nowhere. King looped an arm under his neck, pressing into his throat, and cut off the blood flow to the brain.

Then he squeezed with everything he had.

It didn't take long.

It was far from a pleasant experience, but it was the least painful way to kill the man with his bare hands. Despite Afshar's hostile intentions, King found no pleasure in drawing out suffering unnecessarily. So he held the choke for a long minute after Afshar had slipped into unconsciousness, ensuring that he died. Holding it even a few seconds after the opponent passed out could cause massive brain damage.

King left no room for speculation.

He climbed off the body silently, the muscles in his arms screaming for rest. It took a certain level of energy in a life-or-death battle that he hadn't tapped into for a long time. He found himself intensely tired. He dropped his butt onto the dirt near Afshar's motionless corpse and looked out across the valley.

Adrenalin racing through his veins.

A trio of dead mercenaries on his hands.

How had it descended to this yet again?

CHAPTER 10

After such intense conflict, the Corsican evening was dead quiet.

King wasn't sure how long he sat in the dirt, staring into space, thinking hard. It could have been hours for all he knew. He zoned out completely. Thoughts of violence and anger raced through his mind, sparked by what had occurred.

He couldn't fathom how fast things had unfolded.

He'd been cruising peacefully through the night not five minutes earlier. Now, his whole world had been overturned. He glanced over to the dead mercenary beside him and shook his head.

'Why, you bastard?' he cursed. '*Why?*'

He reached out and slipped a hand into the man's jacket. There was a flat object in the inside pocket. King withdrew a modern smartphone and tucked it into his own jeans. Then he patted down the rest of his clothing, turning up nothing. With his work complete, he pushed Afshar hard, sending the corpse rolling down the hillside, gaining momentum, slowly disappearing from sight.

Afshar clattered and bounced into the darkness, and then he was gone.

As always, it didn't take long for the pain to settle in. King knew he could shut it out in the heat of the moment, but that was nothing more than delaying the inevitable. He felt his ribs burning, his cuts and gashes stinging, his head pounding. He grimaced and picked himself up. He had all the time in the world to feel sorry for himself later.

For now, there was plenty to sort out.

He couldn't go to the police. As usual. A man of King's abilities brought an unparalleled level of violence to any confrontation. There were two men riddled with bullets above him, and another beat and choked to death below. He thought back to a pair of hitmen he'd killed in the backwoods of Australia, and felt a wave of deja vu.

Once again, he begrudgingly accepted that a panel of jurors would be hesitant to believe the argument of self-defence in a situation like this. It meant things would change drastically. His car was a wreck, resting halfway down the hillside. There wasn't a chance he could move it, or hide it. It had been purchased under his own name — the same name he'd purchased the villa in Calenzana with.

He swore loudly, unable to help himself. The curse ripped through the valley, echoing as it broke the night's silence. He got his feet under him and began the painstaking process of climbing back up the hill, heading for the road. As he did so, something very close to an anxiety attack began to form, deep in his chest.

His breathing quickened. He closed his eyes, and for a moment he felt like crying. He spat another glob of blood into the dirt near his feet and pressed on. The new life he'd forged for himself had always felt too good to be true.

He'd originally chalked the feelings up to a change in setting. He wasn't used to peace, and he had to grow accustomed to it, that's all...

He couldn't have been more wrong.

In a fluid chain of events, his retirement had been torn to shreds. He couldn't stay in Corsica. There wasn't a single scenario in which he could imagine that playing out to his advantage. Every avenue led to arrest, and a lengthy trial which he was likely to lose, given his imposing nature and the savagery with which his enemies had been brutalised.

He passed the crash site. The Mercedes was battered into oblivion, its entire chassis beat to shit, shattered glass dotting the ground all around it. King took one look at it and shook his head in disbelief, surprised he'd survived the crash relatively unscathed. The bodies of Afshar's goons were sprawled across the dirt. With his senses still reeling, he couldn't make out much more than the fact that they were both dead.

It was too dark to discern where exactly his bullets had struck them. He knew the first guy had died from the direct impact of King's shots. He had no idea where he'd hit the second, but the man must have bled out from his injuries. There was nothing else to see.

King ducked into the destroyed coupe and retrieved a few personal items he needed for what lay ahead. His phone, wallet, and keys to the villa. The smartphone had been resting loose in the cup holder at the time of the crash, and as a result its screen had been shattered in the carnage.

He left everything else in the car. None of it mattered.

He stole a final glance at his car for the last time, and continued towards the main road.

Calenzana was within walking distance. Maybe not for an unfit tourist, but King had made many a trek in the past. He was hurting in dozens of different places, but it was nothing out of the ordinary. He worked out his priorities as he continued to climb the hill.

Get back to the villa.

Pack a bag.

Disappear.

Nothing he wasn't used to. But this time, he felt it would leave a bitter taste in his mouth.

He'd been rather enjoying his time on the island.

The road was deserted this late in the evening. A warm breeze swept up from the ocean, washing over the quiet mountain road. King stood under a weak streetlight, staring out at the landscape stretching out in either direction. On any other occasion — a beautiful sight.

Now, it was the last thing on his mind.

He turned and set off up the hill, focused on putting one foot in front of the other. It would be a long walk. But he was marching in the direction of a luxury villa — not a terrorist camp, or a top-secret government compound, or a drug-production facility in the middle of the jungle. Those days were long gone. The appearance of Afshar was an unfortunate experience, but it really shouldn't have surprised him given the amount of enemies he'd made in the past. It was an isolated event. The violence had been intense, but that would be the last of it.

He regretted what had happened, but he would move on from it.

He always did.

He sighed and listened to the sounds of wildlife slowly return as the killing and chaos settled into the past.

CHAPTER 11

In the end, it only took a couple of hours.

King reached Calenzana as the hour ticked steadily towards midnight. He stuck to the side of the road, not bothering to try and catch a ride from the occasional car that passed by. There was no chance of anyone picking up a man of his stature in the dead of night. He ignored their headlight beams lighting him up until they'd passed him by. He pressed onward.

The town was deserted as he strolled into its centre. The locals were shut up in their houses, either asleep or close to. He faced no questions or queries from passers-by, because there weren't any to encounter. As the journey came to an end, the pain had all but subsided. His injuries weren't serious. The cuts and bruises would heal. As he stepped onto the gravel trail leading up to his property, he took a moment to gather his wits.

Things could be worse.

He still had a fortune in the bank. He could move freely about until the attention from the three dead bodies subsided. There was no greater conspiracy to end his life. An old enemy had recognised him and tried to finish the job, and King had retaliated. That was all.

But isn't that how it always begins?

He shook off the feeling that there would be more to it than the fight on the hillside, and trudged towards his walled property. A wave of tiredness crashed over him. The standard come-down from an adrenalin high. He shook it off. He could rest when he was on a plane.

He scanned the tag on his keys against the electronic panel by the gate and entered the code he knew off by heart. Gears whirred and the gate began to move, shattering the silence. King stepped through as soon as there was space and made quickly for the house.

Motion-sensor lights flicked on as he crossed the courtyard and headed for the front door. Normally, he would welcome the warm glow, pour himself a drink and settle down for a quiet night in. Just as he had for the past couple of months.

Not tonight.

With his heart pounding in his chest and the blood rushing to his head, he slipped through the front door and made a beeline for the bedroom. He retrieved a large black duffel bag from the closet and began sorting through what possessions were truly necessary.

Not many, he concluded.

He dropped a few changes of clothes into the bag, followed by a laptop and a few books. Looking around the vast home, he realised that none of it mattered enough to bother worrying about. He'd been plagued by the feeling that nothing in the villa truly belonged to him, probably due to spending so much of his life on the move. Now he was abandoning his home once again, yet it felt perfectly normal.

He slung the duffel bag over his shoulder. As he stepped back out into the kitchen, he figured that it should probably feel worse to be leaving behind a multi-million dollar home. Surely it wasn't normal that the change of setting barely affected his emotions. He'd been overwhelmed back on the hillside, but now he was unperturbed.

Darting from place to place was all he'd ever known.

In a way — even though he was leaving behind everything he'd worked hard to achieve — he was returning to normality.

He looked down and saw the blood caked over his arms. His singlet had been shredded by either the crash or the tumble down the hill. He couldn't leave like this. Nothing drew attention more than blood.

He dumped the duffel on one of the kitchen stools and took a quick shower in the deluxe en-suite bathroom. He scrubbed away the dirt and filth, shampooed his hair, and dried quickly. He walked naked into the enormous walk-in wardrobe — still largely untouched — and took a moment to assess his physical condition before getting dressed.

Like he'd predicted — just superficial injuries. Nothing was broken. A large gash had dried on his right forearm, but apart from that he'd emerged from the confrontation with little to show for it. He slipped into a pair of designer jeans and a long-sleeved V-neck T-shirt, thin enough to keep him comfortable in the warm Mediterranean climate. He left thousands of dollars worth of clothing on their hangers and slipped back into the kitchen, leaving his bedroom for what would probably be the last time.

He froze.

He wasn't alone.

A silhouette loomed in the living room, watching him silently.

There was a second Beretta in one of the drawers built into the kitchen's marble countertop, but he would never make it to the gun in time without catching a hail of bullets in the process. That was if the assailant wanted him dead, of course.

Even stranger was that — as the man stepped out of the shadows — King realised he recognised the guy.

'I saw you on television yesterday,' King noted, his voice ringing through the large open space.

Yves Moreau.

The enthusiastic politician folded his arms across his chest and leant back on the edge of the couch, indicating that he had no hostile intentions and wasn't armed. He was dressed in a casual grey suit and an open-necked shirt. His thick hair was unruly, spilling back behind his ears. 'Did you? Very nice. I enjoyed delivering that speech.'

'How'd you get in here?' King said.

'You must be in a hurry.'

'I am. You can tell?'

'Well, you left the gate *and* the front door wide open. That shows me you're leaving.'

'I am.'

'May I take a moment of your time?'

'I'm very tempted to put a bullet in you for having the nerve to walk in here unannounced.'

'Desperate times call for desperate measures.'

King hesitated. 'What do you want? Make it quick.'

Before Moreau could respond, King crossed the kitchen in one fluid motion and wrenched a certain drawer open. He withdrew the Beretta M9 — already fully loaded — and thumbed the safety off. He placed the handgun on the marble countertop and clasped his hands together behind his back.

'That's there in case this turns out to be something else,' he said.

Moreau stiffened when he saw the weapon, and shook his head. 'I don't mean any harm.'

'Don't be offended if I don't take your word for it just yet.'

'What I'm about to say might stir a reaction.'

King raised an eyebrow. 'Oh?'

Moreau's hard eyes bored into him from across the room. 'I know you killed three men a couple of hours ago.'

CHAPTER 12

King snatched the Beretta off the kitchen countertop and had it aimed at Moreau's head before the man could utter another word.

Moreau raised a finger. 'That's what I was talking about when I mentioned a reaction.'

'I should kill you now.'

'But you won't.'

'And why's that?'

'Because I believe you to be a good man.'

'That's a risky assumption. What if I'm not?'

'Then I'd be dead already.'

King hesitated, but his aim didn't falter. He didn't shake, he didn't display emotion. He just kept the barrel trained on Moreau with a steady trigger finger fixed into place. But both he and the politician knew that he would not shoot unless he was antagonised. 'How do you know what happened?'

Moreau rose off the couch and took a single step towards the kitchen. King tightened his finger just a fraction. Enough to get the man's attention. He stopped moving.

'Stay right there,' King said.

Moreau raised both hands, signifying innocence. 'I'm not who you think I am. Those men were here to kill *me*.'

King paused. 'You're sure?'

'I'm the only politician on the island preaching anti-corruption right now,' Moreau said. 'That attracts … attention. I'm sure you can imagine why I have a team of people responsible for my safety. They caught wind over the last few days of a few undesirables floating between towns, asking all sorts of questions. We've been working with passport control for a couple of days. All signs were pointing to one Afshar Nawabi, and a few of his friends.'

'He's dead. Two of his friends are too.'

'I know that. We were tracking his phone via GPS. The wonders of government espionage technology. We were about to arrest him on conspiracy to commit murder. Tonight, instead of returning to his hotel room, he drove all the way out into the hills, spent ten minutes on a hillside, and now he's—' Moreau withdrew a smartphone from his suit pocket and glanced at the screen, '—here.'

'He's at the bottom of that hill,' King said. 'I'm here.'

'So you have his phone?'

'Maybe.'

'I'd be very interested in seeing it.'

'Why should I care what you want?'

'I thought you might want to help out a good cause,' Moreau said. 'I'm close to breaking through to the masses in Corsica. If I can stay alive…'

'None of this concerns me. In fact, it freaks me out. I'd rather be on the other side of the globe.'

'You killed all three of them?'

'Maybe.'

'Then you must be a very dangerous man.'

'Maybe.'

'I could use you.'

King rolled his eyes, exaggerating the gesture so that Moreau could see. 'As what? A hired gun?'

'Afshar had more men,' Moreau said. 'They've clearly been paid to come out here, and I can only guess what their intentions were before they ran into you.'

'Do you know where they are?' King said.

'No.'

'Do you know who they are?'

Moreau shook his head.

'Then it's a lost cause. Give up and go back to your career.'

'You think it'll just end there? Who knows what will be thrown at me in the future? I need your help.'

King was fed up. He skirted round the countertop and picked up his duffel off the nearest stool. He slung it over one shoulder, tucked the Beretta into his waistband and walked across the empty space. He came within a few feet of Moreau and stopped.

'I spent a long time giving people my help,' he said. 'I came to your beautiful island to get away from all of that. I have no idea who you are. I'd never spoken to you until you decided to walk in through my front door. I'm very sorry about your problems but they don't concern me. Right now, I'm concerned with staying out of prison.'

'What if—?' Moreau began.

King held up a hand. 'If what you're about to say has anything to do with threatening me, or bribing me, or telling me that you can make all my problems go away if I help you — then please don't say another word. You might think it's a good idea, but don't bother.'

'And why is that?'

'You don't know who I am.'

Moreau shrugged. 'I would never stoop to such levels anyway. I only came here to see if you could help me get to the bottom of this. I take it your answer is "no".'

'You're correct,' King said.

'Shame.' The man rested against the back of the couch once more. He stared at the ground, unblinking, and for a moment King saw something very close to tears in his eyes. He wiped an eye to compose himself and straightened up. 'No matter.'

King sympathised, but he wouldn't be swayed. He remembered what a man named José had told him in Venezuela. If he wanted any hope of a normal life, he had to turn and flee at the slightest mention of violence or intrigue. And that was exactly what he would do here. He would not be seduced into old habits. 'How long have you been facing threats like this?'

'Ah, a while,' Moreau said, still staring into space. 'I am not a popular man amongst my peers. They pay off all the right people. I do not.'

Something deep inside King twitched. A nerve. A reflex. An old calling. *This man needs help.* He ignored it. 'How good is your team?'

A shrug. 'Good enough, I guess. We're doing great work here. We're close to getting rid of certain corrupt officials. I don't know which ones hired mercenaries, but it just proves that our strategy is working.'

'Well, as much as I hate the fact that you walked in here unannounced,' King said. 'I appreciate what you're doing for the country. And you'll probably keep facing threats, but you need to persist. I think you're a good man — from what I've seen on television.'

Moreau's bushy eyebrows widened and his expression turned hopeful. King brushed him off with a quick shake of the head. 'Doesn't mean I'm going to help you. I've got my own shit to sort out right now. It explicitly involves avoiding situations like this. I'm sorry. But good luck, Yves.'

He held out a hand, and the politician shook it. They met each other's gaze and exchanged a curt nod.

'I'm going now,' King said.

Moreau raised an eyebrow. 'You're just going to leave me here? In your home?'

King brushed past him and made for the entrance hallway, walking fast, determined to commit to his path before he was deterred. He spoke as he strode. 'For all I care, it's your home now. I need to disappear.'

'Why?'

'Like I said, there's things I need to take care of. I can't get wrapped up in anything else. I need to put distance between myself and violent confrontations.'

'You're a troubled man, aren't you?'

'I am,' he admitted. 'And I'd also like to stay a free man.'

King paused at the door, and took the opportunity to survey the villa one last time. It had been good to him, even though his stay had been brief. He'd forged memories within these walls that he would hold onto forever. But he couldn't stay.

'This is worth millions,' Yves called, as if to talk him out of abandoning the place.

'If you get elected while I'm gone,' King said, 'be sure to give it back to me when you're in office.'

'Not a chance. You won't help me.'

'Touché. Goodbye, Yves.'

He stepped out into a balmy Corsican night, regressing into the days of constant motion. This time, though, he had a plan. He would stick to it to ensure he could return to retirement as quickly as possible. It involved the opposite of what he usually did. It meant hiding, laying low, avoiding danger.

Things he was not accustomed to.

But he'd give it his best shot.

He crossed to the garage and unlocked a matte black Range Rover. He'd purchased the car as an off-road vehicle for when he needed to tow the ATVs into the mountains. He barely used it. But his preferred method of transportation was resting halfway down a hillside, completely destroyed.

The Range would have to do.

He slipped into the driver's seat, threw his duffel bag across the centre console and accelerated out of the mountaintop property for the last time.

As he got off the gravel path and the tyres bit the asphalt in Calenzana, King gunned the engine and gripped the wheel a little tighter. It was a one-road journey down to Calvi. There was something he needed to collect from the bar before he made for Sainte-Catherine Airport.

CHAPTER 13

Five hundred miles away in Montenegro, an African-American man sat alone at a table in one of the most luxurious casinos on the planet.

He was slightly taller than average, somewhere around six foot. Underneath the obscenely expensive leather jacket and designer jeans, there wasn't an ounce of fat on his body. He had the lean and wiry physique of a professional athlete. In front of him sat a pile of polished chips, stacked in orderly rows. The man shot a glance at his phone, checking his missed calls, before sliding the device back into his pocket and tossing one of his chips onto the green felt.

The dealer shot him a quizzical glance, but he had been personally cleared by the control room to have a no-limits table opened up for his own use. That's why he was in Montenegro.

'Confirming, sir,' the dealer said, 'that is one hundred thousand euros.'

'I am aware of that,' the man said. 'Now deal the cards.'

The dealer nodded curtly and began to deal.

The man received a queen. The dealer a five. Then a second queen for the player.

A phenomenal hand in the game of blackjack.

He couldn't pass up those odds. He slid another hundred-thousand euro chip across the table. 'Split.'

The dealer visibly blanched at the amount of money in play. He imagined his bosses would not be pleased if the high-roller cleaned him out. He parted the player's two cards, and wiped sweat from his palm before dealing a fresh card to each queen.

A four, and a five.

Awful for the player, unless the dealer busted.

'Fuck,' the high-roller whispered under his breath.

He watched the dealer draw two eights in a row. Coupled with the original five, that gave him twenty-one. The best possible outcome…

The man grit his teeth as he watched two-hundred-thousand euros of his hard-earned cash disappear into the dealer's till.

'Pleasure doing business with you,' he said through a tight jaw, then left before the dealer could respond.

Five steps away from the table, his phone buzzed. He slid it out of his pocket and stared at the incoming number. He didn't know the caller ID. Which meant only one thing.

He answered with a swipe of one finger and lifted the phone to his ear.

'Slater?' a soothing female voice said.

'Speaking.'

'Where are you? This is urgent.'

He looked around before replying. 'Thought we agreed to a week off.'

'Fuck that. We need you back now.'

'What is it?'

'Get yourself to Corsica as fast as you possibly can. You'll be compensated, as usual.'

'Corsica? What's this about?'

'We need you to take someone out.'

'What am I — a fucking contract killer now?'

'That's what you've always been.'

'I wouldn't put it so harshly.'

'I honestly don't care what you think. I told you, this is serious. You should be sprinting for a cab as we speak.'

'Give me some detail, at least.'

'Three dead bodies turned up in a ravine a couple of hours ago. Police are still investigating, but we know who it is. He's killed dozens in Venezuela and Australia before that. This is the last straw. It's time for damage control.'

'Damage control?'

'He used to be one of ours, Will.'

The penny dropped. 'Oh.'

'We let him retire based on the assumption that he'd stay out of trouble. Trouble seems to be the only thing he's got into since he left. We can't have a liability like that running around.'

'Is it King?'

Silence.

'Is. It. King?' Slater repeated, slower, more controlled.

'Yes.'

'You want me to kill Jason King?'

'I want you to try. If you can't, then I don't know what to do. But he can't keep doing this. He's out of fucking control — and you need to intercept him before he leaves the island.'

Slater pressed two fingers against his eyes and sighed. 'I'll do my best.'

'I'll send you everything we know when you're en route.'

'Got it.'

Slater hung up and dropped the phone back into his pocket. He made directly for the exit, passing wealthy socialites and expensive call-girls. The sight reminded him of something. With a grunt of disapproval he made another call, this one to the hotel reception.

A concierge answered in a pleasant tone. 'Good evening.'

'Hello. It's Will Slater.'

'Mr Slater!' the voice exclaimed. 'Are you enjoying your stay?'

'Very much so. But a bit of business has come up and I'm afraid I have to fly out immediately. Would you be able to cancel my reservation for the next two nights?'

'Of course, sir. I shall begin the process of refunding the eight thousand you deposited.'

'Don't worry about it,' Slater said.

'Sir?'

'And there's two women waiting for me in the suite. Please tell them I won't be able to oblige them. Give them some of the eight thousand if they don't approve.'

He hung up without elaborating any further. Another ten feet and he was out of the casino, exiting into a lavish shopping mall. He passed stores for Rolex, Armani and Chanel. The suited-up security guard out the front of the Rolex store gave him a slight nod as he passed by. Slater nodded back. He'd purchased a watch the day before. The staff tended to remember customers willing to drop a working man's yearly salary on a single timepiece.

Slater checked the time before ducking out of the building into a cold night in the Balkans. Soft streetlights illuminated a traditional cobbled path that twisted its way round the enormous complex. He hailed a taxi and slipped into the back seat.

'Airport,' he said matter-of-factly. The driver nodded and peeled away from the footpath.

Already, the two-hundred-thousand was forgotten. It was a drop in the bucket. Slater knew whatever lay ahead would yield a hundred times that amount. If he could successfully take down the most successful operative in his organisation's history, the benefits would be extraordinary. He regretted having to step away from the night he had planned with the two call-girls, but sometimes business held top priority.

When Black Force called, he answered.

Every single time.

He took a deep breath as the taxi bounced across the cobblestone, and did his best to relax. If Jason King was truly as dangerous as legend suggested, then he was in for one hell of a trip.

CHAPTER 14

The Range Rover pulled into the courtyard under the cover of darkness. There were no streetlights in this section of Calvi. King always arrived at the bar after the sun was up and left before it went down. He'd found no need to go to the trouble of installing floodlights or anything of the sort.

He didn't need them now, either.

In the black of night, he slipped out of the vehicle and crossed the gravel to the bar's deserted patio. He'd almost left without returning to this place.

But there was something here that he couldn't leave the island without. Something that he'd tucked away in a safe in Belfast immediately upon retiring, and had only returned to retrieve when he'd been certain of settling down in Corsica. Lucky he didn't have it with him on his previous travels, or it would have almost certainly been stolen or destroyed.

It meant more to him than anything he'd ever owned.

He unlocked the front doors silently, listening out for any kind of odd noise that could signify an enemy nearby. But there was nothing. The bar was well and truly empty. He crossed the room, dodging the faint outlines of tables and chairs in the darkness. He found a particular drawer tucked away in the corner behind the counter and slid it open. The bottom gave out after a slight shimmy and he moved it aside to reveal a tiny hidden compartment. Inside rested a velvet box, just large enough to fit the watch that lay within.

King opened the box and took out the watch. It was decades old, bronze and frail and expensive. The reinforced glass had been nicked and scratched over the years. He'd kept it with him throughout his entire career. Maybe it was a good luck charm. Maybe that's how he avoided death on such a consistent basis. Whatever the case, he wouldn't leave the country without it. It had been given to him over twenty years ago. It carried greater meaning than anyone could know.

He slipped the watch into his back pocket and threw the velvet box away. It landed somewhere in the middle of the room and clattered to a halt. King didn't care where it came to rest. If he wanted to truly bury his head in the sand like José had recommended, it would mean leaving everything behind.

He'd come to terms with that when he choked the life out of Afshar.

He couldn't stay here and risk arrest, or retaliation from any other mercenaries that happened to be roaming the island.

In all likelihood, the three deaths wouldn't have been tied to him, and he could have carried on living his peaceful existence.

But he didn't want to repeat the mistakes of the past.

All the unwanted trouble in his life had come from assuming everything would be okay. This time, he would not assume. He would catch the first flight out of Corsica — abandoning the villa, abandoning the bar, leaving it all behind. He would disappear. It was the only way to ensure that the three dead mercenaries on the hillside would be the last bodies he ever saw.

He chuckled softly in the unlit bar, unable to fool himself. He knew that idea was just a fantasy. Truth was, he wasn't sure if he would ever escape that life.

But he would *try*.

He left the bar without a second thought. He had spent his entire life on the move, which made letting go relatively easy. He didn't get sentimental. In fact, jumping on a random flight seemed to be a return to normality. It certainly hadn't felt natural having a place to call home in Calenzana. Maybe Afshar's appearance had been a sign that this life wasn't for him.

Nonsense.

You'd begun to enjoy yourself, he thought. He couldn't deny that. He would settle down again.

When he was sure that trouble had become a distant memory.

He climbed back into the Range Rover and fired it up. Before he sat down, he took the watch out of his pocket and lowered it into the centre console. It sent a sharp jolt through his chest, a feeling that he knew he had to act on.

He couldn't leave the island just yet, for a number of reasons. Sainte-Catherine Airport was tiny — there would be no overnight flights. From what he could remember, flights began at roughly ten in the morning. Which gave him the whole night to kill. He considered burrowing down in the Rover and getting a few hours sleep, but the memories around the watch nagged at him.

There was something he needed to do.

He put the 4WD into gear and crawled out of the courtyard, navigating the narrow streets of Calvi for what would probably be the last time. He soaked in as much of the town as he could. It had been good to him. For a few months he'd managed to taste peace.

Who knew if that feeling would ever return…

He left the seaside behind and ascended into the mountains, knowing exactly where he needed to go but struggling to muster the courage to continue. There was a small village called Aregno buried in the hills — a thirty-minute drive from Calvi. From the centre of the commune there were sweeping views down to the ocean, much like the view from Calenzana. King had driven through Aregno several times. He'd never stopped — even though that had been his intention.

Maybe this time he would stop.

He remained in brooding silence throughout the drive, coasting along the deserted roads. Every time he rounded a corner he expected to find another horde of mercenaries waiting for him, ready to tear his car to shreds at a moment's notice. Whether he liked to admit it or not, the encounter with Afshar and his men had triggered his combat senses, reviving the sensations of years past. His hands tingled and his chest pounded. It was unclear how long the feeling would last. But he knew he had been primed — switched over to a primal instinct and ready to kill.

As he drove, he thought of Klara. The timing of their fling had been unfortunate, to say the least. He'd truly been looking forward to spending the day with her. He knew he had to throw it all away. He had to discipline himself to forget everything about his life in Corsica. If he stayed here, he would invite trouble. He was sure of it.

Aregno was shrouded in darkness this late at night. The odd window was softly illuminated here and there, but apart from that the commune was silent, save for the warm mountain breeze wafting up from the ocean and whistling over the empty roads. King gently guided the Rover along the main road, slowing and indicating when he spotted a faded street sign branching off down a narrow lane.

He stopped the car in the middle of the asphalt.

He stared at the sign.

He sighed.

In truth, he had never built up the nerve to turn down the street. It was a slim gravel path curving between orderly rows of traditional Corsican houses, but to King it was so much more than that. He mulled over the decision for a long minute, the car's headlights flickering and wavering as they cut through the night.

Then he spun the wheel and turned down the street.

He followed the trail all the way down, until he reached the house at the end. It was a one-storey nondescript place with a terracotta roof and an air of homeliness. The lawn was immaculately groomed — clearly the work of the devoted home-owner. King cut the headlights as he approached the house and depressed the brakes until the Rover halted in the centre of the gravel path.

He killed the engine.

And then something made him stop.

He went to open the door handle but found himself unable to. He couldn't tear his eyes away from the house. All the lights were off. Whoever owned it was asleep.

Ever since he'd first landed on the island he'd been meaning to come here. Now he couldn't find the courage to approach. He couldn't knock. That would be too much to handle. He knew it was the right house, but the doubt and uncertainty that had plagued him for the last two months was barring him from getting out of the car.

He entered a trance-like state. He couldn't tell exactly how long he stared at the house, but eventually fatigue caught up with him. At some point during the night his head fell back against the leather driver's seat and he drifted into a dreamless sleep. He dozed undisturbed, until something jolted him awake in the early hours of the morning. He shook his head from side to side, rattling away the remnants of slumber, and looked around.

On the horizon, the sky was transitioning from black to blue. The sun would be rising shortly. Already his surroundings were brightening. He must have slept for a few hours, at least. The type of tiredness that occurs in the aftermath of a violent confrontation, when every shred of energy in his body had been expended in a brief period of time. His wrist ached, but apart from that he was unhurt from the hillside battle.

A light flicked on in the window of the terracotta-roofed house.

King's heart rate spiked as he saw the glow. It was the first actual evidence he'd seen that proved the house was inhabited.

That meant…

He panicked. With short, sharp breaths he slammed the Rover into reverse and spun the car one-hundred-and-eighty degrees across the gravel. The tyres rumbled on the uneven surface, drawing attention. King accelerated back the way he had come and reached the end of the street. He flicked the indicator to the left and turned the wheel. Before he returned to the main road, he glanced in the rear view mirror, catching a final glimpse of the house that had troubled him so much.

The front door was opening.

A figure began to emerge from the doorway.

King spun the wheel and took off, disappearing from sight, refusing to look back.

Another time. When he had time to process it.

Not now.

A few miles out of Aregno, he spotted a small scenic lookout surrounded by a low cobblestone fence, with views stretching for a hundred miles in either direction. At this time of the morning it lay deserted. King turned into the lot and stamped on the brakes. With shaking hands, he hunched low over the wheel and rested his forehead against the leather.

He burst into tears.

It hurt. He couldn't deny it. He rubbed a sleeve across his damp eyes and let the pain course through him, frustrated and angry and bitter.

Why couldn't he knock?

Why couldn't he get out of the car and approach the front door and confront the person on the other side? He could storm into a terrorist stronghold and kill anyone in his path — but what use was that when he struggled with this basic action?

He knew exactly why he couldn't. He'd built up an internal wall over the years, cutting everything that wasn't his career away. He had to break through that to move on.

And he couldn't.

He stayed in the lot for close to an hour. Every now and then, a salty droplet would run down into his mouth. He ignored it. Over his career he'd displayed a distinct lack of emotions, largely due to the uncanny ability to tune out anything that was not centred around the mission. He knew that letting this out was simply a process of healing. It didn't make it any less raw.

When the sun fully rose, beaming its golden rays over the hills, King sat up and composed himself. He coughed once, hard. He wiped his eyes one last time with his sleeve. Then he continued toward Sainte-Catherine.

He would return to this place one day, when he was a stronger man. He would knock on the door.

Until then, he had to flee.

CHAPTER 15

At dawn, Sainte-Catherine Airport was a ghost town.

Composed of a single terminal, a collection of car rental warehouses and a spacious parking lot, the complex was situated a couple of miles away from the seaside. King pulled into the long-term car park at fifteen minutes past seven, according to the luminescent display on the Rover's dashboard. He selected one of the hundreds of empty spaces and parked quickly. He was keen to board the soonest possible flight. He wasn't sure exactly why he had so effortlessly abandoned the life he'd carved out for himself on this Mediterranean island, but he knew he was doing the right thing.

It had something to do with past experience. Only a month after retiring, King had travelled to a small country town in the backwoods of Australia, where he'd witnessed something he wasn't supposed to. He'd decided to stay then, to seek answers to the questions eating away at his conscience — and it had led to a destructive swathe of violence, death and loss. He feared that Afshar and his friends would only be the start of his troubles if he stayed put and tried to forget the encounter had ever happened. He was already embroiled in the conflict. There was nothing he could do about that.

Except leave it behind.

He got out of the car, tucking the watch back into his pocket and slinging the duffel bag over his shoulder. He left the Rover unlocked and tossed the keys along the concrete. Either someone would be blessed with a free luxury vehicle, or it would be handed over to the police. Whatever the case, King would be a thousand miles away by the time either of those two scenarios played out.

He crossed the asphalt, weaving around the handful of cars parked in the lot, and crossed directly to the terminal. There was no shuttle bus to transport him to the departure gate. Everything was in close proximity. He entered through two glass doors that opened with a whisper as he approached them, and stepped into the high-ceilinged, sparsely populated terminal. Cafés and bookshops and fast food restaurants lined the nearest wall, and on the other side of the enormous room lay a collection of desks — each for a separate airline company.

King paused for a moment, relishing the heavy air-conditioning inside the building, and set off for the other side of the terminal. He decided to simply select a company at random. He hadn't decided a destination yet. He never did.

His entire existence was based on spur-of-the-moment decisions.

Halfway across the room, a set of double doors opened and a stream of tourists began to trickle out into the terminal, mingling with the few dozen people scattered around the various shops. The first arrivals of the day, clearly. King wondered if he'd been wrong. Maybe departing flights were leaving this early…

He saw pasty, unfit Caucasians dressed in cheap sandals and plaid shirts — all of them stressing about nothing in particular. He passed a bossy mother shuffling through her handbag, huffing and panting like her unpreparedness was the end of the world.

'David!' she exclaimed sharply. 'Where the hell is our booking reservation?'

A teenage boy rummaged through his backpack. 'I don't know. Ask Dad.'

King passed them by and continued on, shaking his head at the seemingly normal exchange. Civilian life perplexed him. The pettiness and unimportance of most of the world's problems never failed to surprise him. Booking reservations, lost tickets, cancelled events — it seemed crazy that anyone stressed over anything that didn't involve getting shot at.

Just before he reached the small queue to the check-in desks, he shuffled past a well-built African-American man with intensely white teeth and a military-style buzzcut. He was dressed immaculately in an expensive leather jacket and designer jeans. King made eye contact with him momentarily, and briefly nodded a greeting before he moved past.

Looks like a wealthy businessman on holiday, he thought.

He couldn't have been more wrong.

The fist came out of nowhere. King had rarely met his match in hand-to-hand combat, but he never could have anticipated what came next.

A flurry of frantic movement burst across his vision. Before he had time to lift a finger, something crashed into his gut, sending a wave of white-hot agony through his stomach. He opened his mouth to groan, and another fist smashed his jaw, scrambling his brain.

After the two blows in rapid succession, King saw a shin headed directly for his face, barely half a second after the last punch had cracked across his head. He ducked back, ignoring the pain racking his system, but it didn't faze his attacker. The kick landed square in the centre of his chest, stunning him, slamming the breath from his lungs. It carried such weight behind it that King sprawled off his feet. He lost his balance and toppled to the terminal floor.

He didn't even have time to see who his attacker was.

Another kick — this one similar to a soccer player taking a penalty — drove into his exposed ribs with enough force to send him sliding across the shiny floor. He gasped and retched and blinked away black spots in his vision. Each strike that landed carried years of training behind it. He felt the raw savagery and power in each brutal shot.

He collapsed and exhaled a long breath of nervous air.

The pain was severe, coursing through his body like nothing he'd felt in months, but that wasn't what paralysed King. It was sheer surprise. He always saw *everything* coming. His reflexes were an extreme outlier, which had enabled him such successes as a solo operator in an elite military division. It had kept him alive for years, because he saw blows coming eons before they landed.

But *this* was something inconceivable.

This was a foe who had beat him down like he was a common street thug.

He looked up to see the man in the expensive jacket standing over him. The guy looked calm and composed, like the savage beatdown was just another day at the office. He adjusted the cuffs of his jacket and smiled, exposing his white teeth again.

Around them, panic broke out. Surprised by the violence, most of the surrounding civilians had scattered. Some were screaming. King blocked the noise out.

So did his attacker.

'Hey, King,' the man said elatedly. 'Glad we could finally meet.'

'What the f—'

'Don't move,' the man said. 'I'll just drop you again.'

'Who are you?'

'I thought this would be harder,' the man said, ignoring him. He laughed and shook his head in bemusement. 'I spent the whole plane ride psyching myself up for this. You should have seen the manhunt I was ready to unleash. Then Jason King himself walks straight past me a couple of minutes after I get off the plane. Unbelievable.' He glanced at his fists, which had been bruised and bloodied by the hits. 'You know ... I thought you'd be faster than that, too.'

'Who are you?' King repeated. 'Afshar's pal?'

The guy cocked his head. 'What?'

'Never mind.' King spat blood onto the linoleum beside his head. Already, his cheek had begun to swell.

The man pointed to his face. 'You'll feel that tomorrow.'

'I'm going to keep asking who you are until you tell me.'

'Will Slater,' the man said.

King sighed. 'Thanks. That answered every fucking question I had.'

Slater squatted down so that his face was only a foot away from King's. 'You don't have to know who I am. I was sent here to kill you. And I intend to do so, because it pays well. But

112

I had a plan laid out to acquire a couple of firearms when I arrived here — which clearly I haven't had the opportunity to carry out yet. And I don't fancy beating you to death in a packed terminal with airport security on their way. So count yourself lucky.'

'You seem pretty blasé about all this,' King said through bloody teeth.

'I'm used to it.'

'So am I.'

Slater's eyes bored into him. 'You don't seem insane.'

'Who said I was insane?'

'My employers.'

'And they are?'

A voice cried out from behind, 'Sirs! Please leave!'

Slater wheeled around. King looked past him to see a panicked secretary fumbling with a landline phone.

Slater turned back to let loose with another quip, but by the time he did so King was on his feet. King grit his teeth and clenched his fists.

You were taken by surprise, he told himself. *Won't happen again.*

He charged Slater, bundling him backward, using his considerable size advantage for his own benefit. He knew the man could let loose with powerful and precise shots if he had the distance. Hopefully, by closing the gap, he would disorientate the man.

It wouldn't be so easy.

An uppercut shot through the narrow space between their chests with incredible speed. King saw the blur a millisecond before his jaw cracked and his teeth crunched together and his eyes closed involuntarily. But now he was within range.

And he was mad.

He rolled with the punch, taking most of the serious power out of the connection, then swung with a haymaker of his own. His fist shot through the air like a released piston and caught Slater on the side of the head. The sheer power behind it knocked the man off-balance. He stumbled once and righted himself.

Then Slater burst forward, dropping low, reaching his arms out as if searching for one of King's legs. Hunting for the takedown. If the man's wrestling skills were half as good as his stand-up, King knew he could end up being punched into unconsciousness if Slater took him to the ground.

He dropped his hands, reacting reflexively, determined to stuff the takedown attempt before it could unfold.

But Slater wasn't there anymore.

Fuck, King thought.

He had already committed himself to a downward trajectory by the time the kick came swinging at his head. His reflexes were superb, but he couldn't avoid momentum. He recognised that Slater's fake had caught him out just before he met the full brunt of the man's shin with his own forehead.

A sharp crack.

Disorientation.

The world spinning.

King was on the ground, dazed. Maybe concussed. He couldn't tell exactly what had happened — often a side effect of taking a brutal blow to the skull — but he knew that Slater had taken the upper hand.

Again.

The man was undeniably good. This time, there would be no more fighting. King was out of the equation. Both men recognised that.

King looked around with wide eyes, trying to make sense of his surroundings. Slater adjusted his clothing again.

'Here comes airport security,' he muttered. 'Well, I'm off. I'll see you again very soon.'

He turned and strode out of the terminal, disappearing as effortlessly as he had manhandled King.

Like a one-man wrecking ball.

King sat on his ass. He saw three shapes heading for him, yet they were too far away to properly make out. His head was still swimming. He wasn't sure of the severity of his head injury. Hopefully it wouldn't be so debilitating as to incapacitate him for the next few days. He needed to stay alert if he wanted to survive whatever the hell Slater was going to throw at him.

Whoever he was.

King got tentatively to his feet as the three officials approached. Two men and a woman. One had a semi-automatic pistol drawn and the other two wielded handheld tasers. They looked stern, yet unsure of themselves. He didn't imagine there were security issues at Sainte-Catherine Airport very often.

'Sir,' one of them said in accented English. 'Do not move.'

King wiped his bloody mouth and nose with his sleeve and corrected his balance. 'I apologise for that. My friend and I had a bit of a disagreement.'

'You're going to have to come with us,' the woman said, brandishing her taser menacingly.

King looked at her and raised an eyebrow. 'Why?'

'We'd like to ask you a few questions.'

King pointed at the sliding doors. 'I'll be leaving.'

'Sir...' one of the men said.

King pointed at his gun. 'You think I'm scared of that?'

'I'm sorry?'

'I have at least fifty pounds on each of you,' King said. 'You're not going to stop me by force. I got into a fight — nothing more, nothing less. I'm going to walk out of here now, so if you really want to stop me, you're going to have to shoot me.'

The man with the gun stared blankly at him.

'You ever killed a man?' King said.

Silence.

'You willing to do so?'

Silence.

King turned on his heel and left the terminal, his head swimming, his nostrils streaming blood. He clutched his ribs as he walked. Each step sent a small bolt of pain through his sternum. He winced and pressed on.

There was no noise from the security personnel. At no point did King expect a bullet to punch through his back. The three officials had approached a scenario well above their pay-grade, and it seemed they were now frozen in place, unsure of what the right move was.

Before they could decide, King was gone.

He stepped out into a balmy morning and made for the orderly rows of car parks. As the sun rose higher, the activity had increased. He had to skirt around a row of vehicles to lay eyes on the space where he'd parked the Rover.

It was empty.

King's eyes widened and he wheeled around, searching desperately for a target. In the distance, he saw his car turn out of the lot with Slater at the wheel. The man looked across as he peeled away from the airport and they locked eyes.

Slater touched two fingers to his brow and then brought them down in a mock salute. He grinned and left King stranded at the airport, roaring away into the Corsican morning.

CHAPTER 16

King assessed his options.

There were few.

He had no chance of making it onto a flight here at Sainte-Catherine. The incident with Slater had ensured that. If he tried his luck, he'd be met with a taser. And arrest was the worst possible outcome right now. It was the only reason he was leaving the country.

To distance himself from the heinous crimes he'd committed up near Calenzana. To lay low until both the police had lost interest and the rest of Afshar's mercenary friends had given up on finding the perpetrator.

The nearest airport was in the town of Bastia, close to two hours away from where he currently stood. To get there, he'd need a car and a hefty dose of luck. He didn't fancy his chances of making it halfway across the island without running into Slater.

Who the hell was he?

As King felt the pain intensify in various areas all over his body, he stood immobile in the quiet parking lot and shook his head in disbelief.

The encounter had been undeniably jarring. Not so much due to the pain he was in, but because of the *ease* with which he had been dispatched. He didn't often find his physical equal — a man who could keep up with his incredible reaction speed and martial arts prowess. Usually, if any altercation in his life resorted to hand-to-hand combat, he came out on top.

It was the field he excelled in.

And Will Slater had manhandled him.

King hadn't landed a single blow. The experience was so shocking that he felt his hands grow clammy. A cold sweat broke out across his brow. He wasn't sure if it was due to the head kick, or due to something he hadn't felt in years.

True fear.

Even when Afshar and his friends had made an attempt on his life, he hadn't been *scared*. He'd reacted accordingly, implementing his training, ensuring he seized the upper hand in the heat of the moment. But at no point had he thought the three mercenaries were a physical threat to him. This mystery man who he had never seen before in his life had rattled him more than any of the confrontations he'd faced over the last couple of months.

He had to leave Corsica.

He knew he could speculate all day as to who Slater worked for, and why he was being targeted. Yet he knew it would achieve nothing. The truth was he had no hard facts, no evidence whatsoever, and his main priority had to be reaching a plane — whatever the cost.

He shoved his hands in his pockets, wiped his bloody nose on the shoulder of his shirt and headed for the parking lot's exit. On the way he tapped his back pocket, checking the old timepiece was still there. It would get him through the next few hours…

… or he would be torn to shreds as soon as Slater got his hands on a weapon and tracked him down.

Neither outcome would surprise him. The shock of the beating wouldn't fade for a while. Until then, he knew he would be constantly on edge. Even as he walked he flicked his gaze from side to side in paranoid fashion. Searching every nook and cranny for any sign of Slater, or one of Afshar's friends, or a curious law enforcement officer.

How easily you slipped back into the old routine, he thought.

Always vigilant. Always alert. Never relaxing.

Retirement hadn't lasted long.

Two cars entered the lot in unison. King sized up each vehicle as they pulled into a pair of empty spaces. He quickly selected which one to target.

The first car he studied looked like it would fall apart at any moment. An old hatchback, with peeling paint and a sun-faded interior. King dismissed it instantly. Its sole occupant got out and crossed to the terminal, wheeling a cheap stuffed suitcase behind him. He was young — in his early twenties — and he seemed stressed, like he was late for a last-minute flight. King let him pass.

The man didn't need the added hassle.

The other vehicle was a matte black BMW four-wheel-drive. A man in a tight-fitting button-down dress shirt, expensive slacks and cream-coloured loafers stepped out onto the hot asphalt and checked his cufflinks. King noted his designer sunglasses and his wife's pristine dress and heels as she clambered out of the passenger seat. They clearly had money. King saw the man pop the trunk and extract a Louis Vutton duffel bag.

An abundance of money, he thought.

Anyone willing to drop serious cash on a fucking travel bag was definitely financially stable. King made up his mind and approached the couple. He was glad that they were well-off.

Because what came next would set them back.

'Morning,' King said with a smile as he shuffled toward them.

The guy shot him a quizzical glance. 'What do you want?' he said in accented English.

King pointed at the BMW. 'I need that car.'

The man scoffed. 'Funny.'

He looked up, finally taking the time to study King, and what he saw made him hesitate. King knew he was still reeling from the beating Slater had dished out. It would show. He hadn't properly cleaned his bloody nose and lip.

He looked like a homeless junkie, more than likely.

The man stuck out his chest with a false aura of confidence and waved King away like he was a rabid dog. 'Fuck off. Get out of here.'

King outstretched both hands in an apologetic gesture. 'I'm very sorry about this.'

'Fuck off.'

'I can't do that. Give me the keys to the car or I'll hurt you.'

The woman let out a soft gasp, like a tense situation had just become all too real.

Which it had.

King knew what would likely come next. The man — desperate to appear superior in front of his gorgeous wife — would probably let out a little of the adrenalin coursing through his system. But he was an upper-class member of society, and street brawls likely weren't his forte. So he wouldn't resort to punches. Not yet. A shove was the likeliest option.

King prepared for it.

The guy took a fast step, closing the gap between them, and thrust both hands out in the exact move King had predicted would occur.

He flipped a switch and went from annoying bystander to trained killer in an instant. He seized one of the man's wrists in a vice-like grip, moving twice as fast as him with four times the efficiency. He wrenched him down, throwing him off-balance. The guy let out a panicked squawk similar to a parrot in distress as he toppled to the hard ground. King smiled at the outburst.

Everyone reacted to getting overpowered in different ways.

He rolled the guy over with his foot and planted the sole of his boot on his chest, ruining his clean shirt. He squatted and used both hands to flip out the man's pockets in one fluid motion. Before either he or his wife could react, King saw the keys tumble out of his right-hand pocket and jangle to rest on the asphalt. He scooped them up and brushed past the two civilians.

They wouldn't know what had hit them. Sudden blunt force did little damage, but it would be shocking enough. The man's heart would pound in his chest for the next hour, and then everything would be okay.

They'd buy a new car.

The world wouldn't end.

King's would if he didn't get the hell out of Corsica.

He dropped the keys into the centre console, depressed the brake and thumbed the *ON* switch. The BMW roared to life. Before the owner got any smart ideas and decided to give chase, he slammed the car into "DRIVE" and took off, peeling out of the lot.

As he climbed the roads back into the hills, passing the occasional vehicle descending into Calvi, he forced down the cocktail of thoughts bubbling in his mind. Experience in the field had taught him that speculation was useless unless he had serious reason to believe something was the case. He had no idea who Slater was. He had no idea how many other friends Afshar had on the island. He had no idea whether Yves would give up King if interrogated.

He shoved it all away and cleared his head, focusing on the road in front of him and nothing else.

It was a bright morning. The wind howled in through the open windows, drowning out the pleasant music wafting out of the speakers. The owner had good taste. King leant an elbow on the sill and took a deep breath.

He was actually doing it.

Turning away from conflict.

Burying his head in the sand when the going got tough. Just like José had told him to in Venezuela. It didn't feel right, but retaliating would only lead to more chaos.

He'd had enough chaos for one lifetime.

He urged the luxury vehicle a little faster, keen to cover the fifty-five mile drive in record time. Every corner he turned he expected to see Slater standing by the side of the road, fully armed, a ghastly mirror image of Afshar and his men.

Except he knew Slater wouldn't miss.

Whoever the man was, he was a different breed of combatant.

Like King.

CHAPTER 17

He crossed the mainland without incident.

Before long, the drive blurred into another ordinary cross-country trip. King kept one hand on the wheel and turned the music up and — for a brief while, at least — let a slight sense of normalcy return. He doubted Slater would intercept him on the way to Bastia. Unless he'd covertly managed to spot King's vehicle theft and tail him without detection. Which King highly doubted had occurred. He was pretty good at spotting tails, and it would be all but impossible when there was this little traffic on the roads.

A cluster of bustling commotion, Corsica was not.

Even though he knew he shouldn't, he began to grow a little optimistic. He doubted the staff at Sainte-Catherine would rush to radio a description of King to every airport on the island and instil a no-fly-ban on anyone fitting his description. The fight with Slater in the terminal had been violent and disruptive, but it hadn't been enough to warrant that kind of reaction. He would reach Bastia, jump on the next commercial flight to the furthest corner of the globe and continue to enjoy a life without incident.

At least, that's what he told himself.

He couldn't shake the feeling that the emergence of Will Slater wouldn't go away so soon.

It troubled him to have such an experienced enemy. Mercenaries he could handle. Drug gangs and hired goons and street thugs were annoying, but he could deal with them. It wasn't anything he hadn't seen before.

Slater was.

The only person he'd seen move with such fluid efficiency, able to dish out such massive and savage violence…

… was himself.

Who was the man?

He shook it off, knowing no answers would come unless he sought them out. Aware that nothing would cause more trouble than searching for them. He'd done the same thing in the backwoods of Australia — with devastating results. Best to leave things unexplained. Best to leave the bloodshed far behind.

It didn't matter who Slater was.

Staying alive did.

The BMW whispered through the mountain range in the centre of Corsica. King kept his eyes on the road as he weaved between rocky cliff-faces and passed deep gorges. Every so often he glanced out at the terrain and surveyed the land. He glanced down the face of a particularly steep ravine and a shiver ran through him like a bolt of energy.

Large purple welts and bruises had formed across one side of his neck, where the leather seatbelt had bit deep into his flesh during the Mercedes' barrel roll the night previously. As he studied the drop, the area tingled. He remembered the terrifying uncertainty of the crash. Not knowing whether he would live through the next few seconds.

Then again, he'd spent most of his career in that grey zone.

He passed through the most hazardous terrain without any surprises. Despite the lack of action, his knuckles remained white, clenched tight around the wheel. He figured the jarring nature of Slater's arrival would play on his mind for weeks or months to come.

An hour and a half into the trip, he realised he couldn't deny his growling stomach any longer. He'd masked the need to eat and drink for a significant length of time. He was fast approaching his threshold. It had been almost twenty-four hours since he'd consumed anything. Refreshments were required. He wanted to be at peak performance by the time he reached Bastia.

In the unlikely event that Slater had gunned it to the closest airport in an attempt to intercept him, he wanted to be ready for a fight. This malnourished, he didn't stand a chance.

Ahead, a faded street sign rested between a fork in the road. On the left, the asphalt peeled away from the main road, spiralling down towards the now visible coast. King had never been this far north. He was still relatively new to Corsica. He studied the coastline and spotted a small commune on the water's edge, bathed in the morning sunlight. A sizeable marina curved around a bay much similar to Calvi's.

He kept his foot on the accelerator for a moment longer, thinking, weighing up his options.

Fuck it, he concluded. *You were a Black Force soldier. You shouldn't be scared to get refreshments.*

He flicked the indicator on and left the highway behind. The BMW's tyres purred as they mounted the rougher path, handling the cracked asphalt well. He glanced at the street sign as the 4WD whisked past.

Saint-Florent.

Pretty name.

Even though he had been rapidly approaching his third month in Corsica, the beauty and architecture of the towns never failed to impress him. He slowed as he made his way into Saint-Florent, trawling through narrow lanes lined with traditional beige houses, all sporting the familiar schist tiles. He passed cafés and restaurants and a handful of tourist shops.

Eventually he burst out onto the marina — sparkling in all its glory. He paused for a moment at an intersection, surveying the crystal clear water and the enormous pier lined with seaside restaurants, bars and delis. Luxury yachts similar to those resting in Calvi's marina bobbed up and down in the ocean, tied to either the pier or equidistant buoys.

The driver behind him leant on the horn.

King waved a gesture of apology and continued on. He found a busy parking lot close to the marina and spent a few minutes creeping down each aisle, searching for an empty space.

As he did so, he thought of Yves Moreau.

Every single part of him had wanted desperately to help the man, to accept his offer back in the villa and work tirelessly to take down whichever of Afshar's friends remained on the island. King knew it was an instinctive response, hardwired into his system. It's what he had done for decades. It's all he had ever known.

Fighting corruption. Ending lives. Saving lives.

But José's words back in Venezuela had cut deep into his psyche. They'd made him realise that helping others was exactly what had created such a painful and turbulent life for himself. Sure, it satisfied him to succeed. He never felt as alive as when his life was on the line — and he came out on top. A sick obsession, most would say. One developed from years of violence and espionage.

But he'd done enough.

He'd saved enough innocent people.

He'd killed enough savages.

It wasn't his responsibility anymore. That duty to protect others had ended when he stepped away from Black Force. The sole purpose of his retirement had been to find peace. He would never achieve that if he continued to throw himself headlong into danger.

Hence fleeing Corsica.

He found a park at the edge of the lot and slotted the nose of the BMW up to the brick wall. He got out and tucked the key into his pocket and made for the pier.

One quick meal. Then back on the road.

He found a restaurant named the *Saint-Florent Seaside* complete with a long open counter. Bar stools lined the length of the long counter, all facing a centre space populated by chefs, waitresses and bartenders. The stools swivelled, providing a pleasant view of the pier's edge and the bay beyond.

King sat and ordered a jug of water and a pair of club sandwiches. They would satiate his needs until he made it onto a flight, at which point he would probably order everything on the plane. Caving into desires was something he'd recently embraced after a lifetime of denying himself such privileges.

He couldn't help but admit it felt good.

He turned to stare out across the marina. As he did so, a cool barrel jammed into his side, pressing between two of his ribs with considerable weight.

'You really thought I wouldn't be able to find you?' a low voice whispered in his ear.

Slater had positioned himself close enough to mask the sight of the gun from any passersby. Out of the corner of his eye, King saw the man sporting a false jovial expression, as if they were merely two old friends greeting each other after a long time apart.

'I figured you would,' King muttered back.

The steel pressed harder into his ribs. He grit his teeth and rode out the rush of cortisol flooding his veins. Adrenalin was a potent drug. He knew controlling it would be his best bet at survival.

'For a Black Force soldier, I thought you'd be better than this,' Slater said. 'You're an amateur.'

'I'm flattered.'

'You're going to stand up and walk with me. You saw my speed at the airport. If I even get a glimpse that you're not doing as I ask, I'll put a bullet in you. I know you're fast. I'm faster.'

'You should already have put a bullet in me.'

'Not just yet. I'm very curious about you, King.'

'Who are you? You seem to know a hell of a lot about me.'

'Of course I do. You were our best operative before you up and left.'

King froze. Pieces began to fall into place. Who else could match him in hand-to-hand combat, make him look like a fool so effortlessly? Only a member of the most covert organisation on the planet, made up of a handful of soldiers with combat ability far ahead of any of their colleagues.

Black Force.

Slater was one of their operatives.

King had never known the others. Due to his strict demands to operate as a one-man show, the higher-ups never integrated him with the rest of the cohort. He kept a low profile, and carried out the government's wishes. He hadn't even known that there *were* others.

Yet here was another, pressing a gun into his side, nothing but a finger twitch away from fatally wounding him. King assumed that the man knew exactly where his vital organs were, and exactly how to target them with utmost precision.

After all, he himself did.

And Will Slater was the closest he had found to an equal in his long and eventful life.

'You want me to walk with you?' he queried, still perched tentatively on the bar stool, listening to the soft ocean breeze and the hushed murmurings of surrounding civilians. It all appeared so very peaceful. No-one had clued into the tense stand-off happening in their midst.

Slater nodded. 'We're going somewhere a little more secluded.'

King raised an eyebrow. 'I'm sure you're smart enough to know that every second you unnecessarily keep me alive is a massive risk.'

'I'm aware of that,' Slater said. 'It's worth it. I'd like to ask you a few things.'

King flashed back to coming face-to-face with his old Black Force handler — Lars — in the Australian countryside. The man he thought he'd known had been revealed as a monster, hell-bent on releasing a cloud of anthrax over a populated city to compensate for a career kept in the shadows. Now, it seemed Black Force held another traitor in its ranks.

As King got to his feet, he shook his head in bemusement. 'You know, the whole time I was working for our organisation I thought it was pure.'

Slater tucked the sleek black pistol into his jacket pocket in one fluid motion, so fast that King couldn't get a glimpse at the make of the gun. Whatever the case, he knew he was still in enormous danger. He saw its barrel poking against the expensive leather, unwavering, trained directly at King's torso to ensure complete certainty of a hit.

Then the man cocked his head. 'The fuck are you talking about?'

King stayed where he was. 'I didn't realise the lot of you could be bought off so easily. First Lars, then one of the operatives. Money's that important, huh?'

Slater smiled wryly. 'Who do you think's paying me for this?'

'It doesn't matter,' King said. 'Politicians, mercenaries, dictators — I'm guessing it's one of Afshar's friends?'

A pause. 'You couldn't be more wrong.'

'What?'

'You're out of control, King. Command didn't like the amount of bodies you're leaving behind. They think you're a liability.'

It hit King like a truck. 'You don't mean…?'

'This is just another mission,' Slater said. 'Black Force wants you gone. And I'm happy to oblige.'

CHAPTER 18

The knot in King's stomach twisted and turned as he set off back toward the mainland. Slater followed closely behind. The new revelation had come as a gut punch. Afshar and his two dead friends were something else — completely unrelated. Slater was a ghost sent from Black Force to make sure Jason King could cause no further damage.

How had it come to this?

He'd simply wanted to live out the rest of his days in Corsica, undisturbed, confronting no-one and keeping largely to himself. The illusion of a calm existence had been shattered after only a couple of months. He guessed that after wreaking such havoc for so long as a black-ops mercenary, it was impossible to ever truly escape the past, especially because there was so much of it. Sooner or later, someone was bound to come searching for him.

His blood boiled as he thought of the useless suits in Command taking one look at the amount of people he'd killed in his "retirement" and deciding he needed to be wiped off the face of the earth. They didn't know the context. They didn't know that dead men were exactly what he had been trying to avoid by stepping away from Black Force.

'What's your plan?' he said, knowing that the wind would carry his voice to Slater, who matched his pace effortlessly.

He couldn't see the man respond, but he heard it clearly, 'After I kill you?'

'Between now and killing me,' King said. 'You think I'll give you any kind of answers? What do you want to know?'

'Many things. I've never met a co-worker before.'

Ah, King thought. *So it wasn't just him.*

Clearly, Black Force operatives were kept apart, unaware of each other's existence. 'You're playing a dangerous game.'

'I'll take my chances,' Slater said.

The man was confident after the airport encounter. He'd gained the upper hand early and held it. He thought that had exerted enough dominance to remain in control by reputation alone.

Time for King to show him that they were more equal than he thought.

'Command told me you'd be coming,' he said, in a low tone, hushed, like he was privy to secret information. 'Did you check the hills before you came down here?'

A completely meaningless question. King had no idea that Slater would come after him, and no idea that Black Force had been involved. Slater would probably deduce the same. But for that split second — he was confused. His brain would process what had been asked, and his eyes would involuntarily flick to the landscape ahead, wondering whether there really was anyone up there with a gun trained on him…

'What—?' Slater begun.

King spun. Opened his hips. Lashed out. The motion was charged with rabid intensity, helped by the knowledge that if he was a millisecond too slow, he would catch a bullet in the chest for his troubles.

He threw the kick to the mid-section with blinding speed. Years of practice on heavy bags had lent him that power. It thundered into Slater's side with impressive force. There was an audible *crunch* as King's shin made contact with the jacket pocket containing the gun.

Slater's face contorted in agony. He stumbled once, thrown off-balance by the blow. King noted the man's speed as he came back with a punch of his own, but he threw it half-heartedly, still reeling from having the breath knocked out of his lungs.

King batted it away and darted into range, letting fly with an uppercut. Even as he swung, he knew it would connect. The spark that came with a plan unfolding perfectly swelled through him. His knuckles hit the underside of Slater's chin with impeccable accuracy, snapping his jaw back, smashing his teeth together, dazing and disorientating him all at once.

The man lost his footing and fell back, landing hard on his rear, dropped by two devastating shots. It took less than two seconds.

Bam, side kick. Dodge lazy punch, shoot in, land uppercut.

Game over.

King knew it wouldn't take long for Slater to get his bearings and find a target with his pistol. He couldn't let that happen.

Never slowing down, he dove for the side of the marina. His fingers reached for the low barricade running along the edge even before Slater had finished his fall. The man's head whiplashed against the pier's wooden planks as King grabbed hold of the top slat and vaulted over the side.

He fell for a second. Slater and the rest of the marina disappeared from sight. The surface of the ocean rushed up to greet him and then he plunged into the warm Mediterranean sea in a blast of noise and frenetic motion.

He knew it wasn't enough. He had to put as much distance between himself and the pier as humanly possible so that he didn't find himself dead at the bottom of the ocean, riddled with lead. He came to a halt a few feet under the surface. Eerie silence unfolded, in direct contrast to the bustling commotion of the pier. He tread water for a moment, getting his bearings.

The ocean floor branched away in all directions a few dozen feet below him. Saint-Florent's bay wasn't deep enough to escape Slater that way. Besides, despite the SEAL training that he'd undertaken early in his career, eventually he would run out of air. He could hold his breath for three minutes. Maybe four. Enough time to swim a fair distance laterally.

He noticed a cluster of dark objects hovering at the water's surface fifty feet away, closer to the shoreline.

The marina.

That was certainly a way out.

He started to swim almost as soon as he came to rest in the ocean, using a powerful breaststroke and his long limbs to make fast progress. He'd never been a Navy SEAL, but he'd gone through their training. Black Force had worked him half to death in an attempt to capitalise on his incredible reaction speed.

Sometimes, he was thankful for what they'd put him through.

He covered the distance to the boats over the course of a long, tense minute. As he swam, he made sure to descend further from the surface, putting as much space between himself and a potential bullet as he could. At any moment he expected to feel the soul-crushing punch of a round tearing through his skin, piercing his lungs, his heart, his brain.

Would he feel it?

Or would death be instantaneous?

He could only hope for a quick death. The worst he could imagine was a bullet to a limb that incapacitated his ability to swim. He would sink to the ocean floor, bleeding out and drowning at the same time. The thought of such a result urged him forward.

He reached the crusty hull of a speedboat on the marina's edge without a scratch to show for it.

It meant the uppercut he'd landed on Slater had done significant damage. Perhaps the man was still recovering. King knew he had to use every available moment to get away. He was dealing with someone just as adept at combat as himself.

A rare occurrence, to say the least.

He surfaced and took a quick glance up at the pier. There was no sign of Slater. Either he was still recovering from the knockdown, or he had found an advantageous position out of sight and King would soon be dead.

Whatever the case, he had no other options but to press forward.

He studied the nearby speedboat. It was silver, polished to perfection, large enough to hold more than ten people. Luxury vessels weren't King's forte, so he didn't know what type of boat it was, or if it was any good. The brand on the side read *MasterCraft* in bold blue lettering. The number *35* was imprinted toward the back of the boat.

It would do the job.

King swam to the rear of the boat and snatched the small metal ladder. He hoisted himself into the open rear tray, moving fast, desperate to escape civilisation and Will Slater. He dropped silently onto the MasterCraft's floor and assessed the situation.

The control panel in front of him was home to a plethora of indistinguishable switches and levers, and a soft leather steering wheel. King scurried into the driver's seat and flashed a glance over his shoulder.

There was Slater, a few dozen feet down the pier, raising something in his left hand...

A muzzle flash flared and a bullet sunk into the console in front of King. He blanched and dropped into the footwell, covering his head, waiting for the subsequent volley of shots to tear him to pieces.

The report of two rounds ejecting from the barrel echoed down the pier. Screams rose from the restaurants as civilians ducked for cover, probably thinking they had entered a war zone.

But King didn't hear the shots hit the boat.

He paused and stole a look over the edge of the seat, which he'd been using as a temporary barricade. He saw three things.

Slater's shooting arm wavering.

His expression tight with frustration and disorientation.

His torso swaying slightly.

The man was concussed. He couldn't aim straight because King's uppercut had rattled his brain inside his skull, debilitating most of the functions that made him such a deadly operative. The major effects would be suppressible. King had suffered his fair share of concussions on the battlefield, and knew that it was possible to force the symptoms away until he had found safety.

In the heat of life-or-death combat, the human body was capable of extraordinary feats.

Slater was a Black Force operative. He would do the same.

But it gave King a vital window of time in which he could take advantage of Slater's incapacitation.

He vaulted back into the seat. Another round tore into the side of the MasterCraft, but he didn't let it faze him. He checked the choke switch. A key had been slotted into it and left there. King thought it was lackadaisical that the owners hadn't bothered to secure their boat. Then he checked the marina and noticed the entire space was walled off, only accessible to boat owners. They probably thought it was safe in here.

They clearly hadn't expected an ex-Special Forces soldier to approach their vessel via the ocean.

He twisted the key until the 450HP engine roared to life and then slammed down on the throttle control lever. The boat surged out of its space in the water, tearing forwards, heading out to sea. King allowed himself a slight smile as it peeled away from the marina…

An enormous jolt sent him tumbling out of the driver's seat. The shriek of fibreglass tearing and shattering resonated in his ears. He scrambled to his feet, panicking, then shook his head at his own foolishness.

The MasterCraft had still been moored to the pier when he'd taken off at full speed.

Sections of the boat's hull where the rope had been attached had been torn clean off, losing the battle with the pier. Nevertheless, it was still drivable. King sat back in the driver's seat and regained control of the vessel.

He aimed the craft in the direction of the open ocean and surged forward. He didn't look back. Every second he spent close to Saint-Florent gave Slater more time to land the fatal shot. It wouldn't take long for him to recover. King knew first-hand how Black Force operatives worked in the field.

The mission was the utmost priority.

He didn't know where he was headed. He didn't care. He wanted nothing more than to simply escape the crazed anarchy of the situation. He wanted solitude. He wanted to not have to worry about turning a corner to catch a bullet in the forehead.

He kept the throttle down and the engine roaring and pressed on — away from Corsica.

CHAPTER 19

As some semblance of calm was restored, King had a moment to think about what had occurred.

His old employers wanted him dead. It was a disastrous situation. Mercenaries and thugs were irritating, but surmountable. If the most covert and dangerous special forces organisation in the history of the United States were hell-bent on making sure he couldn't trouble anyone else — that was huge.

Slater would just be the first.

If he managed to deal with the man and put him away for good, they would only send more dangerous operatives. Better operatives.

King doubted he could take down the entire organisation on his own.

Black Force had been designed to breed killing machines. King had seen first-hand what one could do. Truth was — if Black Force wanted him gone, then it was inevitable. They

146

would keep hunting him until the end of time. He knew because he would have done the same in their position.

As sea spray splashed overboard all around him, soaking his clothes, he made sure the MasterCraft was aimed in a straight line away from the mainland. Then he got out of the seat and took a long hard look back at the island.

He couldn't cross to another country. He knew that much. He would have to return to Corsica — somewhere far away from Saint-Florent. Some secluded bay in the middle of nowhere. There he could use his skillset to acquire a vehicle and get the hell off this Mediterranean paradise.

Then he realised it wouldn't be so simple.

He saw the small object on the horizon heading out of the same bay he'd come from.

He saw the sea foaming on either side of the craft as it roared after him.

Slater, at the wheel of a similar speedboat.

'Fuck,' King whispered under his breath. He felt the nerves start to creep in. This man wasn't going to quit.

But he'd known that.

Slater was the same as him.

He killed the throttle. It didn't take long for the MasterCraft to slow in the water, settling quickly. The roar of the engine churning through petrol subsided. He had time to consider the options.

Slater was headed straight for him, determined and driven. He wouldn't stop until either one of them were dead. But King knew he couldn't kill the man. Besides the fact that it would be next to impossible given Slater's expertise, he knew that if he killed a Black Force operative, there would never be any kind of retirement to speak of. He would spend his life on the run, until they caught up to him and tore him to pieces for what he'd done.

If Slater died, King would never have a chance to clear the air.

So you run.

He twisted the wheel until the MasterCraft was facing Slater's approaching speedboat. He wasn't sure how reckless the man would be. Would he throw caution to the wind and aim to ram King's boat into oblivion? He wouldn't put it past him. All Black Force operatives had some kind of death wish. They were willing to do whatever it took to complete the mission.

Even if that meant putting their life on the line voluntarily.

Slater's boat grew closer. King made out his muscular frame behind the wheel, hunched over, surging forward at full throttle, gnashing his teeth in anticipation. Slater was wired on adrenalin.

'He's going to ram me,' King muttered, unleashing a torrent of curses directly afterwards.

Now it came down to a matter of timing. Slater's craft was bigger and looked stronger. It probably cost millions more than the MasterCraft. King had little doubt that a direct impact would split his own boat in two, hurling him into the ocean and leaving him completely at the mercy of the Black Force operative.

He had to act like a matador wielding a cape in the face of a charging bull.

When Slater's boat was a hundred feet away, King shifted the throttle slightly and began to trawl to the left. Slater steered his craft to compensate. If they continued on these paths, the nose of Slater's boat would plough into the hull of King's, more than likely demolishing it beyond all recognition. King heard the roar of his engine even from this distance — it was truly a titan of a craft.

At the last possible moment — with his heart pounding against his chest wall like it was set to burst through — King spun the wheel in the opposite direction and yanked on the throttle, shifting it to maximum. His own engine roared and he gripped the leather tight in an attempt to stay standing. The rear of his boat swerved violently, changing direction all at once, sending all loose objects flying across the deck.

He felt the sea spray flooding over the side as the MasterCraft churned in the ocean and kicked up geysers of saltwater. He found himself temporarily blinded, gripping the wheel tight, water pelting against his face and clothes.

The nose of Slater's vessel turned to compensate for the change of direction.

Too late.

King's MasterCraft shot past the other speedboat at a blistering rate, so close that he felt the displaced air wash over him. Their hulls missed by inches. Slater had corrected his course with lightning-quick reaction speed, but it hadn't been enough. King made brief eye contact with the man as their boats passed each other by.

Now King knew he could make it back to land before Slater. Slater's boat was bigger, faster and stronger — but it would take him considerable time to turn the craft in a giant "U". King could spend that time roaring back toward Saint-Florent.

Which was exactly what he did.

He wiped the saltwater out of his eyes and kept the throttle on full blast, making a beeline for the marina from which they'd come. If he could just get back to his car...

A compact burst of air washed over his cheek. He recoiled in abject terror, aware of exactly what that meant. The *crack* of a gunshot came a moment later. The bullet had passed dangerously close to his face, so close he was able to feel the displaced air. He wheeled around in his seat and went pale at the sight of Slater's craft in the distance, still completing its U-turn. The man himself stood at the driver's seat, nothing but a speck, his right arm raised, his aim true.

As King had predicted, his accuracy had returned.

Now King was battling a fully functional human weapon.

He stayed low in his seat, shielding himself from any further shots, and kept one hand tight on the wheel. If he could just keep the MasterCraft pointed in a straight trajectory … perhaps everything would be okay.

The time passed with incredible tension. King listened to the engine's din and the sound of the speedboat slicing through the ocean. Every now and then, a particularly large wave would send him sprawling to the soaked deck, coughing and spluttering. The adrenalin had begun to worn off, quickly being replaced by fear.

'Guess you're going to have to do something about that,' he whispered.

He began to formulate an idea well before he reached Saint-Florent. It was preposterous. Ludicrous. He was asking to be killed in the process. But he knew that something reckless was required to shake Slater free. He had to do something that his pursuer wasn't willing to replicate.

Otherwise, he would never pull away. Slater would stay on his tail until he dropped from exhaustion. He knew that much.

He rose out of the footwell and saw the bay closing in, wrapping around his craft. The shoreline grew closer, carrying a sense of finality with it. If he chose to carry through with the actions he had planned, there would be no turning back once he reached a certain point.

He didn't touch the throttle. It stayed maxed out, tearing through petrol, sending the MasterCraft hurtling towards the beach at over thirty knots. King closed his eyes for a moment. He spent the time thoroughly considering what he was about to do.

'Not many other options,' he muttered.

And that was that. He made up his mind, and committed to the course. He aimed for the least populated section of the beach. Saint-Florent's bay was alive with activity at this time of the day — same as Calvi's. Tourists and locals alike sprawled across the sand, lapping up the Mediterranean sun. Others strolled along the promenade, funnelling into the pier full of restaurants or heading further into the mainland.

King glanced at the pier. It was empty. A handful of remaining civilians scattered, fleeing the scene. Gunshots often caused that kind of commotion. Especially in a place like this.

The panic hadn't yet spread to the rest of the town.

It would.

King gripped the wheel tight and entered the shallow waters of the bay — without any intention of slowing down.

CHAPTER 20

Before he made impact, he checked Slater's position.

The larger speedboat was roaring after him, gaining ground fast. He saw the man behind the wheel, cold determination spread across his face. The unmistakeable look of a Black Force operative in the heat of combat. But he'd never faced anyone like King.

Recklessness was the only thing that would allow King to escape. Slater was too good otherwise. Too experienced.

But he would be unwilling to copy what King was about to do.

He turned back and concentrated entirely on the beach. Already, those civilians covering the sand around his proposed point of impact were in the process of gathering their items. Many had already abandoned their beach towels, sprinting away from the rapidly approaching MasterCraft.

King didn't blame them. It would be a terrifying sight to behold. A large speedboat roaring at full pelt toward their position.

The hull of his boat smashed into the floor of the bay as the water dissipated near the shoreline. It rattled every bone in his body, threatening to throw him overboard. A hideous groaning sounded from all around him.

Then the speedboat burst out of the ocean, careering onto the sand.

The craft had built up so much momentum in the water that the speed carried it all the way along the beach. It only took a few seconds.

King's world descended into madness.

He held tight and tensed every fibre of his being in anticipation for the ride. The boat tore itself apart all around him. Sections of the hull peeled away, smashed apart by the bumps and jolts as it was carried across the beach.

Slowing fast, the MasterCraft mounted the promenade…

… and began to roll.

King felt the hull grating, tearing, shrieking underneath him. He lost his footing on the deck and squeezed the wheel with everything he had. The muscles in his forearms burned with exertion. Then his world began to tilt.

He knew if he stayed in the boat while it rolled across the concrete he would be pulverised. Torn limb from limb. That outcome wasn't on his agenda.

Time seemed to slow as the boat began its roll. Sound and sight and smell and taste blurred into a furious sensory overload. King knew he had one opportunity to abandon the destroyed MasterCraft before he met a grisly demise.

He saw the concrete below his feet. That would do.

He leapt.

For a moment he was airborne, surrounded by fragments of fibreglass and aluminium. He thought he might land in the path of the twisting boat. At least it would be a quick death.

He crashed into the asphalt, landing on all four limbs. The skin tore off his palms yet he barely noticed. Carried by the momentum of the fall, he rolled over one shoulder and spun away from the wreckage, bruising great swathes of his back in the process. Hot pain rolled over him all at once. He slammed into something hard and came to rest — winded, dazed, confused.

With a final explosion of noise, the MasterCraft came to rest — upside-down — in the centre of the promenade, a dozen feet from King's motionless form.

He gave himself three seconds to recover from the impact. It was all the time he had. He looked over one shoulder and saw the gutter which had halted his wild tumble-roll. He was bruised and battered and shocked beyond belief.

But he'd carried out such a brash manoeuvre to give himself a lead on Slater — who would have to spend precious seconds parking his boat and disembarking safely onto the shore.

He couldn't let himself lose the slight advantage he'd gained.

He had time to rest on the plane.

Grunting in agony, he clambered to his feet. His palms and elbows bled freely, most of the skin scraped away by the brutal fall. He made eye contact with a cluster of people gathered at the opposite end of the promenade, staring wide-eyed at what had just occurred.

King thought of events from their perspective.

A man had just run his boat aground at breathtaking speed and proceeded to leap from the destroyed wreck before it crushed him. Then he had picked himself up like nothing was wrong.

King nodded to them, then spat blood on the pavement and hurried away from Saint-Florent.

Towards cover.

Towards escape.

CHAPTER 21

By the time King had disappeared into the claustrophobic heart of Saint-Florent, news of the incident on the pier had spread like wildfire throughout the commune.

The laid-back atmosphere typical of Corsican towns had all but vanished. Locals hurried between tightly-clustered buildings, speaking in hushed whispers, reporting noise of gunshots. King darted from alley to alley, staying in cover, checking his vantage points at all times. The last thing he wanted was to survive the speedboat crash only to look up and find Slater aiming a gun at his head.

He snuck into the lee of a doorway, escaping the sun for a brief moment. He paused and took the time to get his bearings. He had the keys to the stolen BMW somewhere in the soaked pockets of his jeans. If all went well, they would still work. If he could make his way back to the carport without running into Slater — or anyone else looking to end his life — then there was nothing but a short stretch of highway between Saint-Florent and the airport at Bastia.

Then a quick purchase of a ticket on the next flight out of Corsica was all that stood between himself and freedom.

The world was an enormous place. He was confident in his ability to burrow down in the middle of nowhere until all the commotion had blown over and Jason King was all but a distant memory to those that wanted him dead.

But first he had to make it to the middle of nowhere.

He wasn't sure it would be so easy.

He navigated through tight alleyways, growing cautious before every turn, heading in the direction in which he thought the carport lay. He rounded a corner and almost bumped into a tourist family.

'Excuse me,' the middle-aged woman said, her accent British. 'Do you speak English?'

'I do,' King said.

Relief flooded their faces. The couple had two young boys, both sunburnt, both fearful.

'Do you have any idea what's going on?' the man said. His voice wavered despite his best attempts to remain calm. 'We're hearing that there was a shooting on the pier. What have you heard?'

King shrugged. 'I haven't heard anything. I'm sure everything is okay. Are you—'

The woman let out an audible gasp. In her haste, she hadn't bothered to study the man in front of her. Now King saw her eyes dart to the grievous wounds on his hands and the torn flesh on his elbows and the bruising across one half of his face.

She turned to her husband and spoke in a hushed whisper. 'Greg, I think we should—'

King brushed past them, leaving them to ponder what had just occurred.

'Enjoy your holiday,' he said as he hurried away.

He passed several groups of people making for the town centre, fleeing the beach where the trouble had originated. At any moment he expected them to part to reveal Slater hiding behind, ready to shoot.

Ready to kill.

It took five minutes to locate the carport, yet it felt like an eternity. By the time he stumbled into the gravel lot and fished for the keys in his pockets, his heart rate had skyrocketed with tension and fear. There weren't many people on the planet who could evoke such a reaction. He usually considered himself above such nerves.

But Slater was different.

He emptied his pockets, turning up several items now soaked to the core. First was the smartphone he'd prised off Afshar's dead body before rolling him down the mountainside the night before. After the chaos of the last twelve hours, its existence had completely slipped his mind. Clearly water-damaged beyond repair, he shrugged it off and checked the set of keys for the BMW. They appeared no worse for the wear, but he couldn't be sure.

He approached the vehicle and clicked *unlock*.

The BMW's brake lights flashed once — indicating it had responded to the command.

King breathed a sigh of relief and threw the door open. He tossed Afshar's phone and his own wallet onto the passenger's seat and climbed in. The warm interior would be uncomfortable to most after the car had spent so much time under the sun. Ordinarily, King would hurry to fire up the air-conditioner and bring the space to a pleasant temperature.

Now, it was the last thing on his mind.

He leant back against the headrest and closed his eyes, water dripping off him sporadically. He wasn't sure which parts of his body were covered in water and which were covered in blood. He slowly brought his breathing back under control. The unavoidable adrenalin rush of the prior chase would take its time to dissipate. He had no chance of returning to normal just yet.

But he could calm himself a little.

He fired up the engine and reversed out of the space. A stream of men and women alike were in the process of hurrying to their vehicles, worry spread across their innocent faces. He assumed the police were on their way to the marina to ascertain exactly what had occurred.

King didn't care. By then, he would be long gone.

He took the BMW out of the lot and coasted back up into the hills.

You should have known, he told himself.

It had been an awful idea to stop for refreshments. His own ego had masked his judgment. He knew that after a lifetime of meeting adversaries in combat and coming out on top every single time, his opinion of his own abilities had been significantly heightened.

Slater had been a much-needed reality check.

The man was just as smart, just as fast, and just as lethal. King couldn't take a single chance until he was well clear of Slater's wrath. While parts of him were curious about the knowledge of other Black Force operatives, every rational bone in his body screamed to flee.

He reached the same turn that he'd previously taken and continued toward Bastia.

CHAPTER 22

Down in Saint-Florent, Will Slater stood with his hands in his pockets and stared at the overturned speedboat resting in the centre of the promenade.

He shook his head in disbelief. Even though he considered himself reckless at times, he had to admit he had nothing on Jason King. He could throw around his money on the gambling tables like it was nothing — in fact, his two-hundred-thousand euro loss in Montenegro could not even be considered an anomaly given his track record. He could throw caution to the wind on a mission — routinely he put himself willingly in harm's way.

But King's actions had come with such a *carelessness* for his own life that Slater had no choice but to allow him the head start.

He had parked his own speedboat back in the marina and hastily made his way onto the pier and down to the bay. By then, King had disappeared. Slater half-expected to find him dead in the wreckage. The MasterCraft had mounted solid ground so fast and so brutally that he couldn't imagine anyone surviving what had occurred.

He must have abandoned ship at exactly the right moment.

You win this one, he thought.

His jacket pocket began to vibrate. He withdrew the same sleek black smartphone and flashed a glance at the same familiar number scrawled across the screen. He answered with a flick of the touchscreen.

'Progress?' the female voice said instantly.

'I'm working on it.'

Silence. 'Will…'

'What?' he snapped. 'It's a little harder than I expected.'

'We're picking up reports of a confrontation between two men at Sainte-Catherine Airport,' the voice said. 'Was that you?'

'Yes.'

'What happened?'

'I found him.'

'And he's still alive?'

'Yes.'

'Did he get the upper hand?'

'No.'

'Will, what the *fuck* are you doing?'

Slater clenched his jaw and stared out across the bay. 'I told you. I'm working on it.'

'You didn't kill him when you had the opportunity to.'

'We were in the middle of an airport. Did you honestly expect—?'

'*What does that matter?!*' the woman yelled. Slater took the phone away from his ear for a moment until she settled down. 'You're a Black Force operative.'

'And you people have your limits,' Slater said. 'You can pull strings. You can get away with a lot. But I wouldn't fancy my chances of committing blatant murder in the middle of a populated airport terminal. There's only so many strings to pull on foreign soil. Am I right?'

'No,' the woman said. 'You have no idea what we can do. The next time you see Jason King, you blow his brains out? I don't give a shit where you are. Understood?'

'Understood.'

The line went dead. Slater tucked the phone back into his pocket. He hadn't told her about Saint-Florent. He could have shot King right there on the pier and disappeared before anyone was the wiser.

But he hadn't.

Something was stopping him. Something he couldn't quite put his finger on. Perhaps it was the fact that he'd never met another Black Force operative in the flesh. King's mere existence fascinated him. He couldn't kill someone who resembled himself.

164

At least, that's what he was telling himself.

Truth was he simply wanted to talk to the man.

First, he had to corner him.

Slater's head throbbed and his jaw ached and his ribs still burned from the two good shots King had landed on him. It had been years since he'd felt such pain. He was the best of the best in hand-to-hand combat. A true outlier. After the incident at the airport, he'd thought not even Jason King was on his level.

He'd thought wrong.

King had demonstrated that they were even after all. All it took for men at their level of combat prowess was one split second of hesitation, one slight lapse in concentration, to lean the odds heavily in favour of the other man.

Slater tasted blood and fished around in his mouth for missing teeth, running a finger over his gums. The uppercut had truly rattled him. He feared he would feel its effects for weeks.

But time was of the essence.

'Holy shit...' someone behind him proclaimed. A deep voice, accented English, full of surprise.

Slater wheeled around.

A wry smile spread across his features.

In front of him was a pairing he'd seen a million times before. A fast-aging male with a receding hairline, dressed impeccably in a tailored suit, accompanied by a gorgeous young supermodel twenty years his junior.

The things people do for money, Slater thought.

What made him smile was the matte-grey Lamborghini Huracan LP610-4 that the pair had climbed out of to gawk at the speedboat King had left in the middle of the road.

The man turned to Slater, eyebrows raised as if to say, *Are you seeing what I'm seeing?*

Yes, Slater thought. *I'm seeing an empty car. Engine still running. Big mistake.*

He took a step towards the guy. 'Sorry, buddy. Hate to ruin your vacation.'

Perplexion spread across the man's features. 'What?'

Before he could utter another syllable, he had been flung wildly off-balance. Slater kicked low and hard, putting enough force into the blow to knock both the guy's legs out from under him. He sprawled awkwardly to the ground, gasping softly. Slater imagined he hadn't been in a fight in years.

But this was no fight.

Slater brushed past him and ducked swiftly into the driver's seat of the Huracan. He reached up and swung the vertically-raised door down into place. It clicked as it closed. He ran his hands over the luxurious steering wheel crafted of the finest leather and allowed himself a rare moment of joy.

'Oh, baby…' he whispered.

Amidst cries of protest from outside the vehicle, Slater slammed the gearbox into drive and took off along the promenade. The ten-cylinder engine purred, omitting a sound so smooth and pure that for a moment he considered abandoning his career in black-ops and spending the rest of his days driving a supercar around some secluded tropical island until he died of old age.

Then he flashed back to reality and hurtled through the small commune, making a beeline for the hills.

He knew exactly where King was headed. Bastia housed the only airport on this side of the island.

He had unfinished business with the man.

CHAPTER 23

King couldn't help but check his rear view mirror every few seconds.

Everything had unfolded so quickly. He found himself constantly on edge, expecting some kind of attack at any moment. Despite the turmoil of his past, he wasn't used to all this chaos. He'd settled into a peaceful routine that had been quickly and savagely broken.

The BMW entered a section of the highway that cut through uneven, mountainous terrain. On either side, steep cliffs and craggy hillsides rose into the sky. He felt boxed in. Uncomfortable. In danger.

Home sweet home, he thought.

According to the GPS built into the dashboard, he was eight minutes out of Bastia. It wouldn't take long to locate the airport. He was so close to freedom he could taste it.

What if Slater manages to find out what plane you got on? What if he comes after you?

King made up his mind to eliminate all boundaries once he was out of Corsica. While on the island, he promised that he would do his best to avoid any kind of confrontation with Slater. It simply wasn't worth the risk.

But if the man followed him across continents … he wouldn't be so lenient.

If he fled to some yet-to-be-determined country and spotted Slater there, still after him, he wouldn't hesitate to kill the man.

Something on the passenger seat drew his attention. He took his eyes off the road for a moment, glancing across. His eyes widened.

Afshar's phone had lit up. The screen displayed a missed call, which apparently had come through just a couple of minutes ago. The number was unidentifiable. What surprised King the most was that the phone still functioned. He would be the first to admit that he wasn't a technological guru, but even he couldn't keep up with the rate at which these things were progressing.

Waterproof, now?

He reached across and picked up the device, unlocking it with a simple swipe of the finger. As he drove, he flicked absent-mindedly through its contents.

He saw several gambling apps. A couple of international money transfer programs. The messages were empty, obviously cleared after each day.

Smart, King thought.

He clicked on the contacts. Afshar hadn't been so wise in this department. Close to five hundred names appeared in a long list. King scrolled with no real purpose, speed-reading the list of names, wondering if any would jump out.

'Wonder if I've run into any of your friends in the past,' he said to himself.

As he reached the end, a name stood out among the rest.

Yves.

King shook his head in quiet resignation. So Afshar really had been targeting the politician. The desperate man with the plump belly and the thick white hair who had shown up on his doorstep late at night had been right to be suspicious. There truly were mercenary forces after him. He wondered how deep corruption ran in Corsica.

What had Yves Moreau disturbed to become such a target? What was going on in the bowels of this island?

It didn't concern him. None of it did. It was someone else's problem. For the first time in his life, King was ignoring what would probably lead to a shocking discovery.

Out of sheer curiosity, he thumbed the call signal.

Ringing.

He pressed the device to his ear. *Would Yves still be alive?*

He hoped so. The man had shown true fear, yet a sense of steely determination. He would carry on with his righteous task until he either succeeded or died trying. King admired that.

The ringing stopped. The call was answered. 'Hello?'

King paused. It was definitely Yves. The voice was the same as the man who had appeared in his living room the night before.

But the tone was off. It seemed like he'd almost been *expecting* the call.

King didn't respond for a long time. Silence descended over the other end of the line, interrupted by the occasional crackle. He felt a mounting suspicion in his gut.

What if…

'*C'est moi,*' King said, imitating Afshar's voice as best he could, speaking low and hushed. Arabic-accented French.

It's me.

A clear gasp came through the speaker. 'What the fuck!'

King said nothing.

'I thought the American killed you?' Yves said. 'What have you been doing this whole time? We need you.'

A sick feeling coursed through King. He felt like throwing up. In silent fury, he hung up the phone and slammed on the brakes. The BMW's tyres squealed on the asphalt and it fish-tailed to a halt in the middle of the road.

171

*

The Lamborghini Huracan accelerated to almost a hundred miles an hour. With traffic so sparse in this section of Corsica, Slater couldn't help but test the limits of the Italian supercar. He was confident that he would intercept King before the man reached Bastia. There was no chance that King would be travelling at speeds like this.

He entered a narrow section of the highway, where the road began to wind sharply. He slowed, but not by much. A certain exhilaration came with guiding the supercar through twists and turns at breakneck speed. As a special forces operative, he didn't often get the chance to experience thrills like these.

His thrills came in the form of bullets, blood and death.

He rounded a particularly sharp bend as fast as he could, letting out a holler of adrenalin in the process. The Lamborghini would have to be abandoned in Bastia, where it would likely be returned to its rightful owner.

But not just yet.

He tore around the corner and a new, straight section of the highway revealed itself all at once.

A BMW four-wheel-drive had been parked sideways across both lanes, blocking a section of each.

'Oh, fuck,' he whispered, slamming on the brakes.

He hadn't given himself enough time to slow.

The Huracan sent up four plumes of smoke as it struggled to bite into the asphalt. It swerved violently. Slater's stomach fell as he realised he wouldn't clear the BMW's path. He caught a glimpse of a large man loitering in the scrub nearby, watching closely, anticipating what he was now unable to avoid.

One side of the bumper clipped the BMW's rear as the Huracan flew past. Not enough to cause significant damage — but at these speeds, it was the only thing required to cause total pandemonium. He felt the chassis of the supercar lift up on one side and then he was tumbling, his vision blurring. The outside world turned into madness.

He knew he was rolling.

There was nothing he could do to stop it.

He simply closed his eyes and hoped the vehicle's safety features lived up to its price tag.

Centrifugal forces smashed him to one side. His chest bit into the seatbelt, hard, causing him to grunt. Before he could process the impact another devastating punch knocked him senseless, throwing him back into the racing seat. The shocks compounded the headache that had already been throbbing behind his eyes. He moaned in pain — which was cut off by another massive hit.

Finally, the car began to slow. He felt it leave the unforgiving asphalt and roll one final time, burying itself upside down in a row of roadside bushes. He came to rest — suspended by nothing but his seatbelt — surrounded by debris and shattered glass and twisted metal and a rapidly deflating airbag.

Alive.

That's all that mattered.

Blood ran from his mouth, winding down his face and seeping into his eyes. He lifted a hand and wiped it away. As he did so, he felt a numb sensation in his gums. He probed with a finger and confirmed his worst suspicions. Two teeth had been knocked out during the crash.

Somewhere in the haze of pain and discomfort, he struggled to unbuckle his seatbelt. He operated on the sole provision that as long as he was conscious, he had to continue to survive. Laying around feeling sorry for himself would achieve nothing. It would allow King to capitalise. So he reached up, ignoring his screaming muscle fibres. Searching for the unlock function by his waist.

He needn't have bothered.

A figure squatted beside the destroyed driver's window and peered into the vehicle. Slater looked across and saw King staring at him with a mixture of regret and satisfaction. The man held Slater's own weapon in his right hand — a Heckler

& Koch MK23 with an attached sound suppressor. It had been resting loose on the passenger seat before the Huracan's demise. It must have flown out during the impact.

'Think you dropped this,' King said.

Slater gave a final pathetic sigh of defeat and gave up trying to unbuckle himself.

CHAPTER 24

King had observed the crash with wide eyes, never anticipating that his setup would cause such destruction. He had parked the BMW on the other side of the sharpest turn he could find, aware that Slater would be on his tail.

He guessed the man would be suitably reckless in his efforts to catch up to King.

He guessed right.

Even so, he hadn't been expecting to see the Black Force operative at the wheel of an Italian supercar. How Slater managed to get his hands on these luxurious modes of transport so effortlessly, he would never know. Whatever the case, it had sure led to devastating results.

He counted six full revolutions before the Lamborghini came to rest by the side of the road, shattered and beat to hell. For a moment he thought he'd killed the man, and eluded the answers he so desperately desired. Then he saw Slater's struggling form in the driver's seat — and laid eyes on the

Heckler & Koch Mark 23 pistol that spun from the wreckage amidst a spray of debris.

He snatched it up and crossed to the supercar.

A Huracan, he noted as he approached the overturned vehicle. *Its owner won't be pleased.*

Slater's demeanour instantly shifted as King gestured to the sleek black weapon in his palm and let out a quip. He accepted his position. Surrendered to King. Reluctantly admitted that he had been defeated.

'Get it over with,' he muttered, wiping blood off his lips.

King paused. 'I'm not going to kill you. We need to talk.'

Slater had been staring straight ahead, accepting his demise with a resigned finality. Now he looked across and made eye contact for the first time. 'I made the mistake of keeping you alive. You shouldn't do the same. You know I'll kill you if I get the chance.'

'I'd prefer you didn't,' King said. 'We've only been at this game for a couple of hours and look at what we've done to each other.'

'I fail to see your point.'

'I'd say we're the two most dangerous men on the planet. Would you agree?'

Slater raised an eyebrow, then winced as a seemingly fresh wave of pain coursed through him. 'You think pretty highly of yourself.'

'Just facts.'

'Yes, I'd say we are.'

'So let's talk. That's why you kept me alive on the pier. You could have killed me there, just like I could have killed you here. I think we both know that it would be too much of a waste to finish the other off.'

'Fair point.'

'Get out of the car.'

King waited patiently as Slater spent a long minute manoeuvring out of his seat. He cut his forearms on shattered glass as he clambered out of the Huracan. King didn't care. The man had shot at him just half an hour ago. He deserved whatever he got.

He watched Slater get to his feet. They faced each other on the asphalt, two soldiers of fortune, men who could dominate almost anyone on the planet in combat.

But they couldn't bring themselves to kill each other.

King considered what would happen if his judgment was wrong. He almost backed out, but then he made up his mind. He needed the man's help, and holding him at gunpoint would achieve nothing. So he flicked the safety back on the MK23 and tucked it into his waistband. He held up both hands in a show of compromise, palms out, demonstrating that he was unarmed.

'Don't try anything,' King said.

'I might,' Slater said.

'I know you won't. You're fascinated by me, aren't you?'

Slater didn't respond.

'All your life you've been shut off from the other Black Force operatives,' King said, 'and now you're face-to-face with one. Someone like you. That's why you can't kill me. You're intrigued. So am I.'

'It's my job to kill you. I'm still employed.'

'Retirement hasn't been as relaxed as I thought it would be.'

'Evidently. Command picked up on bodies you left in several countries. What the hell are you doing?'

'Trying to survive.'

Slater let out a scoff. 'Playing the victim?'

'I didn't ask for any of this.'

'I'm sure you didn't.'

'I don't know how much Command told you about what went down in Australia,' King said. 'But it involved Lars. Was he your handler?'

'You brought that up before and I thought nothing of it,' Slater said. 'He *was*. Until he disappeared off the face of the earth. I've been told nothing.'

'Best leave it that way. The less people know about what happened, the better.'

'So you're saying none of this is your fault? The dozens of people you've killed? It's all just a crazy coincidence.'

'If I had an answer to that I wouldn't be here. I'd be lounging on a beach drinking margaritas without a worry in the world. But people are dying by my hand. Whether that be coincidence or not, I don't know. Seems like making a lifetime of enemies is finally catching up to me. I can't catch a break.'

'Poor you.'

'I hope you try and get out one day,' King said. 'Before you wind up dead. So you can see what it's like.'

Slater glanced over himself. His designer clothes were tattered. He was battered and bruised and bloodied. Much like King. 'You almost killed me then.'

'I needed to pin you down. So we could talk.'

'About?'

King raised Afshar's phone and wiggled it in the air. 'I need your help with a problem. I told myself I'd back away from any kind of confrontation, but I don't think I can. I could leave you here to tend to your wounds and disappear into another country, but I don't want to. I want to fix this.'

'Fix what?'

'What do you know about Yves Moreau?'

'Never heard of him.'

'You and me both — until a couple of days ago. He's a politician here in Corsica. Big anti-corruption standpoint. He

180

tracked me down and told me he was being hunted by mercenaries — the same mercenaries who attacked me last night. They wanted to shut him up, apparently.'

'The three bodies you left on a hillside?'

'Hired guns. One of them recognised me from a Black Force gig years ago. Unrelated to whatever's going on with Yves.'

'You sure are a beacon for trouble,' Slater said, shaking his head.

'Can't help myself.'

'So — why should I give a fuck about Yves Moreau?'

King pointed at the phone in his hand. 'I fished this off one of the dead guys. Yves' personal number is in it. I called it. He knows the mercs. They're working for him.'

'I couldn't care less,' Slater said.

'I know. But I do. This guy showed up at my house, pleading with me for help. He could have killed me if he had something to hide, but he didn't. I want to sort this mess out. I could use your assistance. Wrap it up quickly.'

'You're an ex-Black Force soldier,' Slater said. 'Do it yourself.'

King gestured at the state he was in. 'I'm a little incapacitated.'

'So am I, no thanks to you.'

'Then we make a good team.'

Slater raised an eyebrow. 'What part of this makes sense to you? I work for the most secretive government organisation in the United States. I'm being paid millions of dollars to kill you. And you want me to help you clean up a personal issue?'

'I thought you might have wanted to do some good,' King said. 'Instead of killing me and ignoring the real problem on this island — which would achieve nothing. Maybe I'm not jaded enough yet.'

It struck a nerve. King saw a flash of something in Slater's eyes, and suddenly he knew. This man didn't have a pleasant relationship with Black Force to begin with. Maybe he wanted out. Maybe he was disillusioned. Or perhaps he simply wanted to discover more about a man who used to work for them.

King doubted he would ever know the true reason, but a few seconds later Slater brushed past him and made for the BMW.

'It's a fair drive back to wherever you came from,' he said, throwing open the passenger door. 'Let's talk on the way there. I may just decide to kill you yet.'

King followed him. 'Don't be so sure. You try anything and I'll rip your head off.'

They ducked into their respective seats, two of the most lethal operatives the Special Forces had ever seen. King completed a three-point-turn and took off the way they'd come, leaving the destroyed Lamborghini Huracan resting idly by the side of the road.

He drove back toward an uncertain fate. He drove toward confrontation. The exact action José had told him to avoid.

But the action he had spent a lifetime succeeding at.

Someone was going to pay.

And he felt right at home.

CHAPTER 25

They spent the first five minutes of the journey in absolute silence. King focused on the road, a million thoughts bubbling through his head, at the same time wary of any ill-fated movement from Slater's side of the car. He was just waiting for a punch to whistle its way toward his throat. He wouldn't blame the man. He was operating on shaky pretences here.

Out of the corner of his eye, he saw Slater checking his wounds. The man moved methodically from limb to limb, assessing each cut and bruise before moving onto the next. He fished through the glove compartment and found a standard-issue first-aid kit. Bandages were slapped onto the most grievous injuries, and the others were cleaned and sterilised with some cotton and a small bottle of antiseptic.

King could tell that Slater knew exactly how to tend to injuries. He moved fast, addressing every major concern before moving onto the minor unpleasantries. King recalled many times on the battlefield in which he had done the same.

He and Slater were much alike.

Finally, when the man threw the used kit in the footwell and took a deep breath, he spoke. 'You could have easily killed me back there.'

'You shot at me and tried to ram my boat out in open ocean. Do you blame me?'

'Just saying, it's an odd way to ask for help.'

'Everything's odd in our field.'

'My field,' Slater said.

King looked across. 'Sorry?'

'You're out of the game, my friend. It's not your field anymore.'

King smiled. 'You keep thinking that. You're the one who's beat to shit.'

'You don't look so pretty yourself.'

'Half of this is from the mercenaries. Don't get too cocky.'

'How long were you in Black Force?' Slater queried. He threw the question out absent-mindedly, knowing that he was beginning to delve into the personal realm.

King wasn't bothered. 'A long time.'

'Specifics.'

'I walked out at the start of my tenth year.'

'Which makes you…?'

'Thirty-three. Yourself?'

'Thirty.'

'You thinking of getting out?'

Slater grimaced. 'I don't know. I'm having thoughts. I'd imagine it's pretty common when you do what we do.'

'How many missions have you been through?'

'I stopped counting years ago.'

'And you're still here,' King muttered. 'Fascinating.'

'Like you said, we're outliers. They select us from the upper echelons of the special forces based on our reaction speed, our ability to make decisions in the heat of combat. They only pick those who are the hardest to kill.'

'Explains why we were hesitant to kill each other,' King said.

Slater nodded. 'We're a rare breed. It'd be a shame to thin out our population. I doubt this Yves guy stands a chance against the both of us.'

King looked them both over. 'We did spend much of the day beating the shit out of each other.'

'About that,' Slater said, cracking his neck from side to side. 'I think I have a concussion. I won't know until later on, but you cracked me good on the pier.'

'You had one before?'

'Several times.'

'Likewise,' King said. 'You know, that's what worries me more than anything.'

'Brain trauma?'

King nodded. 'Bullet wounds can heal. They're superficial. I don't want to spend my whole life avoiding death only to develop CTE and die a crazy old lunatic in a nursing home.'

'How many times have you been concussed?'

'A fair few.'

'Any long-term symptoms?'

'Not yet.'

'Me either.'

'Then we hope for the best,' King said. They passed the trail leading down to Saint-Florent. Even from such an elevated position, it was clear that there was commotion within the commune. Flashing police lights dotted the land near the ocean.

They'd caused quite the ruckus.

Slater rested one foot on the dashboard and visibly relaxed. It seemed the conversation had calmed him down. King knew that they both lived their lives constantly on edge, always worrying where the next attack would come from. If they could trust each other, then this trip could be used to recharge their batteries. He let the tension loose from his muscles and tried to settle into a rhythm.

'I'm curious,' Slater said, 'what made you do it for ten years?'

'Work for Black Force?'

Slater nodded.

'I guess it's an addiction,' King said, letting out a few thoughts that had been stirring in his conscience for years. 'That rush of adrenalin when you don't know whether you'll survive the next few minutes. The closeness to death. It's all a big thrill ride, isn't it?'

Slater cocked his head. 'Odd. I'm exactly the same.'

'Of course you are. I'd say the other operatives are similar too — however many of them there are. Love of your country and duty to protect the homeland only get you so far in terms of motivation. Truth is, we all do it for selfish reasons.'

'Is that why you're getting into so much trouble in your retirement?' Slater said.

'It's very possible.'

'You came from a broken home, I take it?'

'What makes you think that?' King said.

Slater shrugged. 'Don't we all?'

King shook his head. 'My home life was fine. I was powering through a law degree when I decided to up and leave. Join the armed forces. From there, it just kept escalating. And I was fine with it.'

It took a long time for Slater to form a response. 'You crazy motherfucker.'

King smiled. 'I get that a lot.'

'My parents died when I was young. We never had money. I was basically raised on the streets. Taught me mental toughness at a very young age. The Army was the only thing I ever thought of that would pull me out of the hole I was in.'

'I take it you're doing well for yourself,' King said. 'Given what Black Force paid me.'

'Of course. All that government funding has to go somewhere, doesn't it?' Slater said.

They both chuckled. 'What's that saying?' King said. '*Live fast, die young.* They pay us well because they want us to enjoy life before we eventually catch a bullet.'

'You're doing well to avoid that.'

'Not well enough.'

They plunged into the main mountain range and roared on toward Calvi.

*

The apartment building had been half-completed and then abandoned. It barely stood on its foundations, which were quickly withering away. Tucked deep in the outskirts of Calvi, it hadn't been tended to in many years. The paint that had been coated on the half-erected walls had faded away long ago. The entire place smelt of fetid dampness.

No-one cared about its existence.

No-one looked twice at it.

Deep in the bowels of the building, Yves Moreau crossed a small windowless room and pressed a slim smartphone to his ear.

'Have you found out what the fuck that call was about?' he said in rapid French.

'We think it's the American. Police are reporting that Afshar's body didn't have his phone on him. King took it.'

Moreau swore viciously. 'Where is he?'

'That's the strange part.'

'What the fuck are you talking about?'

'He's with someone. Heading back for Calvi. We've rounded up a few witnesses who saw them. Police found a demolished Lamborghini ten minutes ago.'

Moreau shook his head, struggling to decipher the strange occurrences. 'You said something about a boat earlier?'

'Someone ran a speedboat aground in Saint-Florent. Almost killed himself in the process. We think it was King.'

'What the hell is he doing?'

'Do you think he's onto us?' the voice said.

'I don't know,' Moreau admitted. 'I certainly hope not. For all our sake. Who's his help?'

'We don't know. All we're aware of is that he's headed straight for Calvi. He made it almost to Bastia by the time he turned around.'

'He's coming for me…' Moreau whispered.

'We'll kill him.'

'I hope so. I hired you lot for a reason. Demolish this fuck. He can't expose me.'

'On it.'

They ended the call without saying goodbye. There was no time for pleasantries in their business. Moreau crossed the room and threw the door open. He had no time to loiter here.

The goods needed to be transported.

CHAPTER 26

Thirty minutes out from Calvi, King turned to Slater. 'Don't fall asleep.'

The man stirred. He hadn't dropped off yet, but he had been on the verge. 'What?'

'If you're concussed, don't go to sleep just yet. That's the worst thing you can do. You might never wake up.'

Slater nodded. 'I knew that.'

'Not thinking straight today?'

'It's been a hell of a morning.'

King spotted the town in the distance, facing out over the brilliant turquoise ocean. 'I don't think the day's over just yet. This could get ugly.'

'I'm not really used to anything else.'

'Touché,' King said.

He felt the familiar twitches coming back. It began as a strange sensation in his gut then worked its way into the rest of his body one limb at a time. His muscles reflexively tensed. He felt the nervousness of imminent combat. He assumed Slater did too — unless the man was completely deranged.

It wouldn't surprise him.

'So,' Slater said, 'what exactly is your plan here?'

'I'm not entirely sure,' King admitted. 'Track Yves down. Get him to talk. Find out why exactly he's conspiring with the men I killed and why he bothered to show up to my house and spin a false tale.'

'If he's really up to something, then he'll be protected.'

'I can handle that.'

'You sure? You look pretty hurt.'

'I'm sure. But we shouldn't be worrying about that now. I'm curious as to why you're here.'

'What?'

'You have a task. That task is to kill me.'

'I simply haven't been able to locate you yet.'

King looked across. 'That's all well and good, but what happens when you get spotted? What happens when you're unsuccessful?'

'Who says I'm going to be unsuccessful?'

King shook his head. 'If you really wanted to kill me, you could have done it at the airport. Or during any of the encounters since. I could have done the same. Truth is, if we were both really committed to doing that, one of us wouldn't be here. We're too efficient.'

'Okay,' Slater said. 'You're right. I don't want to kill you. But it doesn't have anything to do with you.'

'You shouldn't be taking this lightly,' King said. 'Black Force doesn't take anything lightly.'

'Fuck Black Force.'

Slater spoke the words with such bitter contempt that it all clicked at once. King saw a man disillusioned by his own organisation. A man who had become unwilling to carry out every deed in an unquestioning manner. A man much like himself.

'You want out?' he asked.

Slater shrugged. 'I don't know what I want. I'm sitting here trying to work out what comes next.'

'Don't run from them. They'll find you. They always do.'

'What makes you think that?'

'You found me.'

Slater smiled. 'I won't make the same mistakes you did.'

'How can you be sure? People like us can't just switch off. It's in your blood to fight. It's in mine. That's why there's a trail of bodies showing up. That's how people like us react to confrontation.'

'They sure were painting you out to be some kind of rogue agent,' Slater said.

'It probably looks like I am.'

194

'I hate to think what happens when they're wrong. How many times have I been sent into some place where I had no business being in? How many innocent people have I killed?'

'You'll never know,' King said. 'Neither will I. That's why I got out. I didn't want to add any more to the existing count.'

'When you went AWOL it threw them off,' Slater said. 'You were their best operative. By far. No-one ever stated it explicitly, but the entire organisation went into disarray in your absence. I've been working overdrive lately. Taking most of the workload you had.'

'And you're still here. So you must be their best operative now. They piled the work onto you because no-one else is good enough.'

'If I tell them I'm walking away, I don't think they'll be as lenient,' Slater said. 'Not after you're gone. Not after Lars is gone.'

'You think they'll force you to stay?'

'They can't force me to do anything. But they might consider me too much of a liability. After what they saw you do.'

'They haven't seen me do anything. They saw bodies and they assumed. That's what all this is. One big assumption.'

'That's what I realised,' Slater said. 'That's why you're alive. I saw myself in your position. And I couldn't kill you.'

'Black Force isn't the devil,' King said. 'They have good intentions. I can't put into words how much good I did for them. How many lives I inadvertently saved.'

Slater nodded. 'I know. That's why I've stuck around for so long. But this job burns anyone out. If you couldn't do it anymore, what chance do the rest of us have?'

The rest of us.

King couldn't avoid being intrigued. 'What exactly do you know about the others?'

'Nothing. They told me about you after you left, because they had to explain why my services were in such high demand. But they keep us all apart. I don't know how many there are. I assume you don't either.'

King shook his head. 'Not a clue.'

'Maybe it's best that way. We don't know how many have died.'

'Given our track record,' King said, 'I would assume very few. They only take the best of the best. Unless we're anomalies.'

'I'd say we are.'

'So what do we do about this situation?' King said. 'What happens after I find Yves?'

'If we're alive tomorrow, you mean?'

'Let's assume we are.'

'Okay. Then I slink back with my tail between my legs.'

'What?'

'I'm beat up. I'll tell them you got the best of me. I lost you, and the mission was unsuccessful.'

'What if we cause a scene?' King posited. 'A dozen dead mercenaries show up in Calvi in the aftermath of all this. What do you tell them?'

'I'll make something up.'

'Dangerous game to play.'

'I don't care what they think anymore. I don't know how much longer I'll stick around.'

'You're putting your life in the hands of powerful people. Who knows what decision they'll make?'

'I guess that's my weakness,' Slater said, shrugging. 'Got a bit of a death wish. We all do in this business.'

'I have to let you know that I'm grateful,' King said. 'You had the opportunity to kill me back in that airport. I was a sitting duck. Not many people get that chance.'

'I told you,' Slater said. 'I saw myself.'

'Thank you.'

'Thank you for the concussion. Much appreciated.'

'I could have killed you also.'

'I know.'

They spent the next stretch of time in mutual silence. King felt a newfound respect for the man across from him, and he was sure that Slater felt the same. They were two of a kind, elite mercenaries who had the ability to end the other's life at any moment. Even though they hadn't vocalised it, a sort of truce had come from the knowledge that one well-placed blow was all it took to kill the other. They had refrained from doing so up until this point, and now they had developed a trust.

'We're getting close,' King said. He paused, thinking back to his time in Black Force, to what he had access to. 'You can get Moreau's personal address, can't you?'

'Yeah,' Slater said, pulling out his smartphone and opening an application. 'Shouldn't take too long. Yves Moreau — that his full name?'

King nodded. Sometimes, working for the upper echelon of government black-ops had its advantages. Particularly the advanced methods of surveillance that other departments could provide. He let Slater work his magic, deciding to focus on the surroundings. He sighed. Corsica had been good to him. It was a shame that he would have to abandon the island at the end of this task.

If he survived.

At the moment, Moreau was a mystery box. The politician clearly presented a strong anti-corruption stance to mask something else. Something sinister. Whatever it was, it required the use of a mercenary task force, a group of soldiers of fortune led by Afshar. Who knew how deep his dealings ran…

'Got it,' Slater muttered. 'Fuck me, nice place. You said this guy's a politician?'

'On the surface he is,' King said. 'There's something underneath, though. He lied through his teeth when he met me. I believed him. He wanted me to work for him...'

'Probably thought you could be bought.'

'That wouldn't have turned out well for him. Where does he live?'

'Some kind of pretty estate. Big mansion. Fenced off. Security cameras and the like. If he's got some kind of security detail that we don't know about then this could take some effort.'

King slowed the car and looked across at Slater. 'Why the hell are you doing this?'

'Doing what?'

'Helping me. You don't know this man. You don't know me. I could be a lunatic for all you know.'

Slater tapped the side of his head for added effect. 'It's in our DNA, brother. I help people. I weed out the crooked fucks in society. Been doing it my whole life. And I don't need to ask questions. I rely on instinct. You seem to be pretty fucking determined to sort this guy out. So I'll tag along.'

King turned back to the road and shook his head in fascination. It didn't surprise him that Slater had decided to help him on his quest for vigilante justice. What surprised him was that he would have done exactly the same.

He'd found his equal — something he hadn't even considered a possibility before this.

Slater reached forward and punched the address he'd found into the GPS on the dashboard. It acknowledged him with a high-pitched beep and set out a route to the estate. A digital timer said they would arrive in twenty-two minutes.

'It's the middle of the day,' Slater said. 'Don't think he'll be home.'

'He doesn't have to be.'

CHAPTER 27

The sun rose just after seven in the morning over Washington D.C., bathing the city in a pale orange glow. The south parking lot of the Pentagon had already begun to fill.

At 7:09a.m. a nondescript beige Toyota pulled into a parking space and a mousy middle-aged woman got out. She slung a cheap handbag over one shoulder and hurried toward the looming headquarters of the United States Department of Defence.

Dressed in tan secretarial clothing and sporting a pair of horn-rimmed spectacles, no-one would have looked twice at her on the street. Nothing about her drew attention. She blended effortlessly into any crowd. Which was exactly her intentions. Nobody would be any wiser to the fact that she had been running the most secretive division of government black-ops for the last six months — promoted after the previous' handler's untimely demise.

She entered one of the compartments of a rotating door in the building's side and strode into a vast marble lobby bustling with activity. A security guard nodded as she approached and ushered her quickly through a plain white door. She found herself in a narrow hallway that stank of cheap air freshener and cleaning product. There were no decorations on the walls. There were no noticeable ornamentations anywhere. This section of the Pentagon was kept sparsely utilitarian.

The woman navigated the corridors with the experience of a seasoned veteran and unlocked one of a hundred indistinguishable wooden doors. No labels of any kind. No markings. Everyone in this area knew exactly where they were heading. If they didn't, they would be promptly escorted out.

She opened the door to reveal a group of four men. Two were high-ranking military officials and the others were part of the Presidential detail, sent to receive a report on how the operation in Corsica was unfolding.

Together, they made up half of the population who knew of Black Force's existence.

'Gentlemen,' she said, nodding as she sat. 'Let's make this quick.'

'Where is Slater?' one of the officials said, his voice cutting through the quiet room like a knife.

Straight to the point.

'Corsica.'

'Where exactly in Corsica?'

'We don't know.'

'Can't you track these things?'

'We have a few different means of knowing exactly where our operatives are. He seems to have disabled most of them. Maybe this part of his assignment needs to be carried out at his discretion. We generally let our men do whatever they want. They operate outside the boundaries of the law. They don't exist. You know this. Whatever Slater's doing, I'm sure there's a perfectly reasonable explanation for it.'

'He's going after Jason King?'

'He is.'

The second official piped up. 'And King walked away eight months ago?'

'He did.'

'What's to say King hasn't killed him? He would know how to disable all kinds of tracking devices.'

'No he wouldn't,' the woman said. 'To do so requires all kinds of personal identification methods that King would never have access to. Slater wouldn't give them up.'

'King could have interrogated him.'

The woman paused. 'That simply wouldn't work. You clearly don't understand the level that our operatives are at. They never break. They never stop. They're human weapons.'

'You're describing King perfectly, ma'am. This was a risky assignment to hand Slater. He could very well be dead already.'

'You're right,' the woman said. 'He could. But King cannot be allowed to continue his path of destruction. Who knows how many he's killed in Corsica. The three bodies uncovered by the police could be just the start of a deeper web. He needs to be eliminated. We can't have the risk hanging over our heads. We created a killer, and then allowed him to walk away.'

One of the President's men finally decided to open his mouth. 'Slater is our best operative, correct?'

'He is now,' the woman said. 'Before him, it was Jason King…'

'And if Slater is dead?' the man said. 'What next? Who do we send out?'

'We have other operatives…'

'Who aren't on Slater's level. Or King's. Truth is, our two most valuable assets are in the process of trying to kill each other somewhere in the Mediterranean. I vote we put a stop to this madness right now.'

'It's too late,' the woman said. 'Slater's fallen off the grid. We don't know what's going on. When he resurfaces, we'll know.'

'Send more of your operatives to Corsica.'

'That will create anarchy,' the woman insisted. 'Let them fight. If Slater makes it back, we'll be fine.'

The first military official rose out of his chair, deep wrinkles furrowed into his forehead. 'If he doesn't, we're fucked. We'll have lost our two best operatives.'

'We can always pull more men from Delta. The best of the best.'

'We could. But they're not Slater or King, and you know it.'

There was nothing further left to be said. The four men got to their feet and hurried out of the room with terse nods of farewell. The woman sank into her chair and chewed away at the inside of her mouth. An unfortunate tendency when she was highly stressed.

Which — lately — seemed to be every waking moment.

She waited until the last man had left the makeshift conference room. Then she picked herself up and hurled a pen at the far wall. It clattered off the plaster and rolled to a halt on the thickly carpeted floor.

Truth was, Slater falling off the grid was a much more serious event than she'd given off. He had never been so reckless before.

Whatever carnage the man was wreaking in Corsica, she prayed he made it out alive. Without him, Black Force was nothing. She begrudgingly admitted that King and Slater were the two best operatives the secret world had ever seen. If they lost them both…

She turned her mind off such pessimistic thoughts. As always, there were other operatives in the field. Two were in Bangladesh, and another was deep in the slums of Mogadishu. They awaited further instruction.

She hurried out of the meeting room and made for her office, sending up a silent prayer that Slater would return to her shortly.

CHAPTER 28

On the outskirts of Calvi, a matte-black BMW turned into a private estate with a whisper and coasted along the smoothly-paved roads. It moved slowly, as if its occupants were scouring each house in turn. When they finally found the correct destination, the driver pressed on the brakes and killed the engine.

King stepped out into a literal paradise. Staring at the houses all around him, he briefly regretted not looking for property in these parts before settling on the villa in Calenzana. The estate had been constructed on the side of a gently-sloping hill, so that each house had an equally gorgeous view of the Corsican coastline. He glanced down at where Calvi met the ocean, and revelled in the location's beauty for what would likely be the last time.

After this, a one-way ticket to anywhere else in the world lay in wait.

'I can't believe I'm doing this,' he muttered as he crossed to the other side of the car, stepping up onto the pavement.

'Working with me?' Slater queried, climbing out of the passenger seat.

'No. Doing exactly what I promised myself I wouldn't do. Getting into trouble.'

Slater cracked his neck and rolled his wrists. 'Trouble's the only thing we're good at, brother.'

'There was a brief period where I was enjoying an absence of it.'

'Did it drive you insane?'

'I was beginning to get used to it.'

Slater grinned, flashing perfect white teeth. 'Needed a reality check, huh?'

King shook his head in silent resignation. 'It seems so. This the place?'

Slater checked his phone, then studied the enormous three-storey mansion in front of them, walled off by a substantial brick-and-mortar fence running the perimeter of the property. The fence was easily seven feet tall, but what King could see of the building was beyond luxurious. Pristine glass windows ran the length of the upper level, which he knew would provide stunning views of much of the coast.

Moreau clearly did well for himself.

'Can't tell if he's home,' Slater said. 'If he was, he'd keep the car in the garage anyway. So — if he answers, we talk?'

'We talk,' King said.

For two men about to embark on a home invasion which could potentially see them interrogating a renowned politician, their communication had been surprisingly sparse. Yet somehow, King knew exactly what to do. There was enough experience between the two of them to classify this type of confrontation as near the bottom of the list of dangerous encounters.

Despite that, they knew very little about what lay ahead.

Slater took the lead. He strode up to the solid metal gate built into the security fence and slammed on it hard, three times, loud enough for the neighbours to hear.

'Jesus Christ,' King whispered. 'Keep it down.'

Slater turned to the electronic panel built into the side of the gate and proceeded to tap the *"DOORBELL"* button eight times in quick succession. Then he returned to smashing his fist against the gate with everything he had, rattling it on its hinges.

After ten seconds of controlled chaos, he took a step back, crossed his arms, and waited.

He noticed King staring at him out of the corner of his eye and flicked his gaze across. 'What?'

'You want to draw the attention of everyone on the island?'

'If it makes this guy answer his door, then yes. I want to make sure he's not home.'

He leant over and thumbed the doorbell another six times.

They waited patiently. The street remained deserted. King guessed everyone was at work. It would take either an inherited fortune or an intense work-ethic to afford one of the properties in this neighbourhood. He quickly concluded that Slater's knocking was falling on deaf ears.

It was the middle of the day on a weekday. Moreau would be busy handling his political career.

'He's not home,' King said.

'Perfect.'

Slater reached into his jacket and withdrew something. His frame blocked it from view. He fiddled with it for a moment. King craned his neck in an attempt to catch a glimpse of the object. Slater seemed awfully preoccupied with it. When he finally caught a glimpse of what the man held, his stomach fell.

'What the fuck are you—?' he begun.

Slater didn't listen. He finished removing the pin from a standard-issue M67 fragmentation grenade — the go-to grenade for the United States Special Forces — and tossed it lackadaisically over the gate.

'Might want to step back,' he said, his voice holding the same level of panic as if he were halfway through a Sunday stroll.

King felt the energy that came with an adrenalin rush flood through him. His legs picked up a life of their own. He took off across the road, away from the live grenade. Slater followed in his wake.

Before it went off, King managed a single statement. 'You're fucking insane.'

Slater grinned. 'Thought you wanted a way in.'

The sound hit him first. His eardrums thrummed as the M67 detonated on the other side of the fence. A deep, bass-filled fist punched him in the chest. He felt the shock even from the other side of the road. A large chunk of the brick crumbled to pieces, forced outward by the explosion. Debris smashed across the pavement outside the property.

King grit his teeth as two of the BMW's windows shattered, cracked by the grenade's punch. The metal gate crumpled and spun away.

When the dust settled, a gaping hole lay in the fence. Slater nodded approvingly and headed for the newly-formed entrance.

'Gotta love grenades,' he muttered to himself as he walked.

King snatched his arm. 'I wanted to do this as quietly as possible.'

Slater shrugged, just as nonchalant as always. 'No point wasting time. I have places to be.'

'You'll get us both killed if you keep going like this.'

'You said the guy's hired a mercenary force? This is the quickest way to sort out who he's employing. They'll come straight here.'

'Are we ready for a fight? And where the hell did you get all this stuff?'

Slater yanked the MK23 out of King's belt in one swift motion. King made to seize the man's wrist but he was out of range before the gun could be retrieved.

'This is all I need,' Slater said. 'And I have a contact here. Ex-Paraguayan military. Told me years ago that he owed me a debt. I came knocking.'

'That's all you took off him? A pistol?'

'Thought it was all I'd need.'

'And the grenade?'

'He had that lying around. Couldn't pass it up.'

King sighed. The pair of them stepped over the rubble at the base of the fence and entered a small courtyard. He guessed it was previously untarnished. Now, dust and debris lay over everything. 'Let's hope a pistol's enough.'

'You bet your ass if Yves has any friends on standby, they'll already be notified of what just happened,' Slater said. 'They're the next best thing. We can find out why he needs guns-for-hire.'

'What if we're wrong?' King said.

'You mean, what if *you're* wrong?' Slater corrected. 'I'm just tagging along for this.'

'I never intended to demolish the guy's house before we found out what he's doing.'

'Fuck me,' Slater said, exasperated. 'His house is fine. It's just a fence. He can afford it. You'd think I committed genocide by the way you're talking…'

They stepped onto a secluded patio and approached the enormous oak front door. King tried the handle. Locked, as he expected.

'Okay, so we're past the fence,' he said. 'Now how do you expect we—'

Out of the corner of his eye he noticed Slater bending down to snatch up some kind of object on the edge of the patio. He ducked away as fast as he could. He didn't want to find himself in the path of whatever madness the man conjured up next.

No sooner had he ascertained what Slater was doing before the man hurled a heavy pot plant through the floor-to-ceiling glass window to the right of the door. The pane shattered and caved inward. Slater nodded in satisfaction and stepped through the newfound entrance.

'Unbelievable,' King muttered.

Perhaps you've finally found someone as reckless as yourself, he thought.

He followed Slater inside the home. They clambered over a recliner chair and came to a halt inside a luxurious sitting room, fitted with custom-made leather sofas and expensive framed artwork lining the walls. It reminded him of a similar living room he'd come across in the hills of Venezuela. The owner of that home had lauded over a drug empire.

He wondered what Moreau's particular vice was.

'You think he makes all this money from politics?' Slater said, gazing around the space.

'I'm sure he says he does,' King said. 'But any bet he has a side income. Which is likely why he's employed an army of mercenaries. There must be some kind of big deal going down.'

'We'll find out soon enough.'

They ducked through an open doorway into a massive space containing a living room, a dining room and a kitchen. The ceilings were high. The countertops were spotless. Everything was kept in pristine conditions.

'Think he has a maid?' Slater said.

'Probably. Seems like a busy man.'

'Can't wait to ask him all about it.'

'What if the police show up before his gun-toting friends do?' King said.

'Then we run. You're good at that.'

'What do you tell the higher-ups when you get back?'

'I thought King was hiding inside the property. I was wrong. My mistake. Won't happen again. Sorry, ma'am.'

Slater cut off the mock conversation as he ducked through a connecting hallway and moved methodically from room to room, looking for something in particular. He swung open an ordinary wooden door halfway along the space and nodded approvingly.

'Bingo.'

'What is it?' King said.

'Office. Hopefully he's dumb enough to keep some juicy details locked away in these drawers.'

'I don't have a paper clip,' King said. 'Get me one and I can pick the—'

A gunshot rang out through the house, loud even with the sound suppressor attached. King saw the hint of a muzzle flash ring out from the office. Instincts kicked in.

Slater.

He took off, powering into the room, thinking someone had been lying in wait. As he burst into the small office, Slater turned and looked at him with a furrowed brow. 'What's the hurry?'

He stood in front of a large file cabinet, wielding the MK23 in his hand. A thin trail of smoke wafted from the barrel. The top drawer had rolled open, its lock blasted to shreds by a single gunshot.

'You're an idiot,' King said, allowing his heart rate to settle. 'Warn me before you do shit like that.'

Slater chuckled. 'Didn't realise you were that much of a baby.'

King grimaced and left the man to sort through the documents within the drawer. He could spend his time elsewhere. He'd known Slater for an hour and already the man was getting on his nerves.

He ducked back into the vast living space and crossed to the fridge — an enormous stainless steel number with an inbuilt ice-machine and a small dial that displayed the temperature of each compartment. He opened the right-hand door and searched for anything to eat. After all, Slater had rudely interrupted his meal at Saint-Florent's marina.

His stomach was on the verge of consuming itself.

He found a half-empty dish of leftover lasagna and threw the entire thing in the microwave. Two minutes later he wolfed the majority of the food down with a tall glass of tap water. After not eating for over twenty-four hours, the meal hit a spot that he'd been meaning to satiate for most of the day. He sighed approvingly and finished up as quickly as possible.

At some point, Slater stuck his head out of the corridor. His eyes widened.

'Do you want a massage with that?' he said.

'Fuck off,' King said. 'I was hungry.'

'Yes, sir,' Slater mocked in a high-pitched tone. 'If there's anything else I can do for you, master, just let me know. I'll do all the hard work. No problem.'

He retreated to the office. King couldn't help but smile at the banter. It had been a while since he'd done anything of the sort. He followed Slater into the office just as the man finished rifling through the last few documents in the drawer.

'Anything?' he said.

Slater shook his head, perusing a booklet. 'Political shit. Nothing out of the ordinary. I think our man is smart enough not to leave anything incriminating lying around.'

The screech of tyres on asphalt sounded from somewhere outside. King's ears pricked up at the noise. He felt cortisol rear its head, charging his limbs with energy. 'That sounds like Moreau's friends.'

Slater checked the MK23's magazine and smiled. 'Beautiful.'

They moved like wraiths through the house, King leading the way, Slater following close behind. King felt the fluidity of their actions as he approached the front door. Slater moved exactly where he expected him to, checking each doorway for signs of life, one finger slotted into the trigger guard. He moved like the expert he was.

King had always operated alone, but he recognised the advantages of a cohesive team in that moment, especially if he managed to team up with someone of Slater's caliber. He crept to the nearest window — situated in the sitting room they'd entered from — and peered out through the hole in the fence.

Instantly, he soaked up information.

Three men. Hard, expressionless faces. Grizzled mercs, for sure. Same ethnicity as Afshar. Scars dotting their visible skin. Dressed head-to-toe in standard combat uniform — army boots, dark khakis, long-sleeved polyester compression shirts, bulletproof vests resting over tight fat-free musculature. They had exited an armoured four-wheel-drive with blacked out windows, bringing it to a stop next to the BMW.

Slater saw them too.

Without a word, he raised his MK23. King noticed his mannequin-like composure. When he locked on his aim, he didn't move a muscle. He slotted the same finger back into the trigger guard and moved to unload a series of rounds.

The mercenaries carried MK17 Mod 0 SCAR assault rifles, but all the firepower in the world was no use against a few well-placed shots from a covered position.

King waited for the three men to die.

Then rapid footsteps against the marble entranceway floor echoed through the house.

Someone behind them.

Reflexively, King spun. He was unarmed. Any wild shot would put him out for good. He searched desperately for cover, then dove behind the nearest sofa.

A well-built figure hurried into the room, armed with some kind of carbine. King saw him in his peripheral vision as he rolled for cover.

Slater spun and fired a shot with the reflexes of a trained killer.

The wet sound of a body slapping against tiles sounded through the hallway.

'He came round the side,' Slater muttered.

King pulled himself to his feet just as a hail of automatic gunfire diced through the open window.

CHAPTER 29

The mercenaries were onto them.

Their friends' little distraction had proved advantageous.

Slater recoiled away from the window, avoiding a swathe of bullets. King skirted around the sofa he'd taken cover behind and scrambled for the entranceway. As he crawled, he passed over the body of the surprise guest. He noted the cylindrical hole in the centre of his forehead, already pouring blood onto the tiles. He admired Slater's aim, then dashed out into the hallway.

He was one step ahead of Slater, who was still in the sitting room, flattening himself out across the floor to avoid the barrage. All at once, the gunfire ceased. King's ears rang. He stayed poised in the hallway, listening closely.

He made eye contact with Slater.

'You think they're—?' he begun.

Two things happened at once.

First, a bulky figure leap-frogged through the gaping hole in the sitting room's shattered window. Slater noticed the movement and rolled onto his back, bringing the MK23 up in a controlled arc.

King didn't have time to see what resulted from the exchange, because right beside him the front doors burst open, shouldered inwards by two charging bodies.

Surrounded by frenetic movement, he chose to focus on the most pressing issue.

The last two mercenaries charged into the hallway, running straight into him. He felt their strength and knew it was inferior. He ducked instinctively, avoiding any weapon barrels, his veins pumping and his head pounding from the intensity of the conflict.

He *loved* close-quarters chaos.

Wielding heavy-duty assault rifles in a hand-to-hand fight was disadvantageous. While they were preoccupied with trying to lock on an aim, King could act. He smashed aside one of the SCARs with a well-placed shove and thundered a closed fist into that same mercenary's jaw. He felt the *crack* of breaking bone and shouldered the guy aside, sending both him and his weapon skittering across the floor.

He spun and snatched hold of the other man's SCAR in a vice-like grip, clutching the barrel with white knuckles. In a millisecond's hesitation, he realised that if the gun went off it would burn his palms severely. He wrenched it out of the guy's grip and threw it aside.

The now-unarmed man — who sported a buzzcut and the hint of stubble on his pronounced jaw — swung a vicious combination as soon as King disarmed him, reacting quickly to the change of momentum. King was fast, but he still had to obey the laws of physics. He couldn't pull his head out of the way in time to avoid the first punch.

Thankfully, he rolled with it. The fist crashed against the side of his head with enough power behind it to drop a smaller man, but King jerked his head backwards to take the majority of force out of its impact. He felt the sharp firing of nerve endings across his temple, but he could deal with superficial pain.

And now the man had over-extended in a wild attempt to knock him unconscious.

Counter-punching was a technical feat. It required dexterity, speed and a level-headed approach to combat. Most of the adrenalin had to be taken out of the interaction. King knew he had the ability to complete all three.

As soon as the punch clattered off his head he fired back with a left straight of his own.

Pinpoint.

Load.

Fire.

He hit the man on the button as he was moving in. He felt the guy's jaw rattle under his own knuckles and followed through with the punch, pouring everything into it in turn.

His landed much more effectively than the mercenary's had.

The man met his fist with all of his bodyweight behind it, unable to stop himself from falling into it, carried by the momentum of his own swing.

The mercenary's legs buckled and his eyes rolled back and he dropped like a sack of shit all in the space of a second.

Goodnight.

He spun on his heel, assessing the situation in a half-second. One of the mercenaries was out cold, and the other struggled to his feet, sporting a broken jaw and a bloody nose. His weapon had been hurled off to the side, well out of reach. King only had a couple of feet to close the distance.

And more than enough time to do so.

As he hesitated for only a fraction of a second, he heard an exchange of gunfire from the adjacent room. His chest tightened in worry.

Slater.

He charged forward. The only conscious mercenary saw him coming and threw his hands up feebly, trying to mount some kind of offence.

He needn't have tried.

King grabbed him by the vest with both hands, spun around and hurled him through the fragile plasterboard of the nearest wall. A large section of the material caved inward and the mercenary slammed into the wooden supports in a tangle of limbs.

It would take him precious seconds to pick his way out of that mess.

King hurried into the sitting room.

He laid eyes on a life-or-death struggle.

It seemed the mercenary who'd leapt through the window had landed *on* Slater, disarming the both of them in the violent clash. King had heard gunshots but it seemed no-one was hit. The brawl had turned savage, as both men struggled to secure a weapon faster than the other.

They were sprawled across the carpet, fists flying with significant weight behind them. King took one look at the situation and noticed the MK23 lying nearby, both men scrambling for it with teeth bared. The atmosphere was charged with tension.

In one motion, he leapt over the both of them and snatched up the handgun with one hand. He let his legs go loose, falling to the carpet and rolling in the process, twisting as fast as he could. He made sure he was facing the two men before locking his aim on.

Their bodies were tangled together. Blood spilt from the mercenary's mouth. Slater was cut over one eye.

King had one shot. If he hit Slater, he wouldn't be able to forgive himself.

He let out a single, sharp breath. He steadied his limbs.

The mercenary jerked his head up and stared at the scene unfolding beside them.

The man went pale.

Now.

King tapped the trigger once. The gun leapt in his hands and the mercenary's head whipped back with the looseness of a corpse. All the tension dissipated from his limbs and Slater threw the body off himself in the same split second. The man clattered to the carpet and lay still. A pool of red instantly began to pool around his face.

'Fuck me,' Slater whispered, collapsing back onto the ground and panting heavily. 'I thought I was gone.'

'Fight-or-flight instincts?' King said. He'd felt the same sensation many times before. The ferocious determination to *live*. It turned normal men into savage beasts when their lives were threatened.

Slater nodded. 'Never fun.'

'You'll be tired tonight. It saps the strength out of you.'

'I'm tired now.'

'We have a job to do.'

He rose off one knee and made for the entranceway. The last conscious mercenary was busy forcing his way out of the wall. He fell to the tiled floor, covered in plaster and blood.

A sorry sight.

King raised the MK23. 'Don't even think about moving.'

The guy probably didn't speak English, but he got the message. He nodded and ran a hand through his curly black hair, wincing as he did so.

Behind King, Slater stumbled into the hallway. King heard him exhale sharply as he saw the unconscious man by his feet — and the guy on the ground, disarmed and broken.

'You're something else,' he said.

'Thanks,' King said. 'Nice to redeem myself after you schooled me at the airport.'

'What do we do with them?'

King gently kicked the body of the unconscious man. 'He's no use. Leave him here. The police will sort him out.'

'And him?' Slater said, gesturing to the other guy.

King pondered for a good moment. 'He knows what they're up to. He'll be useful. Bring him with us.'

'Where are we going?'

'Anywhere but here. We just had a skirmish in a residential neighbourhood. Police will be en route.'

Somewhere outside, King heard sirens blaring. They were faint, but it was definitely the cops. It sounded like a substantial convoy, even from this distance away.

'There they are,' he said. 'Let's go. Now.'

'Jesus,' Slater said. 'That was quick.'

'Place like this, you have the advantage of an instant response.'

'Ah, of course. Rich bastards paying to be first priority.'

'That'll be you if you ever get out.'

Slater smiled, shaking his head. 'Already falling into that trap. You should have seen my place in Montenegro.'

'Montenegro?'

Slater waved it off. 'Another time.'

They scooped up the incapacitated mercenary, looping a hand under each armpit. In unison, they dragged him out the front door and into the courtyard.

'What if there's more?' King said.

Slater silently acknowledged the possibility and motioned for the gun. King tossed it underhand. Slater caught it and hurried ahead. He leapt across the destroyed brick wall and swept the barrel in a wide arc around the closest surroundings.

'We're good,' he said. Then he paused. 'Oh, shit…'

'What?'

'Police are faster than I thought. Fuck, *hurry up*.'

King hustled with a newfound sense of urgency, dragging their injured hostage along with him. A gruelling fitness regime and the strength of adrenalin assisted his pace. He rag-dolled the guy over the fence and into the back seat of the BMW, which Slater held open, awaiting the arrival of the new passenger.

King skirted around the rear of the vehicle. As he did so, he flashed a look down the sloping hill, searching for the source of Slater's panic.

'*Shit*,' he whispered, laying eyes on the cluster of armoured vehicles roaring up the road toward their position. All were fitted with flashing emergency lights and the insignia of the French police. He counted at least four cars before ducking into the driver's seat of the BMW.

'That's not good,' Slater said. 'They've seen us.'

'I'm aware of that,' King said. 'You a good driver?'

'I crashed a Lamborghini an hour ago. Not really.'

In any other setting, King would have found the statement hilarious. Now, stern-faced, heart pounding, he fired up the car and slammed it into drive. He mashed the accelerator to the floor. The mercenary was thrown back against the rear seats as the BMW shot off the mark, tearing away from the kerb and ascending the hill amidst a squeal of tyres.

Slater took the MK23 off King, whipped round and jammed its barrel against the man's forehead, keeping him frozen in place. 'Don't try anything, you fuck.'

King saw the leaders of the pack growing closer in his rear-view mirror. They had built up enough speed to ascend the hill faster than he could accelerate. He urged his own vehicle on and swore at the number of police converging on their location.

Moreau must have special privileges when it came to response time. It couldn't have taken more than a couple of minutes for the convoy to reach his private residence. Probably the standard reaction speed when a politician was involved.

He twisted the wheel as they approached the T-junction at the top of the street and the car screamed around the corner, heading into a grid of wealthy suburban avenues. King kept his gaze firmly fixed on the road ahead, taking the BMW to its limits. He tore down a narrow lane and swung the vehicle around another bend not five seconds later.

Then the mercenary in the back exploded into action.

He must have taken advantage of a lapse in Slater's attention. Slater would have drifted his gaze to the police convoy pursuing them, losing concentration on subduing the man.

The MK23 flew past King's face, knocked out of Slater's grip by a well-timed swing. It clattered against the driver's door and disappeared under the seat.

They found themselves defenceless with a furious soldier of fortune in the back seat.

CHAPTER 30

King knew he would be targeted first. If the mercenary had any common sense, he would aim to incapacitate the driver and cause a crash. It carried with it the risk of death depending on how severe the impact was, but it was his best chance at getting away.

Without taking his eyes off the road — which would be a death wish given they were travelling at close to seventy miles an hour — King ducked away from the punch he knew was coming.

It didn't achieve much.

The fist hit him in the jaw, not hard enough to strip him of consciousness but with the well-placed accuracy of a trained fighter. He felt pain flare across one side of his face and he recoiled involuntarily. The car swerved, throwing all its occupants violently around the inside of the vehicle.

King crashed into the driver's door, which would have thrown him out of the car if it had sprung open. He bounced back, locking his grip tighter on the wheel, bringing the vehicle back under control.

Slater spat out a torrent of curses and dove head-first into the back seat, throwing himself into harm's way to protect King from losing control again. King heard the wild sounds of a dirty brawl breaking out. His senses were overloading. Too much was unfolding at once.

He glanced in the rear-view mirror again.

'*Fuck!*' he roared.

The swerve had slowed them down significantly, giving the police convoy time to gain vital ground. The 4WD in front pulled ahead. Its bull bar filled the mirror. King knew an impact was inevitable.

Slater and the last remaining mercenary slammed into the back of King's seat, carried by the brawl. He jerked forwards…

… then the police vehicle obliterated their rear bumper, its bull bar causing massive damage.

The jolt was vicious. It catapulted King into his steering wheel, crushing him against the leather. He rebounded back into his seat but the wind had been knocked from his lungs. He gasped for breath and wrestled to maintain a steady course.

It wouldn't work.

The BMW had veered from the impact.

King's knuckles turned white as the tyres screamed against the asphalt, sending up plumes of smoke. A body crashed into his shoulder and he looked across to see the mercenary launch through the space between seats, carried by the force of the police vehicle ramming them. King took his one hand off the wheel and lashed out.

He caught the guy in the throat in mid-air.

The mercenary toppled head-first into the passenger's seat footwell, his trajectory changed by the punch. His legs splayed awkwardly across King's lap. King wrestled them away, then concentrated on saving everyone in the car from certain death.

The BMW fishtailed across both lanes, narrowly missing a sedan passing in the other direction. He stamped on the brakes and wrenched the wheel.

He heard Slater hurtle across the back seat, slamming into the opposite door. He held on for dear life, riding out the centrifugal forces as the car entered a spin. Smoke billowed from everywhere at once, pouring off the asphalt.

They came to rest in the centre of the road.

Unhurt, but shaken.

King looked out the driver's side window and blanched at the sight of the police convoy heading straight for his door. The pick-up with the bull bar surged ahead once more, aiming for the side of the BMW. If it made direct impact, it would kill him.

He doubted they cared after what had occurred.

He shifted the gearbox into reverse as fast as he possibly could and stamped on the accelerator. What little traction the tyres had left clamped to the asphalt and sent the vehicle careering backward. King's stomach dropped and Slater let out a grunt of surprise.

The police wagon hit the hood of the BMW. A glancing blow. But the vehicle had picked up enough speed to cause massive damage to whatever it touched.

The impact spun their car around like a plaything.

Loose chunks of plastic and metal exploded off the BMW as it twisted around. Inadvertently, they ended up facing the direction they'd been heading in the first place.

King returned the car to drive and floored it.

'We can't take another one of those,' Slater said from the back seat. 'This thing's going to fall apart.'

'I know that,' King said.

The mercenary had finished scrambling out of the footwell, bucking and writhing until he righted himself in the passenger's seat. King sensed Slater diving across the space between them. A thick arm looped around the man's throat and locked into place.

Slater choked the guy into unconsciousness while King drove. The incident with the police wagon had put them in an uncomfortable position. They were now boxed in by the convoy, with the main aggressor vehicle coasting in front of them. Every time King swerved to overtake, the car in front compensated, blocking their path. The driver had good reflexes. King imagined this wasn't his first high-speed chase.

Directly ahead, a narrow laneway branched off from the main road, disappearing between two residential apartment buildings. It was just wide enough to fit a car.

King sucked in air, psyching himself up for what lay next. 'Slater.'

'Yeah?'

'Hold onto something.'

As the police wagon in front tore past the alleyway, King stamped on the brakes, wearing away the rubber on the tyres even further. He wrenched the wheel and aimed as best he could and hoped for the best.

The BMW mounted the footpath at close to fifty miles an hour.

It rocketed across the pavement and shot into the alleyway, knocking off both side mirrors in an explosion of sparks.

King yelled in fear.

Slater released his grip of the unconscious mercenary and grabbed the passenger seat's headrest for stability. The man in front of him slumped over, eyes closed. He wouldn't know if they were involved in a fatal crash.

Lucky bastard, King thought.

The suspension kicked in as they bounced over uneven ground. King jolted in his seat, barely managing to ride out the waves of bumps and crashes. A particularly vicious drop sent him head-first into the roof. He winced and wrestled with the wheel, keeping his foot on the accelerator, making sure they stayed on a straight course.

Then they shot out the other side amidst a spray of sparks. The sound of shrieking metal surrounded the vehicle.

King wasn't sure what was keeping the BMW together, but he thanked the vehicle for keeping them alive.

Barely.

Thoroughly rattled by the treacherous journey between buildings, he pulled them out onto a twisting road that spiralled down into Calvi.

'Get us down there,' Slater said. 'We can lose them in town. It's too congested.'

'On it.'

He brought them back up to max-speed and followed the road, tearing around the bends as fast as he dared. This area was more perilous. Away from the estate, there were no houses boxing them in. No barricades, no railings. Just one wrong turn and a hundred-foot drop to certain death. The BMW was on its final throes. Any more significant force applied to its chassis would buckle it completely.

'Well, that changes things slightly,' Slater said, falling back into the rear seats and sucking air into his lungs in an attempt to calm himself down. King did the same.

It was their first real opportunity to recover from the chaos.

'It doesn't change much,' King said. 'Except now Moreau knows he has a problem.'

'We're nowhere near working out what he's up to.'

'There's no backing out now. There's two dead men up there.'

'There'll be more once I discover what this fucker is doing,' Slater said, venom in his tone. 'That wasn't an ordinary police response. They were looking to ram us off the road and kill us. I'm sure of it. No-one's that aggressive when trying to make an arrest.'

'We work for the government, technically,' King said, allowing himself a quick smile. 'I'm sure we're that aggressive — if not more.'

'We're a different story,' Slater said. 'You think they chase civilians like that? They wanted us dead. Moreau's paying them off, I'm sure of it.'

'Let's not jump to conclusions. Right now, we don't even know if he's doing anything illegal.'

'You never would have turned around if you didn't think he was doing some sick shit. You wouldn't have risked it. You had a straight path to a plane ride out of here. Whatever you found out on the phone — you believe in it.'

'I didn't find out anything,' King said. 'Just that he lied through his teeth when he tracked me down. That's enough to get me fired up.'

'Thought you said you were trying to avoid this kind of thing in retirement.'

'I was. Doesn't seem to be working out at all. I was adamant that this was the day I would put it all behind me. It's why I was in such a hurry to leave Corsica. The old me would have razed half the island to the ground to sort out the mercenary situation.'

'That seems to be what you're doing now.'

King reluctantly agreed. He looked across at the unconscious man in the passenger seat and thought back to the skirmish with the other three mercenaries.

To knocking weapons away and throwing punches.

To putting bad men in their place.

To winning.

Truth was, he'd enjoyed every second of it.

'The old me is back,' he said. 'Don't know if he ever left. Don't know if he ever will.'

CHAPTER 31

It didn't take them long to find a place to hunker down.

King pulled their battered ride into a narrow residential street on the outskirts of the main town and stopped in front of a small one-storey house with a spacious yard and a two-car garage. A huge sign nailed into the grass out front indicated that the property was for sale.

And entirely unoccupied.

'This'll do,' King said.

He climbed out. As his feet touched the pavement he experienced a momentary wave of dizziness. He leant against the car and steadied himself. His head throbbed. His jaw ached. His ribs seared with every hurried movement.

None of which were new experiences.

He had spent half his career in considerable pain. He knew how to deal with it. Ride it out. Power through the unpleasantness until he had completed whatever task lay in front of him.

He would do so now.

He assumed Slater would do the same.

Together they helped the mercenary out of the car, who had woken to a semi-conscious state. They hurried him across the sidewalk and up to the front deck. Now that they were out of the carnage, King could get a better look at the man.

He was tall. Almost the same height as King. He guessed six-two. Well-built. Obviously kept himself in reasonable shape at the gymnasium. He was the perfect example of commercial fitness. Theoretically, he was likely the same size as King in terms of sheer muscle mass. Yet it was clear he trained entirely for aesthetics. King could hurl him around with ease.

King had battlefield fitness.

He thundered the front door open with a single kick. No alarms sounded. A system hadn't even been installed yet. He imagined crime was relatively low in a seaside town like Calvi. They would be more lax to security measures than other areas.

Except Moreau, apparently.

Slater followed him inside, slamming the door behind them. They moved to the empty kitchen — entirely devoid of furniture — and threw the mercenary down on the dusty wooden floor.

He moaned and coughed violently.

'You speak English?' King said.

No response.

'English?'

The guy shook his head. 'No.'

King looked at Slater. 'Please tell me you speak French.'

Slater raised an eyebrow. 'You don't? You live here.'

'Not enough to hold a conversation.'

They established a system where King would talk, Slater would translate, the man would respond, and Slater would relay the message back to King.

'You're working with Afshar?' King said.

The mercenary instantly perked up at the name. He nodded, a little too vigorously. As if he were hoping his leader were still alive.

'You're employed by Yves Moreau?' King said.

No response, even when Slater translated.

Which meant *yes*.

King darted forward, moving with anger and purpose, a fake bull rush that made the mercenary flinch from where he lay cowering on the floor. 'I'll hit you for real next time. Yves Moreau?'

Slater translated again. Begrudgingly, the man nodded.

'What is he using you for?' King said. He assumed the man understood, but got Slater to translate just in case.

The man took a long time to respond. As if he were weighing up his options. He knew he had few. Either he told King and Slater what they wanted to hear, or the consequences would be disastrous. He began to speak, fast and panicked, like he was sharing information that he knew he shouldn't be divulging, no matter the severity of the situation.

Slater said, 'He says he and his friends are set up on a luxury yacht in the Bay of Calvi. He says it's the largest one there. Towers over all the others in the marina. Impossible to miss. They're here to oversee the smooth transition of a shipment and make sure everything goes according to plan.'

'A shipment?' King said. 'What does he mean?'

'He's being intentionally vague,' Slater said. 'Think you should do something about that. Give him a reality check.'

King motioned for the MK23. Slater handed it over. He took a step forward and elevated the barrel, aiming it directly in between the mercenary's legs.

'You hold back one more fucking thing from me,' King said, 'and I'll change your life forever. Tell me what I want to hear.'

The man spat out, '*Femelles.*'

King knew what that meant. His stomach dropped, even before Slater uttered the single-word translation. 'Females.'

'I definitely don't like the sound of that,' King said.

Slater stared at the mercenary for several drawn-out seconds, letting the silence hang in the air, until it reached an uncomfortable length. The mercenary squirmed on the floor. He said something, speaking inhumanly fast, his voice laced with fear.

242

'He says he just does what he's paid to do,' Slater said, refusing to take his eyes off the man. He bored his gaze into the guy until he began to visibly sweat. Pores opened up across his forehead and salty droplets started to trickle into his eyes.

King wasn't about to interrupt. He could feel the rage coursing through Slater.

Perhaps he'd been affected by personal experiences related to human trafficking in the past…

Whatever it was, it didn't seem like there was a positive outcome involved for the mercenary on the kitchen floor. King saw something flash in Slater's eyes. Something primal and furious. He feared that if he let Slater do as he pleased, the mercenary would suffer for an extended period of time.

No matter what his shortcomings were, King didn't want that to happen.

When the mercenary made a sudden, desperate move — his limbs scrambling against the wooden floor as they flooded with panic — King raised the MK23 and shot him between the eyes.

The discharge echoed through the tight space, making Slater flinch. The mercenary slumped to the floor, his expression cold, his face already turning pale. Eyes wide. Mouth open. Staring into oblivion. King flicked the safety back on and slotted the handgun into his waistband.

Slater turned to him. 'That was too quick.'

'Thought you might think as much. We're not here to torture anyone.'

'It would have been my pleasure.'

'You're letting emotions get in the way,' King said. 'I can tell something about that made you snap. I won't be too intrusive. I won't ask questions. But he wasn't the man to take out your anger on…'

'Who are you to say he wasn't? He's willingly aiding this entire thing.'

'We're after the men who run it,' King said. 'We're after Moreau.'

Slater rested a hand on the smooth stone countertop running the length of the kitchen and pressed down hard, letting out some of his anger. 'I haven't had the chance to meet him yet. I can't wait.'

'He's all yours,' King said.

'You happy?' Slater said.

'Why on earth would I be happy?'

'Now you know what he's up to. Roughly. Wasn't that your whole intention in coming back?'

'I'll be happy when he's dead.'

Slater glanced at the corpse pooling blood onto the wood. 'Would have been ideal if we could get a bit more information out of that guy. We just know the biggest boat in the marina is where everything goes down. A little rudimentary.'

'You're right,' King said. 'But he made a move.'

Slater kept his eyes on the corpse. 'You acted pretty quick.'

'You need to in situations like those.'

'He was unarmed.'

'Didn't want to risk it.'

'You didn't kill him to stop me from having my way with him, did you?'

King paused. 'I'm not going to answer that.'

'I don't need you to babysit me.'

'And I'm not going to. We go after Moreau, and you can do what you want with him.'

King crossed to the nearest window and pried open a pair of blinds. He peered out into the yard. The sun had begun its steady decline toward the opposite horizon. He guessed it would set in a couple of hours.

'What's the time?' he asked Slater.

'Almost three.'

'I say we wait until it's dark. Easier to approach the boat that way. And if it's as large as I think it is, then whoever's buying or selling the girls will be staying onboard. That way, they can leave at a moment's notice.'

'You think Moreau's task force is the only people involved in this?' Slater said.

'We don't know enough yet. I vote we get a couple of hours rest. I have a feeling we'll need it.'

Slater crossed to the living room and threw himself down on one of the sofas. 'I was thinking the same.'

CHAPTER 32

King didn't want there to be any chance of their vehicle being spotted out on the street. He pulled the BMW into the driveway and parked it inches away from the closed garage door. A solid wooden fence blocked it from any inquisitive eyes. A passerby would have to stare directly down the driveway to get a glimpse of the BMW's rear, which had been caved in by the impact with the police wagon.

He was surprised the car even started.

He returned to the house, where Slater had closed his eyes. His head had drooped back against one of the armrests. He looked peaceful. King let him be. Enough time had passed to reduce the risk of serious brain injury.

Besides, the man deserved a nap.

King planted himself on the opposite sofa and stared at the ceiling. There was a great deal on his mind. None of it positive. He was furious at himself for throwing all his progress away and willingly diving back into the madness. It almost seemed like he'd been looking for an excuse to turn back and fight. If he'd truly intended to find peace, he could have been halfway over the Tyrrhenian Sea, en route to a thousand potential destinations.

All of them probably entirely devoid of people looking to actively end his life.

Moreau knew who he was. He'd been able to locate King's villa and find a way in fairly effortlessly.

But what had that conversation been necessary for?

The politician had asked for his help in tracking down the remaining mercenaries — even though in truth they worked for him. Why had he bothered to involve King at all? Why hadn't he planted a bullet in the back of his skull when he went to leave the property? That would be the rational solution to finding the man who had killed three of his employees.

King drew frightening parallels to Venezuela, where a drug lord had toyed with him on the grounds of letting out a little rage.

But Moreau didn't seem like an inherently angry man.

There was something more to this.

He would soon find out what that was. For some reason or another, King had been allowed to live. He would utilise that opportunity, as he always did. It only took one slip-up on the part of his adversaries.

Across from him, Slater's eyes flitted open at the same time as he jerked awake, springing off the couch in one tense motion. He looked around the room, wide-eyed. Then he dropped back onto the cushion and let out a giant breath. Easing the pent-up terror in his system.

'Bad dreams?' King said.

Slater looked at him. 'Yeah.'

'You usually get them?'

'Not like that one.'

'What do you mean?'

Slater settled back into the sofa and put his feet up on the coffee table in the centre of the room. 'Sorry, King, but I haven't known you long enough to get this personal.'

King nodded. 'Understood.'

'I might tell you after all this is over.'

'I think I have an idea anyway.'

Slater raised an eyebrow. 'You do?'

King pointed to the kitchen, to the trail of blood flowing steadily along the floor. 'You looked at that man like you wanted to tear his limbs off one by one. I assume as a Black Force operative you're accustomed to violence and corruption and unpleasantness. Something particular about what he said set you off. Something personal.'

Slater's expression glazed over, like he was flashing back to memories long in the past. Memories he'd rather not dwell on. What the mercenary had said seemed to have stirred them out of his subconscious. 'Human trafficking … of that kind. It has particular meaning to me.'

'You don't have to say another word if you don't want to,' King said.

Slater scoffed. 'I know that, King. I'm a big boy. I've got my head on my shoulders. I can tell you whatever I wish to tell you.'

'And I won't be—'

'My mom,' Slater interrupted, blurting out the two words like they'd been swirling around in his head for far too long.

'Your…?' King said, beginning to understand the implications. His skin turned pale.

'I told you I grew up on the streets,' Slater said, staring past King, refusing to make eye contact. His eyes began to water. 'Before that, we never had money. My parents worked odd jobs when they could. It was never enough. We barely got by. So my mother turned to … other methods of employment.'

'I'm sorry,' King said. It was all he could manage.

Slater shrugged. 'Just the facts. She fell in deep with the wrong crowd. Did unspeakable things. Then one day, she vanished. She'd been spending more and more time around the pimps and the dealers and the fiends. They must have seen a tantalising opportunity. She was beautiful. Far too pretty for that kind of work. So I imagined they shipped her off to some third-world country to please a few dictators. Something like that. I'll honestly never know what happened to her.'

'Jesus Christ,' King said, lost in his thoughts, unable to comprehend what that would do to a man. 'How old were you?'

'Thirteen,' Slater said. 'Old enough to work out the most likely outcome. Young enough to not be able to do anything about it.'

'What about your father?'

'He didn't have a spine,' Slater said, his tone suddenly cold, emotionless, detached. 'Sure, he was sad, but he didn't do anything. He probably knew exactly who took her. But what could he do? He was a skinny drug addict.'

'What happened to him?'

'He killed himself the year after.'

King took a moment to respond. His own childhood had been a breeze in comparison to Slater's. He couldn't imagine what that level of grief and distress would do to a young teenager.

Yes you do, he thought. *It created a Black Force operative.*

'When I joined the military,' Slater said, 'I never expected it to lead to this. But then again, I'm glad I ended up in a division like Black Force. It allows me certain … exceptions. Being off-the-record has its advantages.'

King paused. 'Do they know?'

Slater shook his head. 'No. If they did, I imagine they'd use me as a wrecking ball to destabilise international trafficking operations. But if that's all I spent my time doing, it would consume me.'

'I've dealt with traffickers before,' King said, thinking back to his time in the secret world. 'I imagine they would show up on missions every now and then.'

'They do,' Slater said. 'And I can't help myself. I always go overboard.'

'Command hasn't clued in?'

'I'm sure they have,' Slater said. 'But I think they pass it off as just instability. After all, you have to be a little insane to do what we do.'

'What you do,' King said. 'I'm out.'

Slater cocked his head and waved an arm around the place. 'Does it look like you're out?'

King didn't respond.

Of course it doesn't, he thought. *You'll never be out.*

'What about you?' Slater said. 'Your parents still alive?'

King mused on the question for a long while. 'My mother isn't.'

'She died when you were young?'

King nodded. 'Cancer.'

'I'm sorry.'

King shrugged. 'The three of us saw it coming for a long time.'

'You and your parents?'

King nodded again.

'Only child?'

A third nod. 'Yourself?'

'Yep,' Slater said. 'Just me.'

'Dad raised me for the last half of my childhood. He didn't do a very good job.'

Slater frowned, as if he didn't wish to probe any further yet knew it wouldn't be enough to leave it there. 'Was he abusive?'

King shook his head. 'He just wasn't there. Mom's death hit him hard. Harder than I thought possible. He fell into himself. It was impossible to communicate in any meaningful way.'

'Does he know what you do?' Slater said, then corrected himself. 'What you *did?*'

'He knows I joined the military,' King said. 'I think that's the extent of it.'

'Where is he now?'

'I have no idea. I haven't seen him in fourteen years. In all likelihood, he's in the ground.'

Slater paused. 'You ever think about tracking him down?'

King hesitated, then shook his head. 'Not my thing. We went our separate ways. We understood that.'

'I'm sure he'd want to hear from you.'

'I wouldn't know the first place to start looking.'

Slater shrugged. 'I hope one day you try. If my father was alive, I'd be sure to give it a shot. You don't want to find out too late that he passed before you could meet.'

He settled back into the sofa and closed his eyes again, unaware just how profound of an impact his statements had made on King.

King got up and crossed to the kitchen, leaving Slater to get some rest. He glimpsed the body of the dead mercenary on the floor. He ignored it. He had spent too much of his career surrounded by the dead for their presence to bother him. He propped himself up on the counter and rested his elbows on his knees…

… and wept.

CHAPTER 33

He came to roughly an hour later, stirring out of unconsciousness on the sofa opposite Slater. At some point he had clambered off the kitchen counter and returned to the comfort of the cushions. Slater was still fast asleep. The man's stomach rose and fell in his slumber.

King wiped his eyes and moved to the bathroom to clean himself up. He hadn't anticipated turning into such a wreck, but Slater's words had struck a chord with him. He would do his best to hide how much of an effect they had, because that was simply the way he handled things.

But he wouldn't forget what he had been told.

He showered, washing away the blood and dirt and dust covering him from head-to-toe. The previous twenty-four hours had been a whirlwind of action that he was only just coming down from. The freezing water lent him a renewed vigour. It recharged him. Revitalised his system. Now clean, he dried himself before dressing in the same clothes and heading back into the living room.

Slater stirred as he moved across the wooden flooring, which creaked and groaned under his weight. King wrenched the MK23 automatic pistol out of his belt and dropped it on the coffee table between them.

'You well-rested now?' he said.

Slater nodded. 'Good as new. Sofa's a hell of a lot better than what I've had to put up with in the past.'

'Likewise. Is this the only weapon we have?'

'Afraid so. At the time I thought it would only take one shot.'

'You seemed to have no trouble getting your hands on a grenade.'

Slater smiled. 'Like I said, my contact had one lying around. How could I refuse?'

'And you decided to waste it blowing up a fence?'

'Can you think of a better use for it?' Slater said. 'You want to throw it onto the boat Moreau's using? He'll use his goods as human shields and you know it.'

'How do you expect us to take on an army with a single handgun?'

'We don't know how many there are,' Slater said. 'For all we know, we took care of the last four at Moreau's house.'

'I highly doubt that.'

'So do I. But it's possible. Besides, we only need one bullet.'

King raised an eyebrow. 'Oh?'

Slater waved a hand dismissively. 'Kill the first guy. Take his weapon. Now we have two weapons. Rinse and repeat.'

'You make it sound awfully simple.'

'I've been doing this long enough.'

'Don't get cocky.'

Slater rose off the couch and made for the front door. 'I'm not cocky. I'm determined. I'll rip Moreau's head off before I leave. That's a promise.'

King believed him. 'It's not dark yet.'

'We can do some scouting. I can't sit around in this house any longer.'

'We'll be sitting ducks in that BMW,' King said. 'It's hanging together by a thread.'

Slater looked at him like he were a child throwing a temper tantrum. 'For fuck's sakes, King. We'll just steal another car. It's not that hard.'

'I'd prefer not to ruin anyone else's day.'

Slater threw open the front door and hurried outside. 'We'll be ruining several before the morning.'

In the twilight they piled into the BMW and reversed out of the driveway. They left the dead mercenary in the house. Someone would discover him, but by then King planned to be on another continent.

He planned to vanish into thin air after this was done.

'Slater,' he said as he turned onto the main road and headed for the Bay of Calvi.

The man looked across. 'Yeah?'

'Promise me you'll make me leave after this is over. I can't keep getting into this shit.'

Slater took his time to respond. 'You're a broken record, King. If you wanted to get away from all this madness, you would have. It's as simple as that.'

Begrudgingly, King admitted that the man was right. Sooner or later, he had to face the facts.

He feared he would never find peace.

Suddenly, Slater piped up. 'Stop the car.'

'What?'

'Pull over. Now.'

There was urgency in his tone. King wasn't about to argue. Slater knew what he was doing. There had to be a valid reason for the sudden demand. He drifted to the side of the road.

'What?' he said again.

'You should go.'

'What do you mean I should go?'

'You keep talking about getting away from everything. About starting over, and avoiding violence at all costs. That's what you want, right?'

'Yeah.'

'Then go. I'm the one who still works for the government. I'm responsible for eradicating pieces of shit like Moreau. I have everything I need. I'd be happy to carry out what needs to be done. You have no need to involve yourself with this. Hand it over to me, and disappear. If you *really* are serious about retirement, then you won't go a single foot further. You'll get out of the car and let me take over and get yourself to the nearest airport as fast as you can. You'll forget I ever existed. Now's your chance.'

They lapsed into silence. King made sure not to rush his response, because he knew he truly needed to think about what Slater had said. The man was completely right. Intentions and actions were two separate things. He found himself desperate to find solace yet perfectly willing to throw himself back into harm's way at the nearest opportunity.

There was no reason for him to continue on to Moreau.

It had nothing to do with him.

But did it ever?

He took his foot off the brake and pressed onward.

Slater shook his head in disbelief. 'Your call.'

'I've been lying to myself this entire time,' King said. 'I keep saying I want to get away from this — but for what? I'll just find trouble somewhere else in the world. And the whole time I'll wonder if you succeeded in doing away with Moreau.'

'Trust me,' Slater said. 'I'll succeed.'

259

'And I'll help you do so. That's my choice.'

'So be it.'

King let his resolve grow steely. He continued down the road until they ducked in between traditional cottages and multi-storey buildings.

They entered Calvi, and pressed on toward the marina.

—

Night fell over the Quai Adolphe Landry. Streetlights flickered on across the promenade, lighting the way for the small clusters of tourists drifting from the beach to the restaurants, then back to their hotels. Tropical birds shrieked as the sun dipped below the horizon.

A pleasant setting, soothing for all but the white-haired man hurrying along the largest pier in the marina, headed for a gargantuan luxury yacht bobbing in the shallows of the bay, moored to the jetty.

Yves Moreau strode with intense purpose.

His brow had been furrowed for hours, a clear indication of the stress he was experiencing. He had received grave news regarding four of the members of the task force protecting his operation. The ease with which they were being dispatched troubled him endlessly.

Moreau was careful with his money. He always had been. He rarely spent it on unnecessary luxuries — with the exception of the decadent house he owned in the hills. A house which had been effortlessly ransacked by Jason King and his mysterious friend not two hours ago.

They had eluded police capture. They had killed two of his men, knocked one senseless, and made off with the fourth. That mercenary's location had yet to be determined. He had his people scouring the island.

What the fuck am I paying all these idiots for? he thought.

What had begun as a proposition full of potential and financial gain had morphed into an operation of the highest magnitude. His side profession made him hundreds of thousands of dollars a week, which he expertly funnelled into tax havens all across the globe. He was a smart and cautious man. He wanted to spend the rest of his term in office, then disappear into a life of unparalleled luxury. He was saving everything he owned for such an occasion.

He couldn't give a shit who he had to exploit to get there.

Soon, he would be free. The largest deal in his illegal operation's short-lived history was about to unfold. He'd be damned if he let a pair of nobodies throw it all away.

He exchanged a nod with two burly security guards manning the drawbridge connecting the enormous yacht to the dock. They recognised him, and allowed him to pass without a word. He was the reason they were in Corsica. They would not mistake him for anyone else.

He walked through corridors with plush carpet and ornate artwork hanging on the walls. Finally he entered a large boardroom in the centre of the yacht, containing a massive oak table surrounded by more than fifteen antique chairs.

A dark-skinned man sat at the end of the table.

He was of Arabic descent, with a clean-shaven face and a pronounced jawline. He kept his hair short. He didn't look a day over thirty, yet Moreau knew he was in his late forties. He was the owner of the yacht — and the reason for Moreau's recent successes.

Where he came from, Moreau's services were in high demand.

He would shortly provide Moreau with more money than he had ever seen in his life.

In exchange for the goods, of course.

'Are we ready to proceed?' he said, his tone calm and even. He spoke as if he were on the verge of falling asleep. Yet Moreau knew that he chose his words with precision. He never spoke an unnecessary syllable. He was a calculated and cunning man — much like Moreau.

'Yes,' Moreau said. 'I have what was promised.'

'Wonderful,' the man said. 'Bring them aboard.'

CHAPTER 34

King parked the BMW in a secluded lot between two residential apartment buildings. It coughed and spluttered into its parking space and came to rest for a final time with a pathetic wheeze.

King patted the wheel. 'You've been good to us.'

Slater gave him an odd expression before he got out. 'You're talking to a fucking car.'

They exited the four-wheel-drive and King tossed the keys into the gravel. They would no longer be needing it. If they ventured any closer to the marina in it, they would surely be spotted. King didn't want to risk it, and Slater didn't protest as he decided to abandon the vehicle.

They would proceed on foot.

'What if we get arrested?' King said. 'I'm not willing to kill police officers to escape.'

'I'll get us out,' Slater said. 'Black Force has influence.'

'You sure? They also want to kill me.'

Slater winced. 'Noted.'

'I guess the answer is to try not to cause too much of a scene.'

'Yeah,' Slater said. 'Like that ever happens.'

They strode down narrow alleys and through cobbled streets sloping down toward the bay. As the last of the daylight disappeared into the horizon, shops began to shut their windows and the various restaurants serving dinner grew busier. The sounds of nightlife sounded from all around them.

Normality.

People going about their day without a worry in the world. They cared about taxes and budgeting and what people in their workplace thought about them and whether they would miss their shuttle bus to the airport.

King seemed to only care about staying alive.

He and Slater moved through the night like they were a different breed to the surrounding civilians. He couldn't help darting his gaze across everyone in his vision, checking to see whether they were armed. Always vigilant. Always worried about what threat would appear next.

He began to feel like they might make it to the marina without incident when a burly police officer rounded the corner and bumped directly into Slater.

For a moment, the pair of them passed it off as a simple misunderstanding. Slater smiled and murmured an apology in French. The policeman — who sported a thick moustache and the musculature of an aging man keeping himself fit with a healthy dose of HGH and testosterone — nodded back, accepting the statement.

He went to brush past them.

Then he noticed the great purple bruise splotched across King's face and stopped in his tracks.

He studied them in silence. King could see more details were becoming apparent. Their imposing statures. The cuts and wounds dotting their exposed skin.

'Where are you two off to?' he said in perfect English.

King was taken aback by his fluency. 'The bay. We thought we'd get dinner there.'

'Seems like you're not having much fun,' the officer said, gesturing to their faces.

King smiled. 'ATV accident. We both ran into each other on a tour. Hurt like a bitch.'

'Here as tourists?'

Slater nodded. 'We're work colleagues. Thought we'd come see the sights. It's a beautiful island.'

The officer relaxed slightly. 'Sure is. I've lived here my whole life.'

'Your English is good,' King remarked.

'Thank you,' the officer said. 'It's a hobby of mine. Been teaching myself for more than ten years. How's my accent? I'm working on phasing it out.'

'Impeccable,' Slater said. 'Can't fault it.'

'You have a good night, sir,' King said. He moved to brush past the officer.

The man held out a hand and placed it gently on his chest. 'Hold on a second, sir.'

King felt his knuckles tingle. He was ready for anything. 'What's wrong?'

'I'm going to need to see some identification,' he said. 'From both of you. My apologies.'

Slater raised his eyebrows, feigning mock surprise. 'What's this about?'

'Just precautionary,' the man said. 'I'm sure you're fine, but there's been some trouble around these parts over the last couple of days. Getting some strange reports out of Saint-Florent, too. Across the coast.'

'Oh?' Slater said. 'What kind of reports?'

'Strange happenings,' the officer said, shaking his head. 'I'm not too sure what's going on, to be honest. Anyway, they've told us to keep a lookout for men of your description. I'm sure—'

One second, the officer was mid-spiel — and the next he careered back across the footpath, rocked by a devastating uppercut from Slater. King jolted on the spot, surprised by the sudden shift in atmosphere. He hadn't even seen the punch swinging through the air. Slater had thrown it with wild ferocity, letting loose out of nowhere.

Now, he moved in to finish the job and knock the officer unconscious.

King stepped forward and shoved Slater out of the way with both hands. The man had been in the middle of building momentum for a second punch — and hadn't anticipated the abrupt change of direction. Slater skidded on the concrete and toppled over.

Before Slater could right himself, King charged at the police officer and swung a scything fist directly into the man's torso. He targeted the right lobe of the officer's liver. If placed correctly, the liver shot could cause devastating agony — enough to keep anyone preoccupied for enough time to get away. He had landed a pinpoint accurate blow back in Venezuela.

He hoped this strike had a similar effect.

The officer's legs buckled and he dropped to the pavement. A fierce moan spluttered from his lips and he squeezed his eyes shut.

Perfect.

King turned around and hauled Slater to his feet. 'Let's go.'

'What the fuck was—'

He didn't get time to finish the sentence. King hurled him past the police officer, who had curled himself into the foetal position, riding out the waves of pain racking his system.

'What'd you do to him?' Slater muttered.

They rounded the corner the officer had come from moments before the first scream of a witness echoed through the street. For all they knew, King had just viciously wounded an officer of the law. The civilians who had seen the fight take place would be suitably rattled.

'He'll be fine,' King said. 'That pain fades. I didn't want you to knock him out.'

Slater struggled to match King's pace as he strode away from the scene as fast as possible. 'Are you insane? What are you talking about?'

'Unconsciousness is risky,' King explained. 'Who knows what could result from that. You were going to shut his lights out, I could see it plain as day. He might have never woken up. It's a dangerous game to play. Better to hit him in the liver. He didn't do anything to us.'

'You're incredibly preachy sometimes,' Slater said.

King shrugged. 'Helps me sleep at night.'

'Whatever takes the edge off.'

Just like that, Calvi's claustrophobic centre shrank away. They burst out onto a picturesque path curving around the bay. It passed the marina and ran all the way up to the Citadel of Calvi — an enormous walled-off cluster of buildings atop a rocky outcrop. On a tour through the citadel during his first few weeks on the island, King had discovered it was built in 1492.

He doubted he would ever return there after what lay ahead.

The marina was almost full, dotted with hundreds of pleasure crafts organised into orderly rows. The entire space was largely deserted. Most of the occupants were either staying on dry land or out for dinner at any number of the expensive restaurants around these parts.

'Any idea which is our target?' Slater said, perusing the different boats in turn.

King motioned to a craft at the very end of the furthest pier. 'I'd say it's that one.'

'Jesus,' Slater whispered. 'That's a whole new level of wealth.'

The superyacht had clearly been custom-made for whoever commissioned its construction. It towered above all its neighbours, more of a status symbol than for actual function. He couldn't imagine why anyone needed that much space on a boat. King counted five levels to the craft, each one smaller than the last. It had to be at least three hundred feet in length, painted a dark shade of grey.

'Not exactly conspicuous, is it?' Slater commented. 'You'd think if its owner was up to something illegal he would be a tad more … subtle.'

'They probably think they're invincible,' King said. 'Can't wait to show them otherwise.'

Even from this distance, he spotted internal lights shining across the first level of the boat. The deck was illuminated by large floodlights, but its contents were obstructed from view by the tall rim running the length of the boat's perimeter. It lent privacy to whoever was aboard.

'We'll be going in blind,' Slater said, rubbing his scalp with one hand. 'I don't know about this.'

'I thought you were determined to teach this man a lesson,' King said.

'I am. But anger doesn't make me an idiot. We know absolutely nothing about what we'll find — except that Moreau has guns-for-hire … and live hostages.'

'This is what I do best,' King said. 'Let's take a closer look. Don't stare too long. They'll know what I look like, but they don't know you. And I don't think they'll open fire in a tourist destination like this.'

Slater scanned the bay. 'It's too busy.'

'It's always like this,' King said.

'I doubt it. This is prime dinnertime. I vote we get something to eat and wait till these parts start to empty.'

'Less potential crossfire?'

'Exactly. I highly doubt Calvi is the city-that-never-sleeps. We keep an eye on the boat, and if it starts to move out we make a mad dash for it. Sound good?'

'Good call.'

They moved closer to the marina and selected a restaurant at random. It was a quaint number with an open deck and a lively atmosphere. Waiters floated around the customers, taking orders and refilling drinks.

King led the way. He wandered up to the maître d' waiting patiently by the entrance and held up two fingers.

The man nodded and led them to a table at the front. From here, they had a direct view down the length of the pier where their target lay. King took a seat, being cautious not to draw too much attention to himself, and browsed the menu. Slater sat opposite and did the same.

A few minutes later, he flashed a glance down the pier.

It was heavily guarded. Clearly valuing safety over being inconspicuous, Moreau and whoever he was dealing with had made sure the pier was manned by at least four men at all times. They wore nondescript black suits and patrolled the length of the pier in a pre-constructed pattern, arms behind their backs, looking for any signs of trouble. Behind them, the superyacht loomed.

From this angle, King had a better view of the helipad attached to the rear of the craft. He hadn't noticed its existence before. The boat's bulk had blocked it from view. Atop the flat stretch of deck rested a HAL Light Utility Helicopter, painted the same colour as the yacht.

King let out a low whistle as he studied the new sight.

'What's up?' Slater said.

'Check the back.'

Slater turned his head. 'Whoa. You think Moreau will try to get away on that?'

King shrugged. 'I doubt it. He's a prominent political figure. If he flees, the gig is up. I think he'll stay as long as it takes. His contact, however…'

'Who we know nothing about.'

'He owns the boat. He's either buying or selling women. That's all we need to know.'

'You sure?'

'It'd be ideal if we knew more, obviously. But at the end of the day, it's just another man with a gun. I've seen a million of them.'

'You don't know that he's just a man with a gun.'

'They all are, Slater.'

A waitress hovered nearby, looking to take their order but unwilling to interrupt what looked to be a serious conversation. King beckoned her over when he noticed her standing there.

He ordered a sirloin steak with Béarnaise sauce and Slater went for the poulet caramel. The woman nodded satisfactorily, collected their menus and disappeared.

Slater leant back in his chair and spent a moment admiring the view. 'You know, I could get used to this…'

'Retirement's growing on you?'

'It's still a fantasy,' Slater said. 'We talked about this earlier. They need me right now.'

'Always put yourself before Black Force,' King said. 'I learnt that the hard way. Spent far too long in the game. Barely got out alive.'

'Looks like you're struggling to stay away, isn't it?'

'It seems so,' King said, taking a long swig of the chilled table water.

Slater noticed something on the menu and beckoned for a waiter. A squat middle-aged man in a suit and matching cravat hurried over. 'Sant Armettu Myrtus, please. A bottle.'

The waiter nodded his understanding and returned a minute later with two glasses and an unopened bottle of red wine. He and Slater went through the elaborate tasting routine before he scurried away. Slater poured himself a glass and took a mighty gulp.

He saw King watching and raised the glass. 'Try some. It's damn good.'

'We're about to launch an assault on a boat crawling with security,' King explained matter-of-factly. 'Are you insane?'

Slater shrugged and took another mouthful. 'I work better with a buzz.'

'I think your addictive personality is shining through,' King said.

'Maybe so,' Slater said. 'You should see my gambling habits.'

'You sure it's a good idea?'

'I kicked your ass at Sainte-Catherine Airport after four glasses of whiskey on the plane. I think I'll be fine.'

King briefly considered taking the bottle away, but it would only cause more problems. Slater was a grown man. He knew what he was doing. If he willingly decided to consume alcohol before what would likely be an all-out war, then so be it.

'I'm serious,' Slater said. 'Try some. It might calm the nerves.'

'Water for me,' King said.

CHAPTER 35

They spent two hours at the table. The food was good and the weather was perfect. A balmy evening, just the right temperature to make sitting outside a pleasant experience. King found the time passed quicker than he anticipated. He discovered there was much to talk about with Slater. The two of them drew interesting parallels given the nature of their work.

'How do you handle the isolation?' King said as the last of the patrons filtered out of the restaurant's open deck, late into the evening, after the Bay of Calvi had almost entirely emptied of tourists and locals.

Slater drained his second glass of wine and discarded it onto the tabletop. 'Well enough.'

'You're used to it? Spending days and weeks at a time in remote corners of the globe?'

The man raised his hands in an *I-guess-so* gesture. 'Just what I've always done. It stopped driving me mad after a few months.'

'Ever feel like you're missing out on a normal life? We don't get to do what ordinary members of society do. We don't worry about anything other than staying alive.'

'All the time,' Slater admitted. 'It's been on my mind since I started this whole insane journey. Will I look back on Black Force and regret ever accepting a position in its ranks? I really don't know. Have you?'

King shook his head. 'I thought I would. But we do good things.'

'Good?'

'Necessary things.'

'I'm not so sure anymore,' Slater said. 'They asked me to kill you, after all.'

Someone rested a hand on King's shoulder. He turned, expecting to have to drive one of his pieces of cutlery into the throat of a would-be attacker. Instead, the maître d' looked at them apologetically.

'I'm sorry, messieurs,' he said, his accent thick. He must have recognised English as their primary language throughout the evening and done his best to converse in their natural tongue. 'We are now closed. May I get the bill?'

Slater reached into his jacket pocket and withdrew a wad of euros. It looked to be well over a thousand. He handed it over to the man, who bore a look of restrained surprise. 'Monsieur…'

'Keep it,' Slater said. 'I don't need it. I'm out of here in the morning.'

King laughed at the shocked expression on the man's face. He rose out of his chair and slapped the man on the shoulder in turn. 'Enjoy it. My friend isn't always so generous.'

They shuffled off the deck and stepped down onto the promenade. By now it was pitch black. The streetlights stayed on, but they revealed that the Bay of Calvi had largely become a ghost town. Slater glanced around at the absence of pedestrians. He smiled.

'This is perfect,' he said. 'You ready?'

King sighed. 'Seems I always am. Let's go.'

They strolled slowly away from the pier so as not to attract the attention of the security detail. If they loitered too long around the area, King knew they would be seen as suspicious and confronted. As of now, they only had a single firearm.

They reached a wooden bench facing the water and came to a halt.

'Stealth isn't going to work,' Slater said as they sat down.

'Sneaking aboard, you mean?'

'You know it just as well as I do.'

'Yeah. I figured as much. There isn't any way we're doing this quietly.'

'So we're doing it? We've committed?'

King looked at him. 'I'm ready. Are you?'

'There's nothing I want more. Just needed the go-ahead.'

'Anyone on board that boat would be better off six feet under.'

'I whole-heartedly agree.'

'What are you thinking?' King said, scratching his head. 'How do we do this? An all-out assault?'

Slater clasped his hands behind his back as he walked. 'I have an idea.'

'You don't sound too sure of it.'

'I'm not. It's reckless as all hell.'

'I tend to specialise in that sort of thing,' King said. 'You saw what I did back in Saint-Florent.'

'I think I can match that. It's the only way we're getting onto the boat without being torn to pieces.'

King paused. 'What do you have in mind?'

Slater made sure there was no-one in their general vicinity before responding. 'You've got the gun?'

King nodded, tapping his belt.

'Good,' Slater said. 'Wait here. I'll be back in a moment. When I finish, start shooting.'

'What the hell are you—' King began.

Before he could finish the sentence, Slater shrank into the shadows. The man darted into a nearby alley and disappeared from sight.

King let the silence descend over his surroundings and felt the familiar tremors of imminent combat. His heart rate skyrocketed involuntarily. He could never help it. He kept himself calm in the midst of battle, but the adrenalin was always there.

Why the fuck had he been so vague? King thought. *Probably because he thinks I'll try to stop him.*

He ran his fingertips over the MK23 tucked into his waistband and checked that the silencer was firmly attached and the weapon was fully loaded. He leant against a nearby railing and tried his best to act casual, even though the nerves of combat ate away at his insides.

He heard Slater returning before he saw him.

It began with a dull droning noise that cut through the relative silence of the bay and sent a flock of birds soaring out of their perches. King peered into the darkness, staring straight down the promenade, searching for the source of the commotion. He squinted to make out a flash of movement at the very end of the bay.

Then he worked out exactly what he was looking at.

The battered BMW they'd left in the parking lot roared into view, its engine screaming as it accelerated well past the speed limit. It mounted the pedestrian path and rocketed past restaurants and souvenir shops and traditional Corsican houses.

He felt his chest constricting. A wave of nervousness washed over him.

What on earth was Slater doing?

He saw the man at the wheel of the vehicle, his teeth bared, clearly in the midst of a full-blown adrenalin rush. Before he knew it, the BMW shot past his location.

Heading straight for the marina.

King set off at a sprint, clueless as to what Slater was about to attempt yet determined to follow along in his wake and provide support. He drew the Heckler & Koch pistol out of his belt and flicked the safety off as he bolted for the same pier he'd studied for the last several hours.

Ahead, Slater turned the wheel, sending the BMW through a flimsy railing at the very last moment. Its tyres coughed against the uneven ground. The vehicle careered over a waist-high ledge and ground its front bumper into the wooden jetty as it landed. It righted itself and shot off the mark, shooting out along the pier that housed the superyacht.

'Oh,' King said.

Still running, he heard cries of panic. He leapt over a low railing and landed near the entrance to the pier, scrambling to his feet. He looked down the length of it and laid eyes on a fascinating scene.

Slater had set off along the pier at close to fifty miles an hour, veering wildly out of control on the wooden planks yet keeping the BMW in line just enough to stay on solid ground. With no space on either side of the car, the four armed men spread out across the length of the pier were left with few choices.

The pair closest to the yacht were able to unholster their weapons and fire a few rounds at the approaching BMW. The unsuppressed shots rang out through the bay. King flinched as he heard the rounds shatter glass as they struck home in the vehicle's windshield.

They signalled the first proper offence between the two parties.

They signalled war.

The two men closest to the BMW had to jump — or be run over by the charging 4WD. They took one glance at the vehicle bearing down on them and abandoned their position on dry ground. They dove for the black ocean, plunging into the quiet waters of the bay as the BMW rocketed over the space they had occupied moments earlier.

King set off along the pier as fast as his legs would allow.

He knew he had to take advantage of their confusion — or risk catching a bullet for his troubles.

In the distance, he saw Slater press on, heading straight for the last two men on the pier. They exchanged a look … then committed to the same course as their co-workers.

With all four men breaking the surface of the Mediterranean Sea almost simultaneously, the pier had been emptied in the space of five seconds. A course had been cleared leading directly to the superyacht.

'Fuck me,' King whispered as he realised Slater wasn't going to stop there.

He might have been imagining it, but he thought he heard a faint cheer, like a hoot of nervous energy. If Slater really had let out what surmounted to a war cry, then the man was truly deranged. King stared in fascination at what unfolded next.

The BMW shot off the end of the pier, not slowing an inch. It covered the tiny space between the end of the dock and the superyacht's hull in a brief moment. Then it plunged nose-first into the fibreglass hull in an explosion of tearing material. The luxury vehicle came to rest half-buried in the side of the boat, rattling the entire craft in the water, shaking it to its very foundations.

Briefly, King thought he saw Slater leap from the open driver's window and topple head-first into the superyacht's bowels. Unarmed, yet still highly dangerous.

He shook his head at the man's utter carelessness before turning his attention to the four men in the water.

The closest two had only just surfaced. They were in the process of wiping the saltwater from their eyes, clearing their vision. King couldn't see any weapons.

Had they provoked him?

Could he really shoot these men — who had done nothing to him?

What if they were oblivious to their employer's operation?

The answer came a split second later. A gunshot echoed from somewhere in the water and King felt the displaced air near the side of his head as a round tore past, coming within a few inches of taking the top of his skull off. It carried with it an air of violence and brutality that kicked his nervous system into overdrive.

Fuck that.

He raised the MK23 and fired. His aim stayed precise. His hands didn't waver. He clinically spotted the two men treading water below him — unaware as to which one was armed or where *specifically* the shot had come from — and pumped the trigger twice in quick succession.

All at once, their bodies disappeared under the surface.

Direct impacts.

Welcome back, a voice in his head whispered.

Ignoring it, he carried on, leaving the pair to their watery graves. Who was he kidding? These men knew. They were willingly being paid to ensure a human trafficking operation went according to plan. They were as good as dead already.

He quickly found the other two guards, struggling to clamber back onto the pier further ahead. They had yet to spot King converging on their position, preoccupied with the chaos raging all around them. They weren't thinking straight. Some lunatic had just driven his car into the boat they were tasked with protecting. They scrambled for purchase on the slippery pier, consumed by tunnel vision.

King saw their hands reaching for their belts.

He wouldn't make the same mistake twice.

He fired twice — again. Twin coughs emitted from the barrel, but the two muzzle flashes were muffled by the attached suppressor. The guards jerked akin to marionettes in a circus play and toppled back into the water, barely a second after leaving it. King had sent a .45 round through the base of each of their skulls. There was no doubt they had been killed on impact.

They had never seen it coming.

That's something, at least.

He left four dead men in the waters of the bay and slipped quietly inside the superyacht, weaving through the jagged hole Slater had created in its hull.

As he touched down on a wooden path running along the boat's perimeter, a hand shot out of the darkness and clamped around his mouth. He wheeled on the spot and lifted the still-smoking barrel of the MK23, pressing it against the temple of his assailant.

Slater's eyes silently bored into him, urging him not to make a noise. King took the weight of his index finger off the trigger, his nerves tingling at the thought that he had been only a few ounces of pressure off ending the man's life.

'It's quiet,' Slater whispered. 'Think we might be the only ones aboard?'

'I don't know,' King muttered. 'Let's find out.'

From above, a muffled feminine cry echoed down over the lower decks.

'Top deck,' Slater said, his eyes widening.

They hurried for the stairwell.

CHAPTER 36

King led the way, making sure to clear each corner with the MK23 before he hurried forward. The boat was enormous. It would take considerable effort to find anyone on board. There were hundreds of potential vantage points from which any number of Moreau's forces could lie in wait, ready for the two Black Force operatives to come stumbling past.

King heard Slater breathing rapidly. The man was unarmed. King could have lifted one of the dock guards' weapons off them before jumping aboard — but his utmost priority had been on putting them out of the equation. Their firearms had sunk with them to the bay floor, out of reach.

Until they ran into someone else, Slater would remain weaponless.

He found a narrow stairwell that steeply ascended to the upper levels. The cry he'd heard possessed the unmistakeable tone of someone in distress. If there were live members of Yves' operation aboard, protecting them was King's utmost priority.

Save innocents first.

Kill the sick bastards after.

If they could do both at the same time, even better.

He took the stairs three at a time, making sure to keep his head up, navigating with his feet by touch alone. It would be no use fixing his gaze on where he was headed and end up catching a bullet in the top of his skull.

The yacht remained eerily silent.

No doors burst open. No mercenaries spilled into their path, ready for a firefight.

Instead, there was a total lack of action.

'Maybe they really were the last of them,' Slater whispered from behind.

'Moreau wouldn't be that stupid.'

They burst out of the stairwell and raced out onto the upper deck…

… and King spotted a bulky fire extinguisher arcing through the air, aiming straight for his unprotected face.

Without taking his hands off the pistol, he ducked violently, blurring his vision. The next second unfolded without his knowledge of what was occurring. All he knew was that whoever had swung the extinguisher at him had missed. He felt the air whistling above his head. His stomach dropped with the knowledge that a fraction of a second's hesitation would have resulted in a caved-in face.

That had been a powerful swing.

Then he sprawled forward on the deck, stumbling off-balance. Ducking so quickly had caused him to slip. He righted himself and spun around, barrel raised, searching for a target.

Slater was one step ahead.

The attacker had stumbled also, carried by the momentum of the missed swing. He had veered directly into Slater's path, who had been following King onto the upper deck.

King saw Slater thunder a boot into the man's exposed stomach, shattering a couple of his ribs. The mercenary let out a cry of distress and doubled over, crippled by the pain. He was unable to mount any kind of retaliation.

It would be the death of him.

Slater held him at arm's length, simply seizing his collar in an iron grip and extending his arm straight out. King knew what to do.

He fired twice. Once to the torso, once to the head. The mercenary jerked from the force of the impact and went instantly limp.

Slater hurled him overboard.

Due to the nature of the superyacht's construction, the body didn't fall directly into the water. The levels were tiered, so that the entire cluster was shaped like a trapezoid. Therefore the man — already dead — smashed into the lower deck with a grisly thud. King heard the body hit the wood below and allowed himself a grim smile.

It would be an ominous sound for whoever remained aboard.

Slater gestured over King's shoulder. 'I see why he was up here.'

King rose to his feet and spun, taking in the deck's contents all at once. In the commotion, he hadn't had the chance to observe his surroundings. Now he looked out across a wide space taken up by a lap pool, a few dozen tanning beds and a small rectangular building with one side open — converted into a bar.

It was what lay in front of the bar that seized his attention.

Almost a dozen women of various ethnicities dressed in filthy clothing, their mouths gagged with white cloth, their hands and feet bound together by sturdy rope, their eyes wide and panicked. Clearly this was what Yves had hired a small army to protect. He was either selling them, or purchasing them. Either way, the politician was looking to make a profit by any means necessary.

The sight of the group seated on the floor, shaking with terror, made King's blood boil. He nodded to Slater, who tossed him a fresh magazine of .45 ammunition for the MK23. He reloaded and made his way across the deck. The cluster of women watched him every step of the way, some of them making terrified guttural noises through their gags.

They might have thought he was there to eliminate them forever.

King splayed his hands wide open and pointed the barrel of the MK23 skyward. He adopted a calm expression, attempting to demonstrate that he meant them no harm. Most of them visibly relaxed, convinced that they would not be dying just yet.

A few began to weep from the possibility of escaping this hell.

King moved to the closest woman and crouched down beside her. He tore the gag free. She had to be close to thirty, with a toned body and straggly brown hair. She was either Chinese or Korean. King couldn't quite ascertain exactly what race.

'English?' he said.

'Yes,' she responded. 'We all speak English.'

King wandered his gaze over the group. 'Do you all know each other?'

She nodded. 'Same agency. We were here for a photoshoot. We were supposed to fly out tomorrow. We attended a party … earlier this evening.'

King thought back to his encounter with Klara and blanched. She had spoken of the same party. She was here for a…

He studied the group again, searching desperately, praying that he didn't spot what he was looking for.

There she was.

Klara rested at the very edge of the group, her hair dishevelled and her expression one of horror. The gag across her mouth covered half her face, which was why King hadn't recognised her at first. He hurried over and wrenched the cloth off her lips. She spluttered a helpless sob and pressed her head against his chest.

'Cut me loose,' she whispered. 'Let me do it.'

'Do what?' King said, still shocked by her sudden appearance.

'Let me kill him.'

He paused. 'Have you ever killed anyone before?'

She shook her head.

'The first time, it takes a piece away from you,' King said. 'You'll never get it back. Stay here. Where is he?'

'I don't know. Somewhere downstairs. There's a lot more on this boat...'

King felt his stomach twist into a knot. He feared that may be the case, but now that it was confirmed the boat felt like a death trap. There were definitely plenty more mercenaries aboard...

...so where were they?

'Stay here,' King said. 'Watch over them. We'll take care of whatever's downstairs.'

'Can't I come?'

'Only one of us is armed in the first place,' King said. 'If we had more weapons everything would be a lot easier.'

Klara turned pale. 'You're going down there unarmed?'

King waved the gun in the air. 'I'm not. My friend is.'

'Who's your friend?'

'He's...' King spun to locate Slater and introduce him — but the man had vanished. 'Oh, shit.'

CHAPTER 37

Will Slater descended the stairwell like a bat out of hell.

Fury creased his features. Inside, he felt his blood boiling. His skin tingled and his hands shook. The sight of the cluster of women tied up helplessly on the top deck had sent him into a blind rage from which he wasn't sure he would be able to exit.

Distant memories bubbled to the surface, flashing into his head at an alarming rate. He thought of his father coming home to let him know that he couldn't locate Mom. He remembered the long walks late at night, alone, looking for nothing but trouble, searching and wandering aimlessly.

Hoping she would come back.

He remembered the docks in Harlem where he knew she had been taken.

He hadn't had the courage to confront them back then. It had eaten away at him for years. It had enabled him to devote himself to a life of combat. He had become a human weapon since that day. Twenty years ago, he couldn't do a damn thing to stop the fiends who took his mother. He knew where they lived. He knew that they had been responsible for shipping her off to hell.

Now, though…

Now he could act.

He burst out of the stairwell on the ground floor, entering an intricate web of plush corridors and ornate interior decorations. He was a man possessed. The lights all the way along the hallway burned bright. His pace didn't slow. He passed open doorways recklessly, daring *anyone* to cross his path. He prayed that one of the mercenaries — or even possibly Yves Moreau himself — would confront him. He had an arsenal of tools that he couldn't wait to unleash.

He couldn't care less that he wasn't armed.

He didn't need to be.

Halfway down a corridor indistinguishable to any of the others within the superyacht, he heard a noise from one of the neighbouring rooms. Barely audible. Just a faint click of someone bumping against an object.

That would do.

He shoulder-charged the locked door separating himself from whoever was on the other side, aided by the power that came with primal anger. It sprung aside, the lock snapping like a piece of plywood. Splinters flew and the entire door crashed inward, startling the room's three occupants.

All well-built, middle-aged men. All outfitted head-to-toe in combat gear. All clasping high-powered weaponry ranging from automatic assault rifles to heavy duty shotguns.

In that moment, Slater didn't care whether he lived or he died.

He launched into motion. A single high kick shattered the jaw of the man closest to the door. Slater wasn't sure if he knocked him unconscious — or if the man's legs simply buckled from the agony of the injury. But he dropped instantaneously, cascading to the floor of the small office. Slater scooped up his shotgun — a Baikal MP-155K semi-automatic from Russia — and unloaded its contents upon the rest of the room in the space of a couple of seconds.

The other two men didn't even have time to raise their own weapons.

They twisted away from Slater, their blood coating the far wall, turning the cream wallpaper into a speckled mess of crimson. Slater fired the last round directly into the first man's face, tearing the skin right off his skull. He cast his eyes away from the grisly result, threw the empty shotgun away and returned to the hallway.

So much for that little ambush they had planned, he thought.

He surged down the hall like something out of a nightmare, wondering who would present themselves as the next challenge. He would be happy to oblige them. He hadn't even thought about taking the time to arm himself, or take things slowly.

Strategy had been thrown out the window.

He wanted nothing more than to put his bare hands on any *motherfucker* involved in this operation.

He rounded another corner…

…and immediately ducked back into cover.

For half a second he'd entered a vast kitchen and dining room space — home to a cluster of mercenaries with their weapons aimed at the very entrance he walked into. But he knew his reflexes were otherworldly.

They would have seen someone appear in the doorway for a single moment before promptly disappearing.

A volley of shots tore apart the opposite wall. Slater kept himself pressed against cover, his expression deathly stoic. He would simply wait. It would only be a matter of time before their patience would grow thin and the bravest — or dumbest — of the group would make a brazen charge for Slater's last known position.

He'd counted four men during the brief flash of observation.

Easy work.

It took less time than he had originally anticipated for the first man to come sprinting through the doorway, weapon raised, wildly searching for any kind of target to hit in his berserker-like attack.

Slater sent a massive uppercut directly into the soft tissue of the guy's throat, helped along by a healthy dose of animalistic rage. The man's head snapped back, rattling gasps pouring out of his mouth, his lungs scrambling for air after the debilitating blow.

Slater plucked the ArmaLite AR-15 assault rifle out of his hands as if he were a parent scolding a child for picking up a forbidden object. He spun the mighty weapon by the trigger guard until the barrel froze — locked onto the idiotic mercenary who had thought bull-rushing Will Slater was a good idea.

He unloaded a tight cluster of bullets into the left side of the man's chest. Either one or all of them penetrated his heart. It didn't matter how many.

He died all the same.

Slater didn't hesitate for a second. He surged forward, throwing the corpse aside, and stuck the AR-15 around the doorway. He held the trigger down and worked the barrel from side-to-side until the gun clicked dry.

Now.

No time to waste.

He tossed the rifle away and charged into the kitchen, aiming directly for the stone bench with a marble countertop he'd seen positioned in the centre of the space. It would provide ample cover. During his mad dash he threw his gaze from left to right.

Where were the remaining mercenaries positioned?

What state were they in?

He quickly saw that one had been caught by the spray-and-pray. His weapon lay off to the side. He sat — an expression of confusion and fear plastered across his face — bleeding out in the middle of the kitchen, his chest dotted with holes. Completely exposed.

He would be useless in the coming fight.

Another had been hit in the shoulder. He staggered for cover. The last man was unhurt. He held a fearsome-looking rifle in his hands. Ready to use it at a second's notice.

Slater made eye contact with the healthy mercenary before ducking under the bench.

He knew he had the upper hand. This man was paid to look imposing. He didn't know *real* combat. Now, surrounded by savage violence, listening to the sounds of his co-workers hurt and bleeding to death, he would be psychologically affected.

Not many people on earth could completely turn their emotions off in the heat of battle.

Slater could.

He could also use other feelings to his advantage. Like pure rage.

He waited a beat, crouched in the lee of the stone slab, his veins cold and his demeanour calm. He heard the laboured breathing of men all around him and knew they were scared shitless. He thrived off this sort of atmosphere.

The sound of approaching footsteps set him into action. He rounded the bench into open ground, staying low — too low. He almost scraped his stomach on the tiles, moving on all fours, snake-like. The mercenary directly ahead hadn't been anticipating that. His barrel was aimed at chest-height. At empty space. Slater knew he would correct his aim in a second.

But a second was all he needed.

He closed the distance and powered up into the underside of the man's rifle, clattering it loose as their bodies collided. He launched off both legs, using explosive plyometric power to force them both off their feet. They crashed to the floor in a tangle of limbs — where Slater knew he possessed the upper hand.

He scrambled to full-mount, a jiu-jitsu position where the legs straddled the opponent's torso, preventing them from any real movement or defence. A seasoned martial artist could inflict devastating injury from the full-mount position.

Slater prided himself on being exactly that.

He rained down heavy shots, helped by the addition of gravity. His punches broke through the mercenary's guard effortlessly and slammed down into the delicate features of his face, breaking bones, spilling blood, causing agony.

Convinced that his work was done, he rolled off the semi-conscious man and snatched up the rifle he'd knocked loose from his hands.

Another AR-15.

In three clustered bursts of automatic gunfire, Will Slater finished off the three enemies left standing, each at various levels of injury. The lead tore through them, turning them into lifeless corpses.

He let the rifle fall to his side and took in the carnage he had enacted upon the occupants of the boat.

His ears rang.

His pulse raced.

Finally, the anger began to dim.

CHAPTER 38

As King hurtled down the stairwell, wondering just where the hell Slater had disappeared to, he heard swathes of automatic gunfire echo through the walls of the superyacht.

He paused on a step and listened hard. There was a brief moment of silence, then more shots. They seemed to come from everywhere at once. They ripped through the walls, vibrating in King's chest. He thought he heard more gunfire further inside the boat, down on the ground floor.

Someone was rampaging through the ranks...

He could only imagine who that might be.

He hurried to the ground floor and hurdled the last five steps in one giant leap. He crashed to the floor of a corridor leading deep inside the yacht. More shots tore through the silence. King's stomach — previously sinking at the thought of his only comrade dying violently below deck — began to calm.

Because the shots seemed orderly.

Precise.

Like they were all coming from a single man on a violent mission.

He hurried down corridors, chasing the source of the commotion. He passed a cramped office with the door hanging off its hinges. He threw a brief glance inside and his heart rate quickened. Three bodies had been torn to pieces by some kind of heavy weaponry. The walls were painted with their blood.

Slater…

He pressed on, listening to the sounds of violence still raging.

When he finally burst out into a spacious kitchen and dining room, he couldn't believe what he saw.

Slater stood in the centre of the room, panting for breath, riding out the waves of energy coursing through him. Around him, four corpses were sprawled in various positions, all riddled with bullets. Blood covered Slater's hands and face.

The blood wasn't his.

King had trouble putting a coherent sentence together. He surveyed the scene in utter disbelief before blurting out, 'Is that all of them?'

Slater looked at him with ice in his veins. 'I think so. I count twelve dead in total, including the four on the pier and the guy on the roof. Moreau can't have many more men than that.'

'Where is the bastard?' King said.

Slater shrugged. 'Can't wait to find out.'

They each collected an AR-15 and checked the respective magazines. Slater fished a spare out of the combat vest of one of the dead mercenaries and slammed it home.

'Yours good?' he said.

King checked his own weapon. Fully loaded. 'Yeah.'

'Let's go.'

They drifted out of the kitchen and set out to clear the rest of the rooms. King felt the power of the AR-15 in his hands and felt calm. It was a hell of a lot better than a measly MK23.

And look at what you can do with a pistol.

He slammed doors open with a newfound sense of confidence, checking corners, scouring the boat for the monster behind the operation.

As they scouted an empty corridor, King decided to speak. 'What the hell happened, Slater?'

Slater faced forward, refusing to turn around. 'What do you mean?'

'You know exactly what I mean. You just slaughtered seven men in a couple of minutes. Was it the girls?'

Slater nodded. 'We spoke about this.'

'You okay?'

'Lot better now.'

'You should probably get therapy for that sort of thing...' King said. 'That was intense.'

A knock from an adjacent room stopped them in their tracks. It came from the other side of a set of oak double doors, built into the wall. Slater stopped directly in front of them and smiled.

'This is therapy,' he said, and thundered a boot into the flimsy frame.

The doors sprung open. He stormed into the room with his gun raised, and King followed close behind. They trained their AR-15s across a massive boardroom, containing nothing but an oak table and a plethora of surrounding chairs.

Moreau and an unknown Afghani man sat at the other end of the table.

Unarmed.

Like they had accepted their fate.

'I heard the fighting,' Moreau said as King and Slater covered the distance between them. 'Thought at least one of my men might be useful.'

'They probably would have been to anyone else,' King said. 'Unfortunately for you, you triggered my friend here.'

'And he is…?' Moreau said, staring at Slater dismissively, contempt in his tone.

Big mistake.

Slater shifted his aim slightly, turning it from Moreau to the man sitting beside him, and unloaded ten rounds into the guy's skull.

His chair was thrown backward by the force of the bullets. Blood arced from various puncture wounds, covering Moreau's previously pristine clothing. He was dressed in an open-necked dress shirt and a peach-coloured suit which did well to hide his rotund belly. The peach quickly turned red as the body of the dead man crumpled to the floor in a crimson heap.

'*Fuck!*' Moreau cried, clearly disgusted and horrified by the incident. 'You didn't even know who he was.'

Slater shrugged. 'Don't care. He was involved in this.'

Moreau sat rigid, unmoving. His hands began to shake. His cheeks turned pale. 'He was the buyer.'

'So you're selling them?' Slater said. 'That's what this is?'

'Yes,' Moreau said, his shoulders sagging.

King saw the defeat in the man's eyes. There was no way out of this situation. Even if they decided to spare his life, it was over regardless. What had gone down in the Bay of Calvi couldn't be covered up. There were too many dead bodies. Too much blood on King and Slater's hands. The truth of Moreau's real nature would come to light — no matter what he did from this point.

He was done.

'Last night,' King said. 'At my place. What the hell was all that?'

Moreau turned to him. 'Thought you might ask.'

'I can't say I'm not curious. You had the opportunity to kill me, and you didn't take it.'

'I didn't want to kill you at the time.'

'Look where that got you.'

'If I'd known…' Moreau said, staring wide-eyed at the blood covering his suit. 'I would have leapt at the opportunity.'

'Why didn't you want to kill me? Why did you make up all that shit?'

Moreau looked at him with a twinkle in his eye. Like a faint glimmer of hope. 'I thought you could be bought.'

'Ah.'

'You don't sound surprised?'

'I've faced that sort of thing more than you know,' King said. 'Money seems to be the only thing driving people like you. They all think I can be paid off, or dealt with. No-one realises that they shouldn't play games with someone of our caliber until it's too late.' He gestured to himself, then to Slater. 'We're a different breed.'

'I can see that.'

'What would you have got me to do?'

'Finish off these incompetent fucks, if that's what it took,' Moreau said. 'Afshar promised me the highest level of security. Then he wound up dead on the first night at the hands of a random civilian. I wanted to find out more about you.'

'So you took the good-cop approach?' King said. 'Pretended you had a noble cause in mind. Then what?'

'I would have offered you a truckload of cash,' Moreau said. 'And explained what I really wanted from you.'

King allowed himself a grim smile. 'Good thing you didn't.'

'And why's that?'

'Because this whole thing would have been over a lot faster than this. I would have killed you then and there.'

'I still don't know who you really are,' the politician said. 'A hitman? What? Seems you have some kind of moral code — unless someone's paying you to get rid of me and my little operation.'

'No-one's paying me a cent.'

'Then who are you?'

'Someone who despises people like you,' King said. 'That's it.'

He paused, ready to put a bullet between the despicable bastard's eyes and turn his back on Corsica forever. Then he stopped. 'There's a girl upstairs. Her name's Klara. I know her. Is that a coincidence?'

Moreau shook his head. 'Guess that was one advantage of my failed recruitment mission. I came across a scrap of paper on your kitchen counter. Before you came out. It had her name and number on it. Seems like you two had some fun. I did a little research and thought she'd be perfect to add to the collection.'

'How did it go down?'

'The same way it always does,' Moreau said. 'I called her with a promising business opportunity and arranged to meet in the heart of Calvi. Snatched her in broad daylight.'

'Earlier today?'

Moreau nodded.

'Odd coincidence,' King said.

'How so?'

'She would have been at that party tonight. There wasn't any need to move for her early. Risky venture.'

Moreau nodded. 'She would have likely raised a few issues. Usually we screen all our goods before we ship them out. Make sure we snatch the tourists who no-one will ever notice are gone. Her family would have caused an uproar. Many have in the past. It doesn't make a difference. They're in the heart of the Middle East before anyone can bat an eyelid. Largely thanks to the man you just killed. He roped me into all of this, anyway.'

'Trying to divert the blame?' Slater said.

Moreau shook his head, staring into the void. 'I'm a little pessimistic right now. No matter what, I'm done. Death would probably be a relief.'

Slater looked at King and smiled. 'You see what he's doing?'

King nodded. 'Clear as day.'

Moreau looked up. 'And what would that be?'

'You're fucking terrified,' Slater said. 'I've seen a million people like you before. You're silently praying that we spare you, because there's all sorts of loopholes and options you rich fucks have in the outside world. You have a fighting chance if you step off this boat alive. The legal system can be exploited. I've seen it happen before.'

'I disagree,' Moreau said.

'No you don't. And you're making it seem like killing you would be the favourable option — so we're influenced to do the opposite.'

Moreau shook his head. 'I don't know what you're on about. Do whatever the hell you want. But you won't make it off this boat alive.'

'Oh?' King said.

'You won't see the morning,' Moreau said. 'You two might think you have the upper hand because you killed my security, but it goes deeper than that. I own this island. And they'll kill you slowly. I hope you enjoy.'

Slater thundered a boot into the chair between him and Moreau, knocking it across the room, clearing a direct path to the politician. Moreau jolted at the noise. His hands began to shake. He sensed the shift in atmosphere.

King's suspicions were confirmed. The politician had kept up a decent facade, until things got very real…

Slater crossed the room and looped behind Moreau's chair, keeping him in place with a single palm on the shoulder. Moreau whimpered as a muscular arm looped around his throat and tightened like a boa constrictor wrapping around its prey.

'Please…' he whispered.

'I hope you enjoy,' Slater said.

He squeezed.

King turned away as the first pathetic gasps began to crawl out of Yves Moreau's throat.

CHAPTER 39

When it was done, they left the bodies where they lay and retreated to the hallway.

King had no qualms with the police discovering Moreau's corpse amidst this madness. His reputation would be forever tarnished. He would be universally viewed as a monster after what he had been a part of came to light.

Those were the things that brought King satisfaction, even though the effects of his actions could not be undone.

Slater shook out his limbs as they left the boardroom. Veins protruded from his exposed forearms, his energy depleted after the exertion of choking a resisting grown man to death.

It was undeniably a slow, brutal way to kill someone. The victim knew what was coming and — when faced with someone as skilled as Slater — were powerless to stop it. It would have been soul-crushing to be in Moreau's position.

Good, King thought. *He deserved nothing less.*

He thought of the hundreds — if not thousands — of women Moreau must have shipped off to third-world countries before this. How many were still alive? Slaves to the highest bidder. The thought sent chills down his spine.

How can you sit back and put your feet up when problems like this are just as prevalent as ever?

The thought had been nagging away at him for the entire length of his retirement. He wasn't sure he could keep it at bay any longer.

They reached the hole in the side of the superyacht, passing the destroyed BMW now resting on its side, halfway inside the boat. King peered out first, staring down the length of the pier, wondering if the onslaught had attracted much attention.

It had.

He saw blue and red flashing lights from the end of the pier. A single police sedan, parked horizontally, preventing anyone from escaping via land. A smart tactic. Two officers with their guns drawn were hurrying down the wooden jetty, heading for the boat. Even from this distance King could see the fear on their faces. It must have sounded like a war zone from their position.

And they were running into the thick of it.

King stepped out onto the deck, dodging twisted fibreglass. He kept his hands pointed skyward, palms open, clearly demonstrating that he posed no threat.

'You sure about this?' Slater said as he followed King out of the boat. 'This looks bad.'

'Of course it does. But those women up top need to be taken care of. We can't just abandon them and disappear.'

'Fair enough.'

The officers noted their presence and jerked in surprise. The man on the left screamed, pouring out rapid commands in French. He shook his pistol in their direction, wondering if the breath he was taking might be his last.

My God, King thought. *They're seriously on edge.*

The pair of them kept their hands raised.

'We're unarmed!' King yelled. 'Don't shoot! Don't shoot!'

Slater yelled similar statements in French. For a long, drawn-out moment, nothing happened. The tension ran thick in the air. King stared down the barrel of the officers' guns and silently prayed that they weren't overly trigger-happy.

'We are Americans,' King said, very slowly. 'Special Forces. We work for the government.'

'We speak English,' the officer on the right said. 'You don't have to talk like that.'

The pressure eased off a little. The first exchange between the two parties had taken place — and no-one was dead.

Slater stepped forward. 'Myself and my partner work for a division of the United States Special Forces. We're not here for business. But we came across this scene and were forced to retaliate. I'm sure that this can be solved diplomatically. It'll be a lengthy process, but we need to co-operate here.'

The man on the right had short grey hair and a muscular frame that made him look younger than he actually was. King guessed he was in his fifties. His badge read *ROUX*.

The other guy was youthful. He appeared to be in his late twenties. Probably green. He wasn't able to still his shaking hands. He had mid-length brown hair tied back in a ponytail and deeply tanned brown skin. His last name was *MERCIER*.

King assessed the pair and guessed the likelihood that he and Slater would end up dead.

Quite slim, probably.

Roux seemed experienced. His hazelnut eyes flicked over the scene with a calculated efficiency. He took everything in at a glance, and made on-the-fly decisions based on what he saw. He listened closely for signs of commotion within the boat and — after a moment of contemplation — decided to proceed.

'Show us,' he said, refusing to stow away his weapon.

King didn't blame him. 'Through here.'

They ushered the two officers through the same hole they'd come from and stepped back into the intricate maze of the boat's interior. He and Slater made sure to go first, taking the utmost precaution to appear non-threatening. The last thing they wanted was a bullet in the back after making a wrong move.

As he walked, he considered what the next move would be. Would it be best for he and Slater to slip away at the next available opportunity, now that the boat was secured by the police? He wasn't sure whether they would be thrown in jail for the rest of their lives. After all, they were operating in no official capacity.

Would Black Force come to the rescue?

He hoped so. He had done great work for them. He hoped they wouldn't throw their two best operatives to the wolves.

Well, one best operative — Slater. And an ex-employee.

King led the small party to the boardroom. They threw the doors open and gestured to Moreau's corpse.

'You know who that is?' he said.

Roux pushed past Slater so he could get a good look at the body. He processed the scene with a steely expression. 'I do.'

Something inside of King twitched. Some kind of primal nerve that signified danger. He wasn't sure exactly what had triggered it, but he knew never to doubt the sensation when it reared its ugly head. It had saved his life more times than he could count. He observed the utter nonchalance with which Roux studied the body, the lack of reaction.

That didn't phase him as much as the younger officer, Mercier.

The man had stumbled upon a bloodbath not long into his career as a police officer, and he was casting his gaze over the surroundings with a cold detachment. Not exactly standard operating procedure for officers of the law. He wasn't shocked by what he was seeing. Rather, he was nervous. King saw a bead of sweat flow from his hairline to the bottom of his chin. The man subtly shifted his trigger finger. Previously he had employed impeccable trigger discipline, keeping his index finger on the outside of the guard.

Now, as he saw Moreau's body, he slipped his finger onto the trigger.

A tiny action — he probably thought he could get away with such a manoeuvre.

Slater saw it too.

What felt like an eternity elapsed before anyone made a move. King entered a state of hyper-awareness, his vision flicking between each officer's weapon, wondering when the inevitable would come.

Moreau's words rang in his ears.

I own this island.

Roux made the first move. He probably thought he had all the time in the world to blow their brains out, eliminating the last pair of witnesses from the scene. After all, he was probably still on Moreau's payroll. It's what the man would have wanted.

To protect his reputation.

King assumed that Roux and Mercier had paid little attention to the fact that they had classed themselves as Special Forces. A certain confidence came with wielding a loaded gun against an unarmed adversary. They would have thought everything would go swimmingly.

How wrong they were.

King darted forward as soon as he saw Roux bring his weapon hand up. He intercepted the swing at a fifty-degree angle, clamping his hands around the man's wrist while the barrel of the standard-issue French MAC 50 handgun stayed pointed at the floor. Roux fired a shot, deafeningly loud in the confined space. It startled Mercier into action. He raised his own identical weapon, following the lead of his superior with nervous energy crackling all around him.

Slater was on him in milliseconds.

The inexperienced officer didn't stand a chance. He let out a gasp of shock as Slater crashed into him from behind, knocking him across the room in a shocking display of violence. He flew off-balance, MAC 50 tumbling away.

King felt Roux's strength, but he knew he could handle it. He kept a firm grip on the man's wrist with one hand, and punched him in the exposed throat with the other. His accuracy rang true. Knuckles crashed against flesh and Roux spluttered from the impact.

King wondered if the man had ever taken a blow quite like that.

The man's grip loosened instantly. From there it was as simple as plucking the handgun from his palm and spinning it by its handle.

In a second, King had the barrel aimed firmly between the older officer's eyes.

He had learnt many lessons over his long career, but none quite as important as the one he was about to employ.

No mercy.

There were two live enemies in front of him, both corrupt, both determined to kill the only men left in the slaughterhouse that the superyacht had become. They had to protect their boss's dignity. If the truth about his side business came out, his name would be forever tarnished.

King would not let them try again.

He killed Roux with a single 9mm round to the temple that penetrated his skull and sunk into his brain. Death was instantaneous. Moving like a robot, he effortlessly switched his aim to Mercier and shot the officer in the throat before he could snatch up the AR-15 assault rifle he had come to rest by.

He felt nothing. No sympathy. No discomfort. After hearing Moreau's words about the number of women he had already sent off to slavery and death, King wasn't perturbed in the slightest with killing those who had kept him in power.

Just as quickly as the encounter with the officers had begun, it came to a brutal end.

'This is fucked,' Slater whispered, scratching his head at just how deep the corruption ran.

CHAPTER 40

'You heard what Moreau said, right?' King said. 'He was confident that we wouldn't make it off the island alive. I'm starting to believe him.'

'How many more people can he throw at us?' Slater said.

'As many as he wants, I'd say.'

'Not anymore. He's no longer with us. No longer there to give orders. Surely, his employees would take some time to gather themselves. Find a new leader.'

'We don't know that,' King said. 'We don't know anything. He could have an entire system in place in the event of his death. I say we get out of here before shit hits the fan.'

'What about the girls?'

'We bring them. I can't imagine anything going their way if they were taken into custody as witnesses. I don't trust anyone on this island after what we uncovered.'

'How do you propose we do that?' Slater said.

'Do what?'

'Bring them with us.'

'We get them off the boat. Give them cash. Tell them to lay low. I don't know…'

King dropped to the carpet of the boardroom and rested his head against the wall behind him. He sucked in air, almost at the point of hyper-ventilating. 'What do you do when the entire island is on this man's payroll?'

'We don't know that,' Slater said. 'Those could have just been two bad eggs. Paid to keep an eye on the marina while the deal goes down and ensure all goes according to plan.'

'You really believe that?'

'Not one bit.'

Slater paused, like he wanted to say something yet was hesitant to come out with the information. King noticed. 'What?'

'I need to show you something,' he said. 'Found it on the boat.'

Slater led him down a trio of identical corridors until they came across a luxurious waiting room. They entered the space, which was outfitted with a pair of leather sofas facing one another and an ornate cigar chest propped on a small oak table.

'Looks like some serious business goes down in here,' King noted.

'I'd say so,' Slater said, gesturing to a duffel bag wedged underneath the table. 'Found this when I was clearing the rooms.'

King crossed to the bag and zipped it open. He gazed down at a sea of green notes. All American dollars. At least a million. Maybe more. Dirty, laundered blood money. He didn't care who it belonged to. Every possible owner of the bag was dead.

'That's a lot of money,' he said matter-of-factly.

'I think I'm going to need it,' Slater said.

King wheeled around. 'I can't say I like where you're headed with this.'

'I want out.'

'Of Black Force?'

Slater nodded. 'It's something I've been considering for a while.'

'I know. I can tell.'

'I can't do it the way you did.'

'Why not?'

'They'll kill me.'

'You sure?'

'I don't want to risk it.'

King tossed the duffel bag over. 'I don't have any need for it. I've got enough. But I'd say you do too.'

Slater shook his head. 'If I disappear, they'll freeze my accounts.'

'You'll start a new life?'

Another nod. 'You know as well as I do the amount of contacts you form over a career like ours. I know people. All over the globe. I'll be okay.'

'I'm sure you will,' King said. 'Will Black Force?'

'I couldn't care less.'

'You should,' King said. 'Without them the world would be a worse place.'

'I've grown a little skeptical of believing in that.'

King said, 'I'm not going to stop you. Frankly, I'm not sure if I could. But think long and hard about what you're doing.'

'I have.'

'And?'

'And now's the perfect opportunity to flee. I've killed my avenues of communication. I won't switch them back on.' He turned his gaze toward the ceiling. 'And I know how to fly a chopper.'

King raised his eyebrows, realising how Slater intended to disappear. 'Oh.'

'Yeah,' Slater said, picking up the duffel bag. 'This should get me through until I start a new career.'

'What will you do? I can't see you working as a bartender.'

Slater shrugged. 'I don't care. At this point, I just want to start fresh.'

'Black Force takes its toll on everyone, doesn't it?'

Slater nodded solemnly and stared at the floor. 'Sure does.'

They walked side-by-side in silence to the stairwell. King didn't bother to try and convince Slater to stay. He had a rare insight into what was churning through the man's brain. He had experienced many of the same feelings during the tail end of his career. The constant stress and unease and danger. It took its toll, no matter how much they enjoyed it. No matter how much it fuelled them with energy.

In the end, everyone burnt out.

They ascended to the far end of the top deck, stepping out onto the vast helipad constructed on the superyacht's tail. The HAL Light Utility Helicopter rested in the centre, gleaming in the moonlight.

'Didn't even think these things were in production yet,' Slater said. 'Weren't they in development for the Indian Air Force?'

'I think when you're a multibillionaire, you get whatever the hell you want,' King said.

'It seems so,' Slater said. He turned around, grinning. 'Maybe you'll see me on the cover of Forbes one day. I'll shoot for the stars.'

King laughed. 'I hope not. I'd advise you to keep your head down for the rest of your life.'

'I concur.'

'So this is it?'

They faced each other on the open deck of the boat, with the warm breeze coming off the ocean lashing at their clothes. King felt a sudden, uncharacteristic pang of sadness. He hadn't even spent a single full day with the man standing across from him, yet it felt like they had shared a decade's worth of memories. Maybe that was due to the shared experiences that almost no-one else on the planet could relate to, or perhaps it was simply the bond of battle that King had experienced with so many fellow soldiers in his pre-Black Force days.

Slater offered a hand. King shook it. The man's grip was firm.

'I know we spent half the day trying to kill each other,' Slater said. 'But you're a good man, King.'

'I don't think either of us ever intended to do that,' King said. 'Whatever our "instructions" were.'

Slater nodded. 'I'm not sure why. But I was never close.'

King tapped the side of his head. 'We're the same, Slater. Killers with a burning desire to help.'

Slater nodded, then his eyes turned vacant. 'My desire's gone. I can't mask it.'

'I know. I can see.'

'What will you do with yourself now?' Slater said. 'Continue your vacation?'

The question caught King off-guard. He took his time to reply. 'I don't know. I'll figure it out tomorrow. Right now, I need some sleep.'

'And I need a fresh start.'

'I hope it's everything you want it to be,' King said, then smiled. 'I hope it's nothing like mine.'

Slater smiled back, then swung the door of the chopper open. He threw the duffel bag loaded with cash into the co-pilot's seat and clambered inside. 'You take care of yourself. There's not many people like us. We're a rare breed.'

'Will,' King said, causing the man to pause. They looked at each other from across the helipad. 'Don't get caught.'

Slater raised two fingers to his brow, then brought them down in a mock salute. 'Roger that, sir. Guess it's lucky that being a ghost is my specialty.'

He slammed the door closed and fired up the HAL. King watched with his hands in his pockets. The rotor blades whirred and the downdraft threatened to knock him off his feet. He backtracked a few steps, avoiding most of the wind's power. Slater lifted off the helipad and worked the controls. The chopper banked in the air and soared away.

In the space of ten seconds, Will Slater was gone.

King stood alone on the helipad, listening to the sudden calm in the aftermath of the chopper's deafening flight. He saw its grey chassis melt into the night. It disappeared less than a minute after takeoff. He felt something again. Like the only person who could understand his pain had vanished.

Now, it was back to solidarity. Back to bottling up how he felt. He wasn't annoyed by the notion.

In fact, he'd been doing it for years.

It had simply been a pleasant reprieve being able to relate to someone about the work he had to carry out in the past.

He turned away from the views over the midnight-black bay and made for the other end of the deck. He ascended a short flight of stairs and stepped out onto the same area he'd seen previously, before Slater's furious rampage.

The women stood clustered together, all free from their bindings. Clearly, Klara and the Asian woman had done well to cut their friends loose. They visibly relaxed as they saw his face, probably worried that one of the remaining mercenaries would head for the roof and eliminate their chances of ever tasting freedom again. King looked out at shaking hands and terrified expressions. A few kept their composure, remaining stoic even in the face of such grave danger.

'Listen up,' he called. 'You all speak English?'

They nodded in unison.

'Okay,' he said. He took a deep breath, struggling to formulate sentences that would adequately explain the situation they faced. Finally, he simply decided to tell the truth. 'This is precarious. The man who was responsible for your capture is dead, but he had some serious connections. Myself and my partner already ran into a couple of cops who had … other intentions.'

'Was that your partner who took the helicopter?' one of the women said.

King nodded.

'Where'd he go?'

'Even I can't tell you that,' King said. 'I wish I could.'

'Who are you two? Police?'

'No.'

'Army?'

'No.'

He met Klara's gaze, and something flared behind her eyes. She knew he was something else. Something rarer. A hidden understanding lay there.

Did you kill people? she had asked back in the villa.

Now she knew.

'Look,' he said. 'I could spend all night explaining what I am. Or what I used to be. But we don't have time. I don't know how long it'll be until more police show up, but I'd place bets on it happening soon. And there's really no way to tell if they'll be honest upstanding citizens or more of Moreau's friends. You and I would be dead before we could work that out. So you all need to run.'

A brunette European woman still dressed in an evening gown let her mouth fall open. 'Are you saying the police will kill us?'

'I don't know,' King said. 'I honestly have no idea. I can't say they won't. Laying low is your best bet.'

'We don't have our purses, or our phones,' another woman said. 'They stripped us of everything when we were snatched.'

'How did they do it?' King said.

The Asian woman stepped forward. 'Everyone at the party was in on it. You could sense something was up in the air. It was supposed to be this upper-class function full of high-profile names, but there weren't many guests apart from us. We clued onto it when a few girls got drowsy before the rest. They spiked our drinks. A few of us started to panic and they pulled out guns. Herded us into a van and brought us here. It all happened so … fast.'

'How close were we to—?' the European woman said, her eyes welling.

King shook his head and let out an anxious sigh. 'Very close. If this boat left the dock, no-one would have ever seen you again.'

Several whimpers sounded from the group. King would have reacted similarly if he had been in such a position. The sheer helplessness they had faced sent dread through his chest.

And anger…

Suddenly, he knew what needed to be done. It had been a long time coming, but the mental image of these women being carted off to a ghastly fate flipped him over the edge. He made a resolve — inwardly — and committed to it. Then he tossed it to the back of his mind. His troubles weren't over yet.

'When did they take your things off you?' he said.

'In the van,' Klara said. 'They threw them altogether in a plastic bag.'

'Did that come on board?'

'I can't be sure.'

King clenched his teeth together and mulled over what to do. 'Wait here.'

CHAPTER 41

He descended once again into the bowels of the superyacht.

It felt like entering a graveyard. The boat's interior had the aura of death about it. It hung in the air like something physical, something he could touch. There was a different kind of quiet in the aftermath of a battle. The sort of absolute silence which signified that everyone in the immediate vicinity had died a grisly death.

He passed rooms littered with the dead, casting his eyes away from the bodies. It wasn't that he was squeamish. He had seen the effects of point-blank shotgun blasts many times during his career and hadn't been phased. But lingering on so much carnage and violence would only bring him back to that past that he was trying so hard to forget.

Or was he?

He had a lot to process. Everything from the appearance of Afshar to the revelation that Black Force wanted him gone to the discovery of Moreau's depravity had sent him on a wild ride that he was only just starting to come down from. It had made him reconsider many things.

He wasn't sure if the decisions he made after this would be beneficial to his health.

But he had to make them nonetheless.

He burst into the kitchen where Slater had effortlessly murdered four soldiers-of-fortune and gagged as he inhaled. The unmistakeable smell of faeces lingered in the air. A natural response to being shot non-fatally. Yet every man in this room had been subsequently killed by Slater's follow-up shots.

Was Slater a good person?

Should he have allowed him to fly off to a new life, unpunished?

King didn't know. This field of employment had so many grey areas that he'd given up on trying to form a black-and-white opinion of someone's moral compass long ago. He knew his own was muddled beyond belief. Sure, he wanted to help people — but he killed many in the process.

He would never solve the puzzle of delivering vigilante justice … so he chose to ignore it.

He did what he felt was right.

Nothing more, nothing less.

He scanned the marble countertop in the centre of the room and found exactly what he was looking for. The plastic bag of personal items, lying out in the open. After all, what was the use in hiding it? It would take a small army to penetrate the mercenary force defending the yacht. Moreau and his mysterious Middle-Eastern buyer would have felt secure inside the floating fortress.

In the end, it had only taken two specialists.

Next time, pay for better help, King thought.

But there wouldn't be a next time. A 9mm hole in Moreau's forehead ensured that.

He snatched up the bag and returned to the top deck, where the women distributed the possessions amongst themselves until they all had what they needed.

King made sure he had the attention of the group before he spoke. 'Listen up. You get as far away from Calvi as you possibly can. Call whoever you need, do whatever you need to do to get yourself home. But don't trust the authorities. Dye your hair, use fake tan … whatever. But stay safe. Okay?'

They nodded. He led them down through the superyacht, selecting a course that would ensure they saw as few corpses as possible. They clambered out of the hole in the side of the boat in single file, amassing on the pier as a group. King followed behind.

Additional police had yet to arrive. Maybe they had been instructed to hang back by Roux and Mercier, who probably anticipated that they would need to eliminate certain witnesses.

Corrupt pieces of shit, he thought.

The empty police sedan was still parked at the end of the pier, its doors hanging open, its lights flashing over the deserted bay. An ominous sight. King hurried the women down the pier, away from the slaughterhouse. He took a final look back at the yacht, its hull butchered by Slater's wild intrusion with the BMW, its helipad conspicuously empty.

He feared the investigation awaiting whoever stumbled across its contents. A whole lot of good men would lose a hell of a lot of sleep over what went down.

At the end of the jetty, the European turned and looked King in the eye. 'Thank you. So much. Whoever you are.'

'Best to forget I ever existed,' King said, but he nodded his understanding. Several of the other women nodded their thanks, yet most were too traumatised by what an ordinary evening had turned into to respond. They hurried away into the night, some staying in groups, others branching off alone.

One stayed back.

Klara.

As soon as the others had dispersed into Calvi, she threw her arms around King. He held her tight and breathed her scent, devastated that she had become involved in the madness that was his life. He felt her heart pounding in her chest, and her arms shaking as they looped around his neck. He kissed her, pressing his own chest against hers.

When they parted, she seemed a little calmer.

'I still don't know who you are,' she said. 'But this was insanity.'

'I was looking forward to seeing you today,' King said. 'It was the first time I felt truly happy in a long time. Then everything went to shit.'

'We can still see each other. I'd like that.'

'I can't do that to you, Klara.'

'Huh?'

'This wasn't an isolated incident.'

'All of that?' she said, gesturing in the direction of the boat they'd come from.

King nodded. 'That's my life. I don't try to make it that way, but sooner or later it just leads back to chaos.'

'Because of your past?'

He shrugged. 'If I knew, I wouldn't get myself into situations like this.'

'You're a complicated man,' she said, forcing a smile.

He smiled back. 'I am. Adds intrigue, I guess.'

'I don't know if I can handle much more intrigue.'

He wiped the smile off his face as reality hit. 'You should go, Klara.'

She met his eyes and he could see tears forming behind them. 'I thought, you know … that we had something. Even if it was brief.'

'So did I,' he said. 'Truly, I did. But that was while I lived here. I can't stay on this island. I don't know where I'm going after this.'

'Come to Sweden.'

He smiled. 'I'd like nothing more.'

'So just do it.'

'I can't.'

'Why, Jason?' she said, her tone strained. 'You going to go looking for more trouble? I thought you were retired.'

'I am.'

'Then come with me.'

He lapsed into silence. Truth was, his idea of paradise was returning to Klara's home country. He could just imagine the things they could do.

How happy he could be…

But his life had become a pattern. Everywhere he turned, violence and death followed. He saw it as a part of himself now, something unavoidable. And now there were fresh thoughts bubbling in his mind. Thoughts he couldn't ignore.

'You've got a hotel here, right?' he said.

Klara nodded, her blue eyes piercing into him. He saw hope in them. There would be hope in his own if he hadn't made up his mind back on the yacht. 'Go there and lay low. There's something I need to take care of — that I can't avoid any longer. Wait there, and I'll call you.'

She scoffed. 'You're going to leave, aren't you?'

He bent down and pressed his lips into hers again, feeling their fullness. Her taste made him want to abandon every dangerous thought he had, but his conscience was ingrained deep. He knew what he needed to do. It wasn't the pleasant thing, but it was the necessary thing. 'I'm a man of my word. I'll come back. But there's something on the island I need to address.'

'What?' she said.

He thought of a low one-storey house in the hills of Aregno. 'Something personal.'

CHAPTER 42

King slunk back to the superyacht, taking care to make as little noise as possible. He approached the tail end of the BMW, hanging half inside the boat's hull and half dangling in thin air. He released the trunk's latch and it floated open, making barely a whisper of noise.

He climbed in.

He'd forgotten to retrieve his most important possession.

He opened the glove compartment with a single pull. It drifted up, and he gazed at the contents within. His phone, which he'd thrown in after the surprise call with Moreau back on the highway. And — more importantly — the old watch.

He fished out both items and tucked them into his own pockets. Then he snuck away from the marina — and possibly the entire town of Calvi — forever.

He walked the streets in the dead of night, finally free from the intense burden of pressure. The previous twenty-four hours had been a whirlwind of action. It felt like the old days. He knew how to handle that sensation — to ride with the sharp twists and turns that often came when revelations were unfolding at breakneck speed. But now he could finally let go. He could wander aimlessly. He had nowhere to be, no responsibilities to take care of.

But despite that, he couldn't get the thought of Slater's disappearance off his mind.

It would have ramifications. They wouldn't be apparent all at once, but from what he'd gathered, Black Force had been stretched thin enough as it was. Losing their best operative would prove disastrous.

He wondered if Slater's absence would have far-reaching consequences.

He hailed a cab on the outskirts of Corsica and bent down to the passenger window as it pulled to the sidewalk. He saw a burly dark-skinned man with both hands on the steering wheel, eager to pick up another customer this deep into the night's darkest hours. King briefly considered throwing him out of the driver's seat and tearing away in the cab. After all, it had worked so well for him previously.

But he'd blatantly disrespected the law enough for one day, at least.

He peeled a few water-damaged euro bills from one of his pockets and handed them over to the driver, still damp. 'They're not in the best condition, but they're all I've got. You okay with that?'

He'd handed across well over a hundred euros. The driver didn't speak English, but he nodded approvingly. King gave him the address — which he knew off by heart — for the small house in Aregno and let his eyes drift closed as the cab peeled back onto the road.

Within seconds, he was asleep.

He was jerked awake by a soft hand on his shoulder. He started, rattled by the physical contact, expecting a bullet to follow shortly afterwards. Instead, he stared through blurry eyes at the cab driver — looking suitably shocked — who politely let him know that they had arrived at his destination. He nodded his thanks and clambered out of the car, shaking off the fear that had coursed through his body at the thought of being murdered in his sleep.

The cab roared away into the darkness.

It had dropped him at the very end of the familiar gravel street. Even though he had been here many times before, he'd never formed the courage to complete the task ahead. He thought back to the previous night — to the figure opening the door. He had reversed away then. Backed out like he always did.

Now, he would follow through.

He would do what he had been meaning to do ever since he stepped foot in Corsica.

This was the sole reason he had chosen the Mediterranean island as his home.

Because he knew — sooner or later — he would have to confront the past.

With Slater's words echoing in his ears, he set off along the gravel. His pace slowed as he approached the house. Killing he could do. He thought nothing of throwing his life on the line to save others. The knowledge that at any moment a bullet or stab wound could shut his lights out paled in comparison to what lay ahead.

This was a particular confrontation that he'd hoped he could avoid forever.

He walked up to the door. Down the narrow path leading to the front porch and past a few orderly rows of pot plants.

Neat, he thought. *Just the way he used to keep things.*

Some things never changed.

He rapped once on the door before he could stop himself. Now it was too late. He was committed to stay the course. He figured it was close to three in the morning, but he knew that if he put the encounter off for a second longer — he would psyche himself out forever.

This was his one shot.

He heard footsteps. His heart thrummed in his chest. He felt the rapid beat of it roaring in his ears. His stomach dropped. His limbs grew numb. He hadn't felt a reaction so visceral before in his entire life. Something about this moment shattered all his senses.

The door opened.

A man stood before him. It had been a decade and a half since they'd seen each other. Old age had receded his hairline and added more grooves and wrinkles to his forehead, but apart from that King thought he hadn't changed one bit. He had grown a sturdy moustache. His physique was a little saggier, a little depleted by time, yet it still had the same musculature that King had always remembered. The broad chest. The wide back. The kind eyes.

The strength that he'd grown up with.

'Hey, Dad,' King said, unable to help the tears from spilling down his face.

CHAPTER 43

Ray King.

Truth was, King had followed Slater's advice closer than he thought. He'd managed to track down his old man months before — back when he was employed — utilising Black Force programs to scour the Social Security databases. He'd discovered that his father had moved to Corsica after he'd left for the military, alone and retired. There he had coasted along, living a peaceful existence, never venturing into trouble. Keeping to himself for the most part.

King had fully intended to fly directly to Corsica as soon as he left Black Force for the last time. To make amends. To repair what had been broken by his departure.

Yet — when Corsica had finally fell into his sights after an eventful trip through Australia and Venezuela — he'd come up against a mental and emotional roadblock, the likes of which he'd never experienced before. Every time he got close to meeting his father, he backed out. Terrified of what his old man would think of him. Hesitant to even let his father know that he still existed.

He had cut himself off emotionally from the man all those years ago, when he'd left for the military. The two had never been overly close. His father hadn't truly understood why he was committing himself to a life in the armed forces, but he had let him go all the same. In the small town of Green Bay, Wisconsin, the two had hugged in front of a plain weatherboard house that King had spent his childhood in — and then he had left forever.

Now, fifteen years later, he was back.

At first, Ray didn't respond. His mouth flapped open and closed, akin to a fish out of water. He stared across the doorstep at the hulking, six-foot-three, two-hundred pound ball of muscle that was Jason King. King imagined he would be trying to draw parallels between the man standing in front of him and the lanky teenager who had run off to the military all those years ago.

King held out a hand and opened his fingers, splaying his palm out. The watch rested within. 'Remember this? You gave it to me. Twenty years ago. I've still got it.'

Ray looked long and hard at the timepiece, his eyes misty. He still said nothing. Then he launched through the doorway and threw himself into King's arms.

King held his father for the first time in over a decade, and cried.

They wept together, riding out the waves of emotion. King remembered breaking down at the scenic lookout near Aregno the previous morning, frustrated that he would never be able to overcome the first hurdle. The simple act of walking up and greeting the man in front of him.

Now he had.

His father pushed him away and held him at arm's length, looking him up and down, shaking his head in wonder. 'Jason…'

It was the first word he had spoken. He still had the same deep, booming voice that King had grown up with. When Ray King spoke, people listened. He talked with confidence and bravado even when he tried not to. People trusted him. He trusted them.

King wondered why he had moved all the way here.

He wondered many things.

But he smiled knowing he had all the time in the world to get answers.

Ray ushered him inside, noticing his bumps and bruises all at once. He closed the door behind him and hurried him through into a quaint living room. The carpet was thick, the decorations were plentiful, and the sofa was soft. It had the unmistakeable aura of *home*. King threw himself down at one end of the sofa, thoroughly exhausted, both physically and emotionally. The mere act of facing his demons and knocking on the door had taken more strength than he cared to admit.

He was so tired.

Ray sat down at the other end of the sofa. For a long while, neither spoke. They looked at each other with fascination and wonder in their eyes. King could tell his father was in a state of shock. He must have thought his son was dead…

King felt the tears coming on again and choked them back. He stared at his old man … and felt a warm smile creeping over his face. 'It's been a while.'

'It has, my boy,' Ray said. 'It really has.'

'I can't believe it's really you.'

His father chuckled. 'I must say, I'm having a hard time processing it myself.'

'How are you?'

Ray fixed his eyes on King and reciprocated the same warm smile. 'I'm happy, Jason. I'm truly happy.'

'So am I, Dad.'

'Military?' Ray said. The Kings had always been men of few words. His father shared the same straight-to-the-point, no-nonsense type of sentence structure that he used himself.

'Yeah.'

'This whole time?'

'Ninety-five percent of it.'

'You got out?'

'I did.'

'Was it your choice?'

'It was.'

'So you're done.'

King stopped in his tracks. 'It's complicated.'

Ray waved a hand. 'Ah, don't worry. We have plenty of time to talk about that. The only thing that matters is that you're here.'

'You've been here?'

'Coming up on five years,' Ray said.

'Any particular reason?'

The man shrugged. 'Green Bay carried a lot of bad memories. I'd walk around and see places that your mother and I had been…' He trailed off.

'Fresh start?' King said.

His father looked up and smiled. 'Fresh start.'

'Enjoying yourself?'

'More than anything. What the hell are you doing here, in any case?'

'Retired,' King said. 'Got a place up in Calenzana.'

His father raised his eyebrows. 'Didn't know the military paid that well.'

King smiled. 'They don't. Only certain … sections do.'

'Were you…?'

'Special Forces.'

'Oh my God.'

'Turns out you raised a goddamn deadly son,' King said with a chuckle.

They both laughed.

'I don't think I had any part to play in that,' Ray said.

'Good genetics, I suppose. They help.'

'Are you fast?'

The question took King by surprise. 'What?'

'You react quick? On top of things before anyone else?'

'Yeah…' he said. 'How'd you know?'

Ray shrugged. 'Had it my whole life. Not sure if it might have helped you in your … endeavours.'

King blanched in disbelief. 'So that's where I got it from…'

'It helped?'

'It did more than help, Dad. Turns out I'm an outlier in reaction speed. Close to a hundred milliseconds, or something like that. They tested me years ago.'

'I'll be damned,' Ray said, shaking his head. 'That's probably why you're here today.'

He rose off the couch and entered the small kitchenette attached to the living room. 'Can I get you anything? Water, tea, coffee?'

King smiled. 'I'm good, Dad. Just glad to be here.'

Ray returned the smile. 'Glad to have you.'

CHAPTER 44

By the time they finished talking, the sun had risen outside.

King was hesitant at first to open up about the true nature of his career, but it didn't take long for the walls to come crashing down. Truth was, he'd been looking for someone to talk to for years about what he'd done. First he thought Slater might be able to fill that void, but the man had clearly been struggling with his own demons — and disappeared accordingly.

He began with his introduction to the Delta Force and his subsequent promotion to a secret division kept entirely off-the-record. He told tales of hunting drug gangs in the Amazon Rainforest, stalking enemy outposts in the freezing mountains of Siberia, waging war with the cartels in the bowels of Mexico's slums…

As he delved further and further into the past he'd tried so hard to forget, he couldn't help but struggle to believe his own stories. They seemed so unreal … so fake. Yet he knew they had happened, because he carried the memories. He would for life. The things he'd been through would not be easily forgotten.

Not now.

Not ever.

Ray listened with intense concentration, rarely interrupting, letting King unload the various experiences that had been swirling through his mind for years, haunting his dreams. The thing that bothered King the most was how close he had come to death hundreds upon hundreds of times … and how *hard* it was not to dwell on those experiences.

Every night, he flashed back to those close calls, the narrow encounters where a split second determined whether he lived or died. He replayed them over and over again in his mind until he broke out in cold sweats, and stumbled into the various kitchens he'd lived in gasping for water.

He feared it would never go away. But now he had someone to talk to about it.

As birds cawed outside and daylight crept through the living room's small window, King finally brought his tales to a close. He sat back in disbelief, surprised that he had opened up so easily. He hadn't intended to tell his father any of the more harrowing encounters over the course of his life.

He hadn't wanted to trouble the man.

But now — looking at Ray process the load of information with calmness and sincerity — he realised he simply hadn't wanted to bring the scariest memories back to the surface.

'How do you feel?' Ray said after King had finished.

'Free.'

'How many people have you told what you just told me?'

'Zero.'

Ray whistled softly. 'You know you're a brave man for opening up, right?'

'I don't feel that way. I feel like it's best if I don't burden anyone with what I've been through.'

'You needed to talk about it. And now you have.'

'What do you think?'

'About what?'

'Everything. All of what I just told you.'

Ray shrugged. 'What's done is done. I couldn't stop you leaving for the military and I expected to never see you again in the first place. At least that's in the past. You're done now. You can move on with your life. You helped countless people and now we can move forward.'

'About that...'

Ray froze. 'Jason...'

'Something's come up, Dad.'

'What on earth are you talking about?'

'I've been made aware of a new situation.'

'And that is?'

King paused, wondering if he should bother revealing this information too. 'Not even Black Force knows yet.'

'Something that happened here? In Corsica?'

King nodded.

His father frowned. 'Spit it out.'

'The only other Black Force operative who is anywhere near my level has gone AWOL.'

'You've met him?'

'I have.'

'He's like you?'

'He is.'

'And they have no-one else? You're sure of this?'

'They have others. This man was adamant that he was the only thing holding the operation together. Without him, the inexperienced operatives will have to take on the toughest tasks.'

'And he walked away?' Ray said. 'Willingly? Even though he knew this?'

'He'd burnt out,' King said. 'Just like I did. I could see it the entire time. He couldn't go another day living the way he was. So he dropped everything and ran.'

'Like a coward.'

'I did the same, Dad.'

'At least you told those in charge. You did things the official way. The right way.'

'It makes no difference. When we're done, we're done. This man had to pick up the pieces when I left, too. Now I assume others will try to do the same.'

'But you don't think they can?'

King shook his head. 'No, I don't think they can. What happens when they can't pull off the missions? What happens when a nuclear device falls into the hands of terrorists and there's no-one there to stop it?'

'It doesn't matter,' his father said. 'It's not your responsibility.'

'It is,' King said. 'They need me. If only for a little while. Until someone takes my place.'

'Who?'

'I don't know.'

'Jason...'

'I know this isn't what you want to hear. Your only son resurfaces after fifteen years of waging war. You're thrilled that he made it out alive. And now he's throwing himself straight back into it?'

'Those are precisely the thoughts I'm having.'

'And I'm sorry.'

'You don't need to apologise to me.'

'No, I do. This wasn't my intention. I wanted to build our relationship again. But all this has happened in the last day. I know what I need to do.'

'You believe in it?'

King nodded.

Ray let out a deep sigh, releasing years of pent-up emotion with it. 'Then go.'

'Dad...'

'Jason, it's your choice. I've never managed to influence your decisions, and look how that ended up. You turned out to be the greatest combat operative in history, by the sounds of it. If I had my way you never would have left Green Bay and maybe we all wouldn't be here today. Who knows where the world would be if you didn't do the things you did.'

King found himself taken aback by the comments. No-one had ever put it to him that way before...

'I couldn't be more glad that you left,' Ray said. 'It's harsh, but the things you've accomplished... who am I to get in the way?'

'You're my father.'

'And I'd like to continue to be,' Ray said. 'I'm so happy that you came here. It feels like that's what I was waiting for the entire time — I just didn't know it.'

'I'm never going to just leave again,' King said. 'You know that.'

'I know.'

'We'll stay in touch.'

'I know.'

'But I'm needed. You know I am.'

Ray sighed. 'I know.'

'This probably makes it worse. Now you'll know I'm out there.'

His father leant over and rested a hand on his shoulder. 'At least I got to talk to you. I would much rather know you are in danger than not know anything at all.'

King wrapped a powerful arm around his father's back and pulled the man tight. They embraced for a long while. He lost track of time. When they parted, both men had tears in their eyes.

'I'm proud of you,' Ray said.

It was all that was necessary. It was all King needed to hear. He got off the couch and crossed to the kitchen. Snatched up a tall glass and filled it with tap water. Downed the whole thing. Refreshed and rejuvenated after a night of outpouring emotions and rest, he outstretched a hand.

'I hope you understand why I can't stay for long,' he said.

'I do.'

His father seized his palm in an iron grip. They shook. That was the one thing Ray had taught him at the earliest age — have a firm handshake.

King strode down the length of the hallway and opened the front door. He stared out at the quiet residential street in the heart of Aregno and paused. It might be the only pause he would get for the next while. Especially if things went as he anticipated.

He was sure they would.

He didn't exactly attract the calmest types.

He spun and saw his father standing behind him, watching his every move.

'I'll come back,' King said. 'I promise.'

'Another fifteen years?' Ray said with a wry smile.

King chuckled. 'I'll aim to make it fifteen days. See where they need me, and put the boot in their asses to get moving on finding replacements. How's that sound?'

'Sounds pretty damn good, soldier.'

'Bye, Dad.'

'Bye, son.'

King started down the street, but at the last moment turned back again. 'No good luck?'

Ray raised an eyebrow. 'If you needed luck, you would have died years ago. You've got something else. You don't need a single wish from me.'

King laughed. That was the Ray he knew.

He left the street feeling like an enormous load had been lifted off his shoulders. He walked, accompanied by a sensation he hadn't felt in decades.

Inner peace.

CHAPTER 45

He walked thirty minutes out of Aregno, strolling absent-mindedly until the village shrank away and was replaced by scrubs and arid plains and clusters of dense forest. The Corsican landscape was something to behold. He let everything out of his mind as he put one foot in front of the other, focusing on nothing more than the road ahead.

Ten minutes into the hike, a beat-up old hatchback coasted to a halt directly alongside him. A middle-aged man with a deep tan stuck his head out the window.

'Hey!' he cried. 'You want ride?'

'I would. Thank you.' King smiled at his friendly nature and broken English. He skirted round to the passenger seat and ducked inside. 'You going to Calvi?'

The man threw his hands in the air in an exaggerated gesture. 'Ah, yes, of course! Calvi! Lucky day, my friend!'

The journey didn't take long. King let the wind pour in through the open passenger window. He relished the sensation, feeling the salty seaside air against his cheeks, aware that some third-world hellhole more than likely awaited him next. He would enjoy every moment of Corsica while he had the opportunity.

As they drove, the man talked the entire way in French, supporting his tales with animated hand gestures and actions. He knew that King didn't speak the same language.

Maybe he just wanted someone to talk to…

King listened and nodded along, occasionally joining the man in laughter when he let out a gut-wrenching bellow after sharing a particularly hilarious anecdote. King didn't fake it. He was truly happy, and found the laughter effortless. After months of stalling, he had finally found the nerve to meet his father.

And he was intensely glad that he had done so.

He gave the man the address to the hotel he thought Klara was staying at. She had mentioned it off-hand during that night in the villa. It felt like an eternity ago. In reality, it had been a little over twenty-four hours in the past.

When shit hits the fan, it happens fast, he thought.

It seemed his life had become long periods of nothing with intense bursts of action and chaos dotted throughout.

He wondered if he would survive the next outburst…

It was a beautiful day in Calvi. The old man dropped King off on a street corner with a cheery wave and a smile full of missing teeth. King returned the gesture and stepped away from the vehicle. He found himself surrounded by daily life in Corsica. Tourists and locals went about their business with an air of happiness that came with living in an exotic paradise.

King spent a full minute staring at his surroundings, observing their carefree lives. They had no knowledge of the evil and filth that lurked under the surface of this island. That was nothing exclusive to Corsica, though.

Bad people existed everywhere in the world…

Which was why he needed to do what lay ahead.

First, though, he had unfinished business. He found the place he was looking for and stepped into a lavish air-conditioned lobby complete with high ceilings and marble columns.

Nice place.

He walked past pasty tourists lathering themselves in sunscreen and peeling the tags off freshly-purchased swimming trunks. A male receptionist greeted him in a pleasant tone as he approached the front desk.

'Good morning, sir,' he said, ignoring the purple bruise splotched across one half of King's face. 'What can I do for you?'

'There's a woman staying here,' King said. 'Her name's Klara. She'll be expecting me. My name's Jason.'

'Not a problem, sir. Do you know if she's in her room?'

'I think so.'

'I can phone her room and see if she wishes to come down?'

'Please do.'

King sat as the man punched in a number and spoke in a hushed tone into the receiver, relaying what King had told him. The call only lasted a few seconds before she hung up.

It only took her a minute to reach the lobby. The elevator doors chimed open and she hurried out in a blur of motion, a tropical sundress covering her lithe frame. King couldn't help smiling when he saw her. It was an emotion he was quickly becoming used to — genuine happiness.

Something inside him darkened when he realised that it wouldn't be that way for long.

He rose off the stool and looped one arm around her shoulder. They made for the elevator as fast as the social norms allowed. When they hurried aboard, Klara punched the number *17* and the doors swung shut.

They fell on each other in a tangle of limbs. He couldn't get enough of her. He ruffled her hair as they kissed, feeling every sensation of her body against his. When they reached their floor they composed themselves, just in case any innocent families happened to be waiting for their same elevator.

The corridor was empty.

They spilled out and Klara led him wordlessly down to the one-bedroom room she had secured several nights ago. As the door closed behind King, they fell on each other in an irrepressible frenzy. Hours passed, and it seemed the intensity and passion would never end. When it finally did, they lay side-by-side, naked, panting, shocked at just how animalistic they had become.

'What the hell was that?' Klara whispered, dotting his chest with small kisses. 'I've never felt like that.'

'Me either,' King muttered, staring at the ceiling.

'You think it was a release?'

'A what?'

'You know,' she said, propping herself up. 'Like after all the stress. I'd never been so truly scared in my life before yesterday.'

'Did you get any sleep last night?'

She shook her head, and King saw her eyes flicker. She was on the verge of tears. He held her tight.

'No,' she said. 'I just kept playing it back. The way they threw me into the van. I would have known nothing but pain if they shipped me off. I never would have made it back.'

'I'll never let you get into that kind of situation again,' he said.

She looked at him, unblinking. 'Does this mean...'

'I have to leave,' King said. 'For a short time. For work. Unprecedented things have come up. I honestly don't have any control over it.'

'You do,' she said.

362

'Technically, I do,' he said. 'But I'd never be able to live with myself if I ignored my thoughts. I need to go away for a while. But you've made me truly happy, and I know that's too rare to pass up. So I want to see you again. I'd love to come to Sweden after I finish my work.'

She beamed. 'I'd like that.'

'Are you okay with that?' he said. 'I don't want to keep you waiting.'

She leant over and pressed her lips to his forehead. She held them there for what felt like an eternity. Then she peeled away. 'As I said, I'd like that.'

He hesitated. 'You're not curious as to what I'll be doing?'

She smiled. 'You wouldn't tell me anyway.'

He laughed and swung one leg off the bed. 'You know me too well.'

'You're going *now?*' she said, astonished.

'I can't wait,' King said. 'If I do, I'll psyche myself out. I already did that with something personal here in Corsica. I can't keep waiting. I need to move.'

'How will you stay in one place?' she said. 'After it's over? It seemed to work out so well for you here.'

He tossed her the sundress. 'I think you might be able to help keep me grounded.'

She flashed her pearly white teeth. 'Oh? Falling for me, I see?'

'I think so.'

She hadn't been expecting his response to hit so hard. He could see that. She worked her way into the sundress, never taking her eyes off him, her eyes brimming with intensity.

'You'd better fucking come to Sweden,' she said as he finished dressing. 'You've got my hopes up now. Don't go and die on me.'

King winked. 'Not dying seems to be my specialty.'

'I can agree with that,' Klara said.

They made their way downstairs, holding each other in the elevator, knowing that it would be a while before they saw each other again.

Yet King felt oddly determined to make his way back to her. He had never felt like that before...

They kissed a final time in the lobby, not caring who looked on. King held onto her supple lips for as long as he could. Then he stepped away and didn't look back.

He hurried out into a balmy summer's day, his pace measured and even, his nerves fluttering.

What came next would either be the death of him ... or the start of a new phase in his life.

He fished the mobile phone out of his pocket and entered a number he knew off by heart.

It was answered on the second ring.

'Hello?' a stern female voice said, cool yet inquisitive.

'Command?' King said.

'Who the hell is this?'

'It's Jason King,' he said, hailing a cab for Sainte-Catherine Airport. 'I think it's about time I got back to work.'

JASON KING WILL RETURN…

Read Matt's other books on Amazon.

amazon.com/author/mattrogers23

Made in the USA
Lexington, KY
22 February 2017